Murder on Moon Mountain

A LISTED AND LETHAL MYSTERY

I0601420

Jean Harrington

PRESS

Kenmore, WA

CAMEL
PRESS

For more information go to: www.coffeetownpress.com
www.jeanharrington.com

This is a work of fiction. Names, characters, places, brands,
media, and incidents are either the product of the author's
imagination or are used fictitiously.

Cover design by Aubrey Anderson

Murder on Moon Mountain
Copyright © 2018 by Jean Harrington

ISBN: 978-1-60381-649-6 (Trade Paper)
ISBN: 978-1-60381-650-2 (eBook)

Library of Congress Control Number: 2018947674

Printed in the United States of America

Praise for the Listed and Lethal Mystery Series

"Bitchy back-biting, and even greed and murder are here, but so are goodness and kindness, real girlfriends, and even true love. [....] *In Murder On Pea Pike*, with deft strokes, Harrington sketches Honey and Amelia's thin lease on success in a town without boundless choices or resources...."
—Cathy Downs for Reviewing the Evidence

"Harrington does a splendid job of describing the absurdity of human nature and takes full advantage of her delightful characters in this quirky murder mystery. She uses their unique peculiarities to create a lively and thrilling story that is equal parts amusing, kindhearted, and engaging. [....] Murder on Pea Pike is bursting with southern charm and sultry atmosphere. A splendid series debut that won't disappoint readers who love old school murder mysteries."
—Michael Thomas Barry for *New York Journal of Books*

"[An] amusing series debut [with a] lively cast."
—*Publishers Weekly*

"The author Harrington has an eye for the ridiculous in human nature, and she takes advantage of her characters' foibles to concoct a spirited, suspenseful tale with equal measures of comedy and compassion."
—Phil Jason, PhD, for *Florida Weekly*

"...a fun whodunit. Whether you like them or not, the characters are quirky and entertaining. Honey is a likeable diamond-in-the-rough, and it is fun to watch her character evolve into a more sophisticated woman."
—Reader Views

To all my new-found Aurora friends

Acknowledgements

Kudos to Jennifer McCord of Camel Press for her many helpful insights and dedication to this story. Thanks also to Dawn Dowdle of Blue Ridge Literary Agency. And a big shout out to Thorndike Press for publishing *Murder on Pea Pike*, the first book in the Listed and Lethal series, in a large print, library edition.

Chapter One

*G*ood Lord Almighty. The place had been trashed. A three million, five hundred thousand dollar mansion on Moon Mountain, with a view of the Arkansas River. Addresses in Eureka Falls didn't get any better than this.

And look at it now.

Beer bottles, soda cans and empty pizza boxes were flung around the great room willy-nilly. A trail of red wine leaked along a velvet chair, ending in a puddle on the marble floor. Overhead, a pair of jeans swung from the chandelier, and jaunty as a flag, a U of A T-shirt perched on an ivory silk lampshade.

In front of the fireplace, two matching sofas the length of freight trains faced each other. The one with its back to the entrance had a sneaker parked on an arm like it had every right to be there.

That must have been some party.

I sniffed the air, a nasty mix of stale beer, leftover food and sweaty clothes. Though I hadn't met the owner, a Mr. Barry McHale, he was a highly praised man-about-town. Well, regardless of his social standing, if Mr. McHale wanted to sell his super-sized cottage, he'd better get a cleaning crew in here fast. Needing to let my realty office know about the mess, I rummaged in my tote for the cell. As usual, it had dropped to the bottom of the bag.

Not caring if my heels clicked like rifle shots, I stomped across the marble floor to the sofa, set the tote on the arm next to the sneaker—and screamed.

Stretched out on his back, arms flung over his head, a naked man lay there sound asleep, giving me a clear view of everything he possessed. At my scream, his eyes opened for an instant, then fluttered closed.

"Geesh, not so loud." When I screamed again, his lids opened wider and, shielding his eyes with a hand, he struggled to sit up. "What are you doing here, lady?"

Fumbling in my bag for the cell, I inched toward the entrance. "Don't you know? I'm with Ridley's Real Estate. Honey Ingersoll's the name."

"Yeah?"

"Are you the owner of this house?"

He stood, clutching a pink satin pillow to his groin, a move that did nothing to hide his matchstick legs or the pot belly sagging over the satin.

No answer.

I found the cell, yanked it out of the bag and thumbed in 911. Before pressing "Talk," I asked one more time.

"Are you Barry McHale, the owner of this property?"

He paused, scratched something under the pillow and said, "Nope, I don't think so."

Chapter Two

Without waiting for Mr. Mysterious to lose his grip on the pillow, I dashed outside and punched in "Talk." After minutes that felt like hours, a siren wailed along Bluffs Boulevard. Moments later, a Eureka Falls PD cruiser swerved onto the circular drive and screeched to a halt.

The cruiser door opened and out stepped Sheriff Matt Rameros. He crossed the pavers kind of easy like—a mountain man on a hunt.

I ran down the driveway to meet him.

"You call 911, Honey?" he asked. "Some kind of trouble here?"

"Yes," I said, my voice breathless for some reason. "I think there's a squatter in the house. He's naked as a jay bird. Or at least he was."

The glimmer of a smile flitted across Matt's face. "Understood." He motioned to his partner who was still in the cruiser, busy on the radio. "Let's go, Zach."

Deputy Zach climbed out of the car and, together, like one of those ol' time posses, they disappeared into the house while I waited by the cruiser trying hard not to bite my nails and ruin my new French manicure. What a way to take on a listing. Maybe this was an omen, a sign that someone the likes of me had no business dealing with a property that looked like it belonged to Prince Charles. Though, actually, I was only here because of some real bad news.

Two hours ago, my boss, Sam Ridley's daddy collapsed. Just like that—boom. In a rush to get to the hospital, Sam handed me the alarm code to the McHale house and said, "The owner's out of town, but he's flying in today for this meeting. Show him the visual tour and answer his questions. Tell him I'll be in touch as soon as possible."

"But—"

"And get his signature on that contract."

"Suppose he—"

Too late, Sam was already halfway out the door. So here I was, in a peck of trouble without …

"Hi, there," a woman called, poking her head over the fancy boxwood hedge that bordered the McHale property. "Why the cop's car? What's going on?"

Startled, I blurted, "There's a squatter in the house."

"No kidding. How exciting." She slipped through a narrow gap in the shrubbery and came over to chat, dressed—or as my momma would say, undressed—in a fire engine red bikini, a red scarf tied around her hips, its fringe swaying with every step she took.

No doubt about it, she had the kind of body bikinis were made for.

Holding out a diamond-studded hand, she said, "I'm Carmen DeLuca. I live next door, and you are?"

"Honey Ingersoll. I'm with Ridley's Realty."

"Oh, right. Barry's determined to sell the place." She heaved a sigh that sent the bikini bra on a trip around the Ozarks. "I'll miss him when he leaves here. We're very good friends."

"I see. Mr. McHale and I haven't yet met, but I'm looking forward to it."

"Oh, you're in for a thrill. Everybody's crazy about Barry."

I stiffened as the front door swung open. Escorted on each arm by one of the officers, Mr. Mysterious stumbled out in the same jeans, T-shirt and sneakers he'd tossed around the great room. Far from showing signs of guilt, he was hopping mad.

"I'm telling you I never broke in. I was *invited* in. By the man himself."

"Yeah? What's his name?" Deputy Zach asked.

"I don't remember. He kind of mumbled it."

"What's he look like?"

"You know, a guy."

They had reached the cruiser. "That'll stand up in court. Watch your head," Zach ordered. He hustled the man into the back seat and locked him in.

With a nod at me and a warm glance at Carmen's bikini, Matt said, "We'll book him for breaking and entering. If the owner decides to press charges, we'll need your statement, Honey. Either way, it's safe to go back in now. The place is empty."

He touched two fingers to the rim of his uniform hat, winked at me without letting Carmen see it and got behind the wheel of the cruiser.

As the car drove off, blue lights blazing, I heard laughter and party shrieks wafting across the boxwoods. Smiling, Carmen said, "Things are heating up. High time." She half-turned to go then swiveled back. "Why don't you join us? Any friend of Barry's is a friend of the Velveteen Vixens."

"The *who*?"

She laughed. "Oh, a bunch of us so-called trophy wives who hang out together. A photographer's shooting a reality show about us." She wrinkled her nose. "Well, it's just a pilot at the moment. He has to sell it to a producer. Not everyone could make it today, so we could use another body."

I held up my ringless hands. "Thanks, but no thanks. I don't belong in a show like that. I'm just a working girl."

"So are we, Honey, so are we."

Somewhere in my tote, the cell rang. For once, I was able

to find it fast.

"Is this the Ridley's agent?" a man's voice growled into the line.

"It surely is. And you are?"

"Barry McHale. Call me Barry. My apologies, but I'm still in Little Rock. The plane's been delayed. If we leave in a half hour or so, I'll call you back. I hate to ask, but can you wait?"

"I've set the day aside for you, Mr. McHale."

"Is that Barry?" Carmen asked. "Let me speak to him."

I held up a finger. "I'm at your house, Mr. Mc ... ah, Barry. Have the police contacted you about the break-in?"

"I just spoke to them. Sorry you had to deal with that. Be with you as soon as possible."

"Please don't hang up. Someone wants to talk to you."

With her back to me, Carmen purred into the phone so softly I couldn't hear what she was saying, then, "All right. Be happy to. You'll like her, Barry ... blonde ... oh, about twenty-five, I'd say." A few more murmurs and a cozy type laugh before she hung up and handed me the phone. "Barry asked me to keep you entertained. So come on over and meet the gang. Or at least part of it."

"Oh, I don't know, I'm on duty here."

"You sell real estate, right?"

I nodded.

"Then think of this as networking. Penelope Richie's on the cusp of a divorce. As soon as it goes through, she gets her ex's house."

"But—"

"No buts about it. Without old money bags, she won't be able to keep it. And who will she think of when the time comes to sell?" Hands on hips, she paused.

"Real estate sales don't usually happen that way."

"Really? How long you been doing this work?"

"Going on five years. First for the Winthrop Agency. Now for Ridley's."

"And you haven't heard that connections are king?"

"That's one notion."

"Oh, you're not convinced. Too conservative." Her glance swept over me, taking in my navy blue suit—polyester and linen—my starched white shirt and sensible pumps. "That explains the suit. It's so ... so... *Arkansas*. Why advertise where you're from?"

How downright annoying. Why was I chatting with her, anyway? Well, because from the sound of that phone call, she and Barry McHale, owner of a squatter-trashed, multi-million dollar property were bosom buddies. I didn't want to make an enemy out of her. But the feeling didn't last long.

Disgusted with my wimpiness, I womaned up and said, "Arkansas is a beautiful place. I like it here. Though for a while there I was thinking of leaving. Nearly did too. Thought I needed a change of scene because of a—"

Uncertain of how much to tell, I paused. She filled in for me. "A man?"

"Yes, Ma'am."

"Say no more. When it comes to men, a girl can't live with them, and she can't kill them." She stopped as if mulling that one over. "Too bad." She crooked a finger, beckoning me forward. "Come join the Vixens." She shrugged, giving the bikini another ride. "Who knows? This may be the most profitable afternoon of your life, but first we have to ditch your suit. And I have just the thing in mind."

She wiggled her red-tipped finger again. I sighed, and like the good Lord hadn't blessed me with a mind of my own, I followed her through the break in the hedge. On the other side, we stepped into a garden fringed with dogwood trees in bloom and smelling like gardenia water had been spilt all over the lawn. For the second time that day, my breath caught in my throat. I had stumbled into Eden.

A wall of glass doors at the back of the huge, white residence opened onto a terrace leading, one stone step at a time, to a gigantic, heart-shaped pool. Yes, heart-shaped, like a great big box of Valentine's candy. In it, up to her waist in the bluest water you could ever hope to see, her dark curls swept into a tumbled topknot, a pixie-faced girl held up a champagne flute.

"Higher, Penelope," yelled a man in flip-flops and shorts, his red hair scrunched in a ponytail. "Flaunt it." He peered out from behind his camera for an instant. "Your mother teach you how to flaunt?"

She stuck her tongue out at him and hoisted her glass even higher.

"Now drain it," he ordered.

She did, in one gulp and tossed the glass over a shoulder into the deep end of the pool.

"Excellent," he said, lowering the camera. "Now how about a little more action? Jump up and down, say something. *Move.* Don't just stand there. *Emote.*"

"I have to get the glass before somebody steps on it."

"It'll wait."

"You're the boss. Here goes with my best Actors Studio performance. Lee Strasberg here I come." She waded toward the shallow end—the pointy bottom of the heart—and dripping like a sea goddess, slowly climbed the ladder. All the while the guy with the camera was shouting, "Good. Good. Pause. Flick the water out of your eyes. Bend over a little. Excellent. Excellent. Keep on coming. Come to Daddy. Come on. That's good. That's good. A little more action now. A little more action."

"More action? Really?" She shrugged shoulders pink from the sun. "Okay. Here goes." Reaching behind her back, she unhooked her bra clasp and with a *whoosh* sent it flying through the air into the pool with the champagne glass.

Not a word from behind the camera. The pigtailed guy was too busy photographing Penelope's titties.

Like him, I was speechless as she bounced up the rest of the pool steps, blowing air kisses at us all.

"Oh for heavens sake, Penelope, put your bra back on" Carmen said. "What will Honey think? Besides, Jesse can't use that footage anyway. Can you, Jesse?"

He lowered the camera. "Afraid not. Too bad. Best shots of the day." He grinned. "Like they say, less is more."

Before the girl dove for the deep end, Carmen introduced us. Red-headed Jesse, a man in his mid-thirties maybe, said, "*hello there*." Then faster than a hound chasing a rabbit, he snapped my picture. "You're a very pretty girl. I'd like to see you in something other than a suit." Saying "suit" like it was a four letter word.

"Come on in the house with me, Honey," Carmen said. "I'll loan you a bikini."

"Oh, I don't think—"

"Don't be silly. We're short two girls today, and Jesse's film needs more eye candy. So be a good sport. You can talk to Penelope later. Besides, now that Barry McHale's putting his house on the market, maybe I'll sell this one too." A calculating smile and, "So think of it as an informal viewing. Look around while you're inside."

"Thank you, I'd surely love to."

Why not? After all, I reckoned, what did I have to lose? Which only shows what a babe in the woods I was.

Chapter Three

UNLIKE MY QUICK peek at Barry McHale's trashed interior, this time, as I followed Carmen into her house, through one drop-dead room after another, I had a real honest-to-God tour.

In the kitchen, with its high-toned, stainless steel appliances from Europe and its gigantic, marble-topped center island, I met Sophie, the housekeeper. When Carmen introduced us, Sophie nodded in a shy way, like country women are apt to do, and kept on arranging little snacky tidbits on a silver tray.

"Bring those out to the patio as soon as they're ready," Carmen told her. Then waving a hand, she drew me into the great room. A soaring, white-walled space, it was furnished with canvas-covered chairs and sofas and hung with big, bright oil paintings the likes of which I'd never seen before. She said they were jungle scenes from South America. And like Carmen herself, they were both hot and cool at the same time.

As we strolled into yet another room, I said, "Your home is way beyond beautiful."

She shrugged off my compliment. "It used to be important to me, but I'm beginning to think I could live without it." We'd reached her rose and white master suite. She spread her arms wide. "None of this stuff talks to me." A finger pointed at the ultra-king bed. "And I sleep alone." She winked. "Most of the time."

When she didn't, was it Barry McHale who kept her warm?

Anyway, the thought slipped away the minute she swung open the door to a closet roughly the size of my rental apartment. On the left, shelves to the ceiling were stacked with shoes; a hundred pair at least and next to them an awesome handbag collection better by far than the one at Belinda's Boutique. Shelves across the back held folded piles of sweaters and tops, and to the right dresses, pants and gowns were arranged by color. A closet to die for.

As I stood there in my plain business suit, mouth hanging open, Carmen padded over to the center island.

"I keep swimsuits in with the lingerie."

After opening and closing two or three drawers, "Oh, here it is," she said, handing me a sky blue bikini. "This'll be perfect on you."

Clutching the two little scraps of cloth, I wasn't so sure and stood there frozen.

"Go ahead," she urged. "Put it on."

Strip naked in front of a woman I'd only known for a few minutes? "I don't think so."

She laughed. "What's the matter, Honey? You shy or something?"

Heat rushed into my face. "My momma raised me that way." I shrugged. "What can I say?"

She laughed, something she did a lot. "Fortunately, my momma did not. Okay, I'll leave you alone. Come down after you change." Reaching into the lingerie drawer again, she took out a blue scarf. "A *pareo*," she said, handing it to me with a twinkle in her eye. "For your modesty."

I took it, grateful, until I realized I could see right through it.

She left with a, "Ta-ta, we'll be out by the pool. If you need anything, ask Sophie."

I went into her rose-tiled bathroom with its party-sized tub, striped off the suit and slipped into the bikini. Though the fit was looser than on Carmen—especially the top—it was snug enough not to fall to the floor, and for what it was worth, I tied the *pareo* around my hips. In case Mr. McHale tried to reach me, I plucked the phone from my purse and strolled barefoot out to the pool.

"Here she is." Jesse lifted his camera. "Va va va voom!"

"Oh please. I'm just trying to cooperate."

"In all things?" His eyebrows arched into bushy red caterpillars.

I didn't bother to answer him, and keeping my stomach tucked in … well, it was pretty flat anyway … I untied the scarf … I mean *pareo* … draped it on a lounge chair, set the phone on top and dove into the pool.

"Hey, not so fast," Jesse yelled as I stroked up and down. "I need some poses." *Poses?*

No way. I'd been ordered around by enough men.

I ignored him and continued my laps, letting the cool water soothe my vexation. "Look at her go," Penelope said. "She swims like a fish."

I doubted anyone would care to know my daddy had kept his trailer parked near an abandoned quarry. Growing up, I swam in it every summer along with the other local kids.

It was great fun, but sometimes I wake in the night, called out of sleep by the fear that I'm drowning in an endless pit. Then shivering and scared, I calm myself by taking deep breaths and remembering I'm alive and well. A survivor. So doing laps in Carmen's pool wasn't a big deal even if Penelope thought so. Finally, refreshed and relaxed, I tossed my dripping hair out of my eyes and started up the pool stairs.

"Hold it right there, Honey," Jesse called.

Oh, darn. That was about the last thing I wanted to do. But Carmen had been so welcoming, I owed her, so I paused and, stomach sucked in, waited for Jesse's instructions.

"Run a hand through your hair," he ordered. "Good, good. Now go over to the table slowly ... slowly ... and pick up a champagne flute. Take a sip ... that's it ... take another one. Now how about a profile shot ... like you're looking up at Moon Mountain over there."

Jesse was after some kind of sexy image, but I wasn't there to party. I faked a sip or two and set the glass back down. Bad enough that I'd meet my client wet and almost naked, but I had no intention of meeting him ga-ga from champagne.

"You married, Honey?" Jesse asked from behind his camera.

"No."

"Ever been?"

I shook my head, sending beads of water flying into the air.

"Why not?"

I heaved a sigh, but it didn't send my bikini top on a tour. That's a talent, sort of like playing the piano. Some people have it. Some people don't.

As I reached for a fluffy towel, intending to wrap it around me, my phone rang.

I grabbed it on the second ring. "Hello."

"Barry McHale here."

Caller ID had already told me so, and besides, how could I forget such a nice, deep voice?

"My profound apologies," he said, "but I can't get away after all."

"I under—"

"Let's reschedule, shall we?"

"Why I'd be pleased to do so, Mr... Barry."

"Tomorrow at nine. My house."

"I'll be there."

Of course I'd be there. What else? Refuse and lose my job?

Chapter Four

THE NEXT MORNING, I drove onto the McHale property fifteen minutes early so I'd have time to return Carmen's bikini. Yesterday I wore it home with my white shirt buttoned over it and the dratted navy suit folded on the passenger seat. Now washed spanking clean, the bikini sat tucked in a gift bag with a thank you note and a bag of Mami's Cheese Crisps. Today I wore my red mini, the one I usually saved for weekends. In case I saw Carmen, I had a point to make, didn't I?

Gift bag in hand, I slipped through the opening in the boxwoods. Gardenia perfume hovered in the air. I inhaled and took a moment to enjoy the scene. The pool, as crazy awesome as I remembered, gleamed in the morning sun, and beyond it, at the foot of the Bluffs, the river sparkled its way to the Gulf. Off in the distance, Moon Mountain, its highest hill swirling with mist, stood guard over us all.

I skirted the pool and strolled across the lawn, thick and soft underfoot. If I left the gift bag on one of the umbrella tables, Carmen would be sure to see it. Caught in the breeze, a piece of red fabric, one of those … *pareos* … fluttered up from between two of the lounge chairs. I hurried over to grab it before it blew into the trees.

Oh no. Oh God Almighty, no.

Like a rag doll someone had thrown away, Carmen lay crumpled on her side, her knees bent to her waist, her head in a puddle of blood. She was lifeless, I knew she was lifeless. Yet needing to be honest-to-God sure, I knelt down and pressed a finger her cheek. Her skin, a strange gray white, felt cold to the touch. To my horror, ants trailed through the blood seeping from her wound. Then something else caused the breath to catch in my throat. Something that didn't make any sense. Stretched straight above her head, her arm had frozen in place, a single finger pointing at the concrete, where two words were spelled out in blood—*under car.*

"Aren't you at the wrong house?" a deep voice asked. I leaped to my feet and whirled around. *The killer?*

A rock star look-alike stood smiling at me from across the pool. How could he smile at a time like this? I stared at him open-mouthed, unable to answer.

"I'm Barry McHale," he said. "Are you Miss Ingersoll?"

I shook my head.

"No? Oh. There's a Ridley's sticker on the car in my driveway. I thought maybe you were—"

"Not now," I said, brushing away his question with a wave of my hand. "Come here."

"What?" Sounding vexed. "I hardly think—"

"Will you please stop running your mouth? Something terrible's happened."

Paying no mind to my tone, he didn't move an inch. "You look mighty fine to me, Miss, whoever you are." His smile widened into a grin.

I ignored the spots in front of my eyes and his suddenly cozy manner. "Stop wasting time. Call 911. *Now.*"

"What the hell's the matter with you, lady?"

"Nothing's the matter with *me.*" I pointed to the body he couldn't see from where he stood. "It's *her.* Carmen."

One slow step at a time, like I was a crazy woman he'd best

be wary of, he rounded the pool and came closer. And closer. Until he saw her. And stopped short.

"Oh God. Oh, my God."

"Right. So will you make that call now?"

He felt his pockets, hasty like. "I don't have my cell on me."

"Me neither. It's in my car."

"Wait here."

Without the strength or will to go anywhere, I watched as he made a dash for the house. A few seconds later from somewhere inside he called, "Sophie! Sophie! Where's the phone? I need a phone fast."

Fast? I glanced down at Carmen. He needn't rush. Poor thing, it wouldn't do her no earthly good at all.

WHAT BROKE LOOSE after Barry McHale called 911 wasn't hell but something akin to it. Carmen's gorgeous property soon swarmed with medics, police, the coroner and finally the Yarborough County Detective, Lieutenant Bradshaw, a fifty-something man in shorts and a T-shirt with U of A's motto, *Never Yield*, stretched across his chest. He looked like a man whose day off had been interrupted.

Sure enough, Sheriff Matt said, "Heard you were out on your boat, Detective. Sorry, but we had no choice."

Bent over Carmen's body, Bradshaw muttered, "Fish'll run another day. She won't." He stood and pulled a recorder out of his shorts pocket. He turned it on and walked over to where I sat slumped on the edge of a lounge chair.

"You're Miss Honey Ingersoll?" he asked, though he knew well enough who I was. We'd met a year ago when he investigated two murders on Pea Pike outside of town.

Still in shock, I nodded.

"Speak up, please, the recorder can't hear nods."

"Yes sir, I'm Honey Ingersoll."

"You found the body of Carmen DeLuca?"

I nodded, quickly following it up with a "Yes."

"Describe what you saw when you entered the property."

After a little pause, I managed to recollect every horrid detail.

"What were you doing here?"

"Returning a bikini."

Like such news weighed real heavy, the recorder slumped in his hand. "Explain, please."

"Well, yesterday …"

When I finished my story, he nodded, but all's he said was, "Anyone hear the deceased invite you over here?"

I didn't even have to think. "Yes, Mr. Barry McHale."

He shut the recorder and dropped it in his shorts pocket. "No more questions for now. You'll get a call when your statement's ready for signing."

Though I hadn't done anything wrong, Detective Bradshaw had me half way persuaded that I had. Something about his cement jaw and those thin, tight lips, and the way he frowned no matter what all you said …

"Am I allowed to leave?" I asked.

"Yes, you're free to go." Over a shoulder, walking away.

A photographer in a police uniform kept busy snapping pictures of Carmen's body from all angles. No red-haired Jesse Raidel enjoying his job, this man was grim and silent. No shouts of "higher, good, good. Come to Daddy." No champagne glasses flying into the pool. The powerful difference made me want to retch.

A man carrying a black medical bag stomped down the terrace stairs and hurried over to Carmen. The coroner. I shuddered and made my way across a lawn that didn't seem so soft and smooth anymore. I'd slip through the hedge and go back to the office, for it surely wouldn't be fitting to conduct realty business on the Bluffs today.

At the curvy end of the pool, I spotted Barry McHale sitting on the edge of a lounge chair, his head in his hands. He looked so lost and alone, I stopped to say good-bye. When my shadow fell across him, he glanced up, tears streaming down his face.

Like he felt shamed to be seen crying, he swiped his eyes

with the back of a hand. He needn't have bothered. My heart went out to him, and I sank onto the lounge by his side.

"I'm so sorry," I said. "You were friends, I know."

He raised his head, the faintest hint of a smile parting his lips. "Friends? We were more than friends. I asked her to marry me. Three times. She kept turning me down, but I could tell she was weakening. Sooner or later, she would have—" He broke off whatever he had a mind to say and stood abruptly. "Today isn't a good time to discuss my property."

"No, it truly isn't."

"Tomorrow, then? Same time?"

I nodded and watched as shoulders hunched, he hurried off and disappeared through the break in the hedge.

Poor man. He needed to rush away and mourn in private. I should leave too, but sat still as a stone without the energy to move … Carmen had refused to marry him—three times, he'd said. Had the third time been one too many? A reason for killing her?

Chapter Five

By the following day, the common sense my momma gave me set in. Barry McHale had been grief stricken by Carmen's death. So why in the world would he kill her? Still, believing I'd better not disrespect Momma's gift, I phoned the office and told Mrs. Otis I'd be at the McHale house all morning. If I didn't call in by noon, to please send Sheriff Matt out looking for me.

Then I hung up and dressed with care. No navy suit. No red mini. Sky blue was my color. So sky blue, then, in a pencil skirt and matching knit top. I added pearl ear studs and a chunky pearl necklace like those fashion magazines were always talking about. Naturally, mine were *faux*, a fancy French word for a bunch of nothing. But according to *Elle*—and I heard tell *Elle* really knew—all that mattered was the effect. Good thing. Effect was a sight easier to come by than money.

Troubled by Barry's sorrow, I didn't know what to expect when I parked on his circular drive and strolled up to the carved mahogany doors. I reached out to ring the bell, but my finger never touched the buzzer.

"Psst. Psst, realty lady. It's me. Frankie Serrito."

Startled, I whirled around, coming face-to-face with the skinny, pot-bellied squatter.

My hand dropped away from the buzzer. "You! What are you doing back here?"

"I was invited. What else?"

"*Invited?* I saw you leave in a police car."

"Oh that. A mistake is all. The cops talked to the man and let me go. I walked back here and hung out by the pool." He upped his chin at the house. "He never noticed me."

"Probably not. The woman next door was murdered yesterday."

As if I was the killer or something, he scurried back a step or two. "Not good. Not good at all."

"Mr. Serrito ..."

"Boy, that sounds nice. Nobody uses my real name any more. It's always 'Frankie this' or 'Frankie that.' Or 'hey you.'"

I glanced at my watch. "Sorry, but I have to go. I have an appointment to keep."

He crept closer. This time, *I* stepped back. He was little and thin, but no telling if he was harmless.

"Let the man know I'm out here, okay? Anytime he wants, I'll babysit the house, starting right now. No charge."

I had to get away from him and pressed the buzzer. To my relief, deep inside, the chimes struck four notes.

"Okay, lady?"

I shook my head. "He doesn't need a house sitter. You'd be wise to leave. The police might not be so nice a second time."

"*Nice?* They roughed me up good. I ought to sue."

"You ought to—"

Barry McHale opened the door, greeting me with a handshake and a half smile that didn't quite reach his eyes. While he didn't look real good, he did look better than yesterday. As I stepped inside, a scurrying in the shrubbery told me Frankie had taken off. Or had hidden from view.

While I hated to wipe the little smile from Barry's face, he needed to know.

"Your squatter is back."

"*What!*"

"He's outside. Just offered to babysit the house any time you like."

"The nerve of the guy, whoever he is. Had the gall to tell the police I invited him in."

I glanced around the great room. The empty cans, bottles and pizza boxes were gone. Nothing hung from the chandelier or the lamps, and the stale odor had disappeared too. But the wine stain had dried on the velvet arm chair.

Barry pointed to it. "Look at my chair. Destroyed. And you should have seen the master bath."

"Maybe you should call the police and have them check around," I suggested, uneasy at the idea of a squatter outside the door.

He shook his head. "No. The less involvement one has with the police the better."

"But—"

He held up his hand. The signal for me to stop talking. "If you cry wolf for minor problems, when you have a serious issue you don't get any action."

"Really?" A strange attitude for a man whose house had been trashed and was ripe for it to happen again. "He's hiding outside by the front entrance, Barry. I really don't think—"

"Not to worry. He's homeless, right?"

"Could be. I'm sorry for his trouble but …" I pointed to the stained velvet. "You were lucky he didn't cause any more damage. Or burn the house down. As beautiful as it is, a showing with a squatter lurking outside isn't a good idea. It's not safe. Especially not after—"

"What happened to Carmen."

I nodded. When he mentioned Carmen's name, he frowned, and I thought he'd call the police right then and there. But he shoved his hands in his pockets and said, "The poor guy probably has nowhere else to go. Given some bad luck, anybody could end up the same way. Me. You."

True. Not so long ago, I'd come scarily close to living in my car—and not the fancy Lincoln I drove today, either. The memory caused my heart to skip a beat, but all I could think to say was, "If he *is* homeless, the county can help him find a place to live. Provide food."

Barry's frown deepened.

"I'm not sweeping this off the porch," I said. "But look at it this way ... suppose I come in with a client and find Frankie's jeans hanging from the chandelier?"

For a moment, Barry didn't answer, just stood there holding onto his frown, his hands still shoved in his pockets. Why was he so hard to convince?

And then I had my answer.

"You must think I'm being stupid," he said, "but the truth is I have a brother who dropped out of sight years ago. Nobody knows where he is or what happened to him. When I see a guy like Frankie, I can't help but think of Tommy. It makes me kind of crazy."

"Oh, I'm so sorry to hear such a ..."

Though I truly was sorry, I didn't say any more. But what if I walked in with a client some day and found Frankie lolling around naked as the day his momma birthed him?

Worry must have been painted all over my face, for Barry shrugged and said, "You're right. The situation needs to be resolved. I'll call 911."

A twinge of guilt shot through me when Matt and Deputy Zach pulled onto the driveway and, after a short search, found Frankie hiding behind the gardener's shed. While Barry and I watched from the front entrance, they hauled him out of the shed, as spitting mad as he had been two days ago.

He spotted us in the doorway and yelled over a shoulder. "Hey, there's the man, ask him. Ask him. He'll tell you I'm a guest. *A guest!*"

The officers ignored his spouting and hustled him toward the car. Twisting in their grasp, Frankie's eyes lit on me. "Hey lady, you call the cops on me? Why? Why treat Frankie like dirt? Nobody does that and gets away—"

They had reached the cruiser, and his threat was cut short. This time, instead of telling him to watch his head, Zach spread his fingers, and using Frankie's scalp like a basketball, he shoved him into the cruiser's backseat and slammed the door.

Matt strode over to Barry, gave him a two-fingered salute and nodded at me. The nod took me in from head to toe, reminding me … well … that he knew I had a little round beauty spot on the left cheek of my butt. But that's another story.

He turned his attention back to Barry. "We'll book him, Mr. McHale, and this time we'll keep him. He threatened Miss Ingersoll here, so it's no longer simple trespassing. Especially not after what happened next door."

I shot a quick glance Barry's way, but his face was as blank as a sheet of unused paper.

Chapter Six

AFTER THE OFFICERS left, Barry made coffee and I slipped the virtual tour disc of the house into his TV. A sixty inch HD. In the kitchen. I never saw the like of it before—I mean, who keeps such a big ol' television set in a kitchen?

He loved how the video showed off the property, read the contract quickly and, between sips of black coffee, signed it with no argument whatsoever. Not even over Ridley's commission at time of sale, though on a property appraised for over a million we only charged three percent, not the usual six. Even so, Ridley's commission could be well over a hundred thousand dollars.

In short, everything went down easy except for one small detail. Barry didn't say a single word about where he'd be moving to next. Strange. Usually a client will give a reason for putting a place on the market, but not this time. I gave a mental shrug and put his move down to a rich man's restlessness. He had his reasons, and with Carmen's brutal killing fresh in his mind, no wonder he'd signed the contract so fast. He wanted out of there, now more than ever.

Our business finished, I tucked the disc and the contract

in my tote. While he walked me to the front door, I said all the usual things about remaining in touch. As we shook hands on the deal, he held my fingers a moment longer than necessary and in that moment, seeing his suffering, I wanted to say how sorry I was about Carmen but somehow understood her death was the last thing he wanted to hear about. So I held my tongue and drove off in a happy-sad mood.

With morning traffic sparse, I got back to the office in less than a half hour. Spotting an open slot on Main Street, I parked and came in the front way. As usual, dear reliable Mrs. Otis sat at the reception desk by the front window. Seeing her there made me feel all was right with the world.

"Morning, sweetie," I said. "Sam in?"

She nodded. "Came here straight from the hospital. Said his dad's doing better."

"Good. I'm glad he's here. We need to talk."

I knocked on his office door, caught a muffled response and walked in. Most days, he'd be starched, pressed and shaved, ready to take a client on a showing at a moment's notice. But not this morning. Baggy-eyed, wearing what looked like yesterday's clothes, he lifted his loafered feet off the desk and lowered his newspaper.

"Heard your daddy's doing better," I said.

A ghost of a smile raised his lips. "Yeah, looks like he's going to make it."

"That's such good news." I reached into my tote and waved the McHale contract in the air. "Here's some more. Signed, sealed and" … I dropped it on his desk … "delivered."

Though blurry-eyed from lack of sleep, his eyes took on a shine. "Excellent."

Those sapphire blues, the ones I used to think were made in heaven for me alone, narrowed as he ran a hand over his stubbled chin. "Now all you have to do is sell it."

You. I'd worked for Sam for over three years now and had been in love with him for the first two. Though I'd fallen out of love—my longing for him gone for good—I hadn't forgotten why he'd hired me away from Saxby Winthrop—to sell real estate. As much real estate as possible.

So I didn't mind that Sam was basically dumping the responsibility for unloading the McHale mansion squarely in my lap. After all, he had a life-or-death family crisis to handle, and besides, I love a challenge. Good thing. Finding a buyer for an over-the-top property in a town like Eureka Falls would be one whopper of a challenge.

Sam was checking to be sure the contract I'd just handed him was properly signed when Mrs. Otis opened his door and poked her head in.

"Honey, you have a call on line two."

"Can you take a number, Mrs. O? Say I'll call back?"

"The man says it can't wait."

Sam glanced up. "Go get it, Honey. You never know ..." His voice trailed off.

"Right."

I took the call in my cubicle, which to be honest, was a poor excuse for an office. "Honey Ingersoll speaking."

"Well, Miss Honey, do tell."

Saxby Winthrop. My former boss and then some. I lowered the phone from my ear and glared at it, half expecting to see snake oil pouring onto my desk.

"You there, Miss Honey?"

"What do you want, Sax?"

"Now don't take on such a cold tone. I've got an interestin' proposition for you."

I hung up.

Thirty seconds later, Mrs. Otis returned. "He's back on line two."

I heaved a sigh. The last person in the world I wanted to speak to was that snake-in-the-grass, but if I didn't, he'd keep calling. Or worse, drop by. For if I knew one thing about Saxby Winthrop—and I knew a lot more than a body needed to—he never gave up. I guess it's what made him such a good realtor.

I hit "Talk" with more force than necessary. "So what is it?"

"Not something I can speak about on the phone, so I'm invitin' you to pay a little call on me."

"Oh really? Whereabouts, your bedroom?"

A chuckle came wafting through the line. "Now shame on you, Miss Honey, for voicin' such a thought." His voice lower. "Though that particular one's always been a favorite of mine."

"You want me to hang up again?"

"No, no. I want you to come to my office as soon as possible. Or" … he paused

… "I could come to you at Ridley's, but for what I have in mind, it wouldn't be fittin'."

"Why don't you just tell me what you want?"

"Sorry, darlin', but I can't impart this information over an electronic device."

"You're joshing, right?"

"Now would I do that?"

Probably not. Humor had never been Saxby's strong suit. Something else I knew about him. Six years ago, when I rode into town on the back of Billy Tubbs' Harley, I thought Billy was my one and only—until the day he gave me a black eye. On the very same day, I walked out on him and went to work for Saxby. In more ways than one. I'm not proud of that period in my life; in fact, I'm downright ashamed of it, but at the time it felt like survival. And to be fair, Saxby hadn't used force, just a lot of sugar-coated words. Who was to blame that I tasted what he offered? On the other hand, he also taught me the real estate business. Then when straight-as-an-arrow Sam Ridley offered me a job as his agent, I gave Saxby notice and seized the brass ring. So I guess I owed him… something.

"Well, darlin', what do you say?" he asked.

"Is Mindy in today?"

"Sittin' right outside my office listening to every word I say."

In the background, a slammed door echoed through the line.

"As long as she's in, all right. I'll see you in a half hour."

"That'll be most convenient," he said, and then the phone

went dead. Saxby always loved having the last word.

I stared at the dial for a moment before putting the receiver back in the cradle. Since I'd come to work for Sam, never before had Saxby called me at the office. Not even once. Clearly, something was up.

Chapter Seven

LIKE RIDLEY'S, SAXBY'S place of business was located on Main Street, but closer to the center of town, next to the newly refurbished Triangle Office Building. A prime location, actually, at the hub of downtown traffic with the name Winthrop Reality picked out in gold on the front window for every passerby to see. The stop light at the nearby corner didn't hurt either. It halted traffic long enough for people to glance over and peer at Saxby's Deal of the Week poster. An idea he stole—*stole*—from me.

This week's deal was a shotgun house, its pale green paint and white trim set off by a shocking pink door. Long on charm but short on indoor bathroom facilities, it was a do-it-yourselfer's dream.

After running a brush through my hair and checking my makeup—looking good being the cost of war in dealing with Saxby—I strolled into the enemy camp.

Secretary Mindy of the long white legs and long black hair smiled and put away her nail file. "How nice to see you again," she said. "I never did forget you." After fumbling in her top desk drawer for a bit, she held up my business card. "I kept it."

Six months earlier, when I recognized Mindy as my substitute in Saxby's life, a burst of sympathy caused me to scribble my home phone number on the back of the card and invite her to call me if she ever needed someone to turn to.

I pointed to the card. "I guess you didn't need me after all."

"There's been a few times I nearly did call you," she whispered, "but—"

She stopped short as Saxby's office door squeaked open. "Well, here you are, Miss Honey. Right on time. Just like a German train."

"Whatever," I said, irritated before I'd even heard what he had to say.

"Come in, come, in," he urged, waving me toward his private office.

"When do you go for lunch, Mindy?" I asked, turning back to her.

She checked her watch. "Oh, not for an hour yet."

"Good to know," I said before sauntering over to Saxby.

"Was that necessary?" he asked, as he closed his door and took a seat behind his desk.

"No. Just making a point." I sat on the client chair facing him.

"Never thought I'd ask this of a beautiful woman, but can't we be friends?"

I shook my head. "Impossible."

Lacing his fingers together over his belly, he blew out a long, resigned breath. "Very well, this'll be strictly business then."

"That's the way I like it."

"You're a hard woman, Honey Ingersoll, hard." He allowed himself a grin. "But then, so am I."

"Oh please." I half rose out of my seat.

Letting go of his belly, he raised his hands, palms showing. "All right, all right. Just creatin' a little levity is all. But I'll be serious." He paused, moisture suspiciously like tears springing into his eyes. "As you know, my momma, Miss Eloise, passed two months and five days ago."

"Yes, I was sorry to hear it, Saxby." My turn to pause. "Even though I never had the pleasure of her acquaintance."

In the two years he and I cohabited, he'd never taken me out to the family manse to meet his beloved momma. Nor had he ever told her he had a live-in girl friend, one she no doubt would've called trailer trash. And who happened to be twenty five years younger than he was. He had simply hidden me away like … dirty laundry or a bad habit.

All this history hovered in the air as he stared at me with his dark, but not smoldering, eyes.

"Yes, losing Momma was a blow. A life-changing blow, Honey. One that's caused me to come to a decision."

"Well that's mighty interesting." My impatience was beginning to rise as it usually did five minutes into a chat with Saxby. "Now if you could come to the point, I'd be mighty pleased too."

Hands back on his belly. "I'm leaving the real estate business. For good."

Now *that* was a shocker, and I sat up a little straighter.

"*Why*, Saxby?"

"To travel, to play golf, to be a … a …what the Frenchies call a *bon vivant*."

"Miss Eloise would surely be proud." I upped my chin at him. "She leave you a pot full of money?"

He sent me a sad, hang-dog glance then shook his head. "You disappoint me, Honey." Though it wasn't easy, he leaned over his desk. "You're forgettin' what I taught you."

No I hadn't. How could I? "Which is?"

"Unless you're discussin' business, you never inquire into a person's financial state."

"Too late. I've already inquired."

His laugh erased the lingering sorrow in his eyes. "The answer is yes, she did. So why should I squander my remain' time grubbing for filthy lucre?"

I stood and hoisted my tote to a shoulder. "You're wasting

my time. I *do* have to work for a living."

I'd half-turned on my heel when he hit me with it.

"I want you to take over Winthrop Realty."

Stunned, I whirled around. "You want me to *what*?"

"I want you to become the new owner." He spread his arms wide. "To assume legal control of this entire enterprise."

Well, that sure brought me back to my seat.

"You expect me to leave Sam?"

"You left *me*," he said reasonably enough.

"The *situation*, as you very well know, was different."

"Conceded," he said. "But tell me this, do you owe Sam a moral or a fiduciary obligation?"

About to say a person's always obliged when hired for a job of work and paid at a fair rate of exchange, but unwilling to give him a reason to argue, I just shook my head.

"Exactly what I thought. So here's my offer: I'll give you the company name, my entire client list, free rent of this office for one year and the services of Mindy—secretarial only, of course. My cut will be ten percent of net profits."

"Not enticing enough," I said, reaching for the tote.

"I'm not finished negotiatin'."

"Oh, no?" I glanced up. He had me intrigued, the sly dog.

"There's a certain mansion on the Bluffs ... it just came on the market ... you know the one."

He couldn't have heard about Barry's place so soon, could he? Not possible. "Which one?" I asked, wary.

"Barry McHale's."

My mouth fell open. I could feel it sag. "You already *know* it's up for sale? How did you find out? It hasn't been listed yet."

Holding his palms pressed together, he spread his fingers wide. "My tentacles reach everywhere."

That fact established, he leaned back in his chair and swiveled, just a man at his ease. "However, due to the murder of the unfortunate woman next door, the McHale property might not be easy to sell ... ." He examined his manicure. I could have told him his nails were too shiny, but I already had, five years ago. "So ..." the swiveling lurched to a stop ... "I'm here to present you with a perfect solution. In short, a buyer."

"*Who?*"

"Me. Saxby Hunter Winthrop the Third."

"*You?*"

"Of course. How many Saxby Hunter Winthrops are there?"

He leaned back, his grin as wide as if he were sitting in the cat bird seat. Which he was.

"There has to be a hitch."

"Naturally. And I'm prepared to tell you what it is. But first, you tell me what Sam appraised the property for? Three? Three and a half million?"

Though creepy as ever, Saxby hadn't lost his touch. "Three, five hundred and fifty."

"I thought that would be the ballpark figure. I'll pay three million, five hundred. You can forget the fifty grand wiggle room Sam tacked on. Assuming the contract McHale signed specifies three percent commission not six, Ridley's will make a hundred and five thousand on the deal. And out of that sum, the consummatin' agent"—I ignored his smirk—"you, Honey Ingersoll, will realize a standard fee of one and a half percent or a bit less than fifty-three thousand dollars.

"Now here comes the stipulation I mentioned: I buy, providin' you buy my business with the terms I already outlined. I'll put them in writin', of course."

"Why?" I asked, limp with shock and determined not to stir from my chair until I had a sensible answer.

"Why do I want the McHale place? Well, for openers, I'm selling my momma's house to a cousin from Tennessee."

"But—"

"I know, I know. It's been in the family since before The War, but I can't bear the thought of livin' out there without Momma present. The memories are like to kill me. The Bluff'll be a brand new start for my brand new life.

"Now if you mean why do I want you to buy the business ...

well ..." his cheeks with their network of fine, whisky red veins turned pink as a girl's ... "the fact is I love you, Honey. Always have. Always will. When we were together, I didn't treat you as I should have, and that knowledge has been gnawin' away at me. So this is a chance to make good by you.

"Furthermore"—he pounded his desk with a fist—"I want to retire, but I can't stand the idea of Sam Ridley bein' the only real estate hustler left in town."

His declaration finished, he reached into a lower desk drawer and—no surprise there—yanked out a bottle of bourbon.

"Shall we drink on it?"

Chapter Eight

Head spinning, and not from bourbon, I reeled out of Saxby's and sat in the Lincoln for a while, mulling over all his surprises.

It was hard to think of the realty game without him in it. The whole Eureka Falls playing field would be changed. And for me to take over his agency, especially under the terms he outlined, had my mind all blown away. Who could have guessed he'd be so generous?

I was tempted, no doubt about it. The notion of being my own boss, free to run my own business, and go as far as I could was exciting as all get out.

The biggest surprise of all, though, was ol' Sax thinking enough of me to suggest such an idea in the first place. I was only nineteen when he made his first offer ... the one that to this day still caused me to feel used and, well, *soiled*, somehow. Maybe that's always the way of sex without love. At least there hadn't been any love on my side. *Hmm.* Why was I gripping the wheel? I let my hands slide to my lap. Had he meant what he said? Had he loved me all along?

Nice to think so. But he loved a guy named Jack Daniels

more. Still did. What mattered now was how his current offer could change my future.

I put my hands back on the wheel and fired up the engine. I needed help, and there was just one place in town where I'd find it—the police station.

DEPUTY ELLIE AT the admittance desk waved me on without asking any questions. I was in and out of the station often enough for Ellie to know me. And to recognize that Sheriff Matt and I were, well, friends. What she probably didn't know was how I had longed for Sam Ridley day and night for three years. But he'd never really seen me, even though I was right there under his feet, so to speak.

I was over him at last, but the memory of that lost love tore at me. He'd given me a job and rescued me, in a sense, from Saxby. How could I even think of leaving Ridley's for any reason under the sun?

Heavy with guilt, I made my way down the hall and tapped on the door to Matt's plywood-enclosed office. Matt wasn't a shrink but the closest thing to it I knew of, so I'd run this all by him and let him put his psychology degree to work on me.

"Come in," he called, lighting up when he saw me. He set down his pen. "Here to sign your statements?"

I took the only other chair, the one opposite his desk. "Yes, and—"

"They're here somewhere, ready for your signature." After a short search of his messy desk, he plucked them from underneath a pile of papers and held them out. "I'm glad you came in. Detective Bradshaw's due here later today, and he'll be looking for them. Anything happening on the Bluffs brings out the big boys."

The Bluffs. Millionaires' Row. Carmen's murder would get VIP treatment. A good thing, but I knew Matt would say every victim got equal justice, and I hoped to heaven he was right.

I took the statements from him and laid them on the desk top.

He leaned over and tapped them. "I suggest you read those carefully before you sign."

"I will, but first can we talk about something?"

He sat back, ready to listen. "Sure. Shoot."

"I'm in trouble, Matt."

His eyes flared wide. "*Pregnant?*"

"Oh for Pete's sake, is that the only kind of trouble a girl can be in?"

He flushed a little and laughed to cover his slip-up. "You unveiled my thinking process, Honey. At least as far as you're concerned." He tilted his chair back on its rear legs. "So tell Matt the Macho. What's the problem?"

"Saxby Winthrop wants me to take over his business."

Matt whistled through his front teeth and dropped his chair onto all four legs. "That's a *problem*? Sounds great to me, depending on the terms, of course."

He listened without interrupting while I told him about Saxby's offer and, when I

finished, said, "So he's basically making you a gift of Winthrop Realty?"

"Pretty much. Can you believe it?"

"With difficulty."

"So?"

"What do you mean 'so'? There's no question about what you should do. Run, not walk, back to Saxby Winthrop the Third's office and tell him you accept his offer."

"You *knew* he was a third?"

"Don't change the subject." A finger aiming at my nose. "For the past year, I've been urging you to start your own business. Pleading with you, even. Begging at times. Because I know you can do it. In short, this is a golden opportunity." He folded his arms and stared across at me.

"Why did you cross your arms?" I said, staring back at him.

"This is a defensive posture. I'm prepared for your resistance."

"You want me to leave Sam, that it?"

With a sigh, he got off his chair to perch on the front of his desk, knees only inches from mine. "That's part of it." I went to speak, but he cut me off before I could get out a single word. "No, humor me here. You carried a torch for a long time, but the truth is Sam Ridley never let you light his fire. I know that hurts, but it's the truth, as you are certainly aware. The mystery is how he could have made such an error with you there, sitting in his office every day …" he shook his head "… but he did. Honey," bending close now, sincerity pouring out of his brown eyes, "doesn't that tell you something about Sam? Something you need to remember?"

"I remember everything, but I'm not in love with him any more. I'm a free woman if that's what all you're getting at."

"Good." His mouth lifted in a smile. "Then what's holding you back?"

"Call it a sense of loyalty."

He snorted. "Have you earned your money these past three years?"

"Yes, I surely have. Why my sales figures are—"

"Spare me. Point made. Fact is, a case could be made that *he* owes *you*. He's been well paid for taking you on. Now, if you're too scared to take the risk—"

My chin came up. "Of course I'm scared. Who wouldn't be?"

"Granted, but bottom line, do I make sense or not?"

Did he? I didn't reply.

"Well?"

He really wanted an answer, so I smiled sweetly and gave him one. "A long time ago someone told me a woman should always agree with a man. And then do what *she* thinks is right."

Chapter Nine

AFTER CAREFULLY READING my witness statements—the truth is I do tend to read on the slow side—I signed them. Then I thanked Matt for his thoughtful input and meandered on home where I spent a sleepless night trying to make sense out of the situation. By the cold light of dawn, I'd reached a decision: I needed to have two meetings today. I was pretty sure the first one would be interesting, but just thinking about the second one had my stomach in a bind.

Before I could roll out my plan, though, a girl with a topknot of wild curls and a green mini sat waiting for me at the office.

"Penelope, what a surprise." I raised my Dunkin' Donuts medium dark roast. "Had I known, I'd have brought one for you."

She wrinkled her little ski-jump nose. "Just as well. The calories."

"You're pretty safe with a black medium dark roast," I said, sliding onto the swivel chair behind my desk.

"Can you guess why I'm here," she asked.

"I can guess, but …"

"My house. The divorce has been finalized. The other day ... in the pool ..." she actually blushed "... I was celebrating my freedom. You don't know what it's like to be tied to somebody you despise."

Oh yes I did. Why we'd both let such a thing happen to us was really the question. But it wasn't a subject a girl should chat up in a realty office, so I just murmured something soothing and sweet-sounding.

"When I was partying in the pool," she went on, her chin wobbling a little, "I never dreamed Carmen would be dead in a few hours."

"How could you?"

"True. Murder's not a thought that flashes through your mind, not even about someone like Carmen. She might have irritated a lot of people, but enough to kill her? I don't think so."

Hmm. Carmen *had* irritated me when we first met, then her welcome had been so warm, I couldn't help but like her.

A wistful, Orphan Annie expression flitted across Penelope's face. "Carmen had it all. Beauty, brains and money. Lots of money." She blew out a breath. "Wish I could say the same ... about money, I mean. Money's always been my problem. Still is. It's why I have to sell the house, but at least there's only a tiny mortgage left. And it's a beautiful piece of property. Everyone says so."

"I'd love to see it."

"Wonderful. I'm free now, if you are."

For a new client? "Of course I am." The meetings I'd planned would have to wait.

"Let's go then." She glanced up at me as she reached for the bag by her chair. "There's something you should know, though. I'm interviewing another realtor before I decide on one. A second opinion, if you know what I mean?"

"A good idea." I slung my own bag over a shoulder. "From a Mr. Saxby Winthrop, by any chance?"

Her eyes, a shade of green that was perfect with her hair,

rounded into two green O's. "Yes. How did you know?"

"A lucky guess." And the only other realtor in Eureka Falls—for now.

ABOUT TEN MILES west of town, Penelope's house was a typical Arkansas farmhouse—on some kind of growth hormone. Up front, it had the wide verandah that called for rocking chairs and a lazy dog or two. Inside, a central hall divided the space into four square rooms downstairs and four bedrooms up.

In the to-die-for kitchen, with its honed granite countertops, state of the art appliances and red brick floor, I said, "This is wonderful."

"It's George all over," Penelope said. "He's my ex. I wouldn't do up a place like this." She pointed to the bricks. "The floor, for instance, I hate it."

"Really?" I said, squeaky voiced. "That's a shame, but you should have no trouble selling. Providing the price is right, of course."

"Let's make it as high as the market will bear." She sank onto a stool by the island. "I need to wring every dime out of this place. Truth is, Honey ..." glancing down to check her manicure "... the house and the Porsche Boxter are all I have. All I could squeeze out of the old skin flint I made the monumental mistake of marrying."

"That's too—"

She held out a finger tipped with chipped red polish. "Even my manicures are getting too expensive. I may have to start doing them myself." She grabbed my hand. "Never, never marry a guy without checking into his finances. George is loaded, but guess what? Everything's tied up in family trusts. I couldn't get my hands on a dime of it. Can you believe that? So stupid of me."

"No pre-nuptial agreement?" A fancy term, in my view, for settling on the money before settling on the sex.

"Sure. We shared everything fifty-fifty. But a pre-nup can't break trusts. I should have had a lawyer with me the day I signed." She heaved a sigh that lifted her bosom like it was a ship on the tide. "Too late now. If it keeps on like this, I'll have to go to work, and my momma … she was Miss Arkansas back in the day … well she didn't raise me to work for a living. Oh." Her hand flew to her mouth. "No offense."

"None taken." Actually, not quite true. But my momma had raised me to watch my manners, which at the moment was about the only reason why I didn't tell Penelope to take her house and stuff it.

She tapped a foot on the brick floor. "So what do you think, pricewise?"

I hesitated. Location, square footage and what other properties in the area had sold for in the past six months or so were really what mattered, not personal feelings. But no way could I say such a thing to a seller who had a lifetime of memories stored up in her home. Or who, like Penelope, just wanted to squeeze every dollar from every floorboard.

"Well?" The foot still tapping.

"I have an idea of what the place will fetch, but to fine tune a price, I need to check Multiple Listings."

"Oh come on, Honey. You must have some idea. Give me your best guess."

I shrugged. "All right. Off the top, I suggest you ask six hundred thousand and expect to get five-fifty or a little less."

Her face fell. "That's *it*? But look at what Barry McHale is asking. And what do you think Carmen's place will go for now she's …"

"Dead?"

"Yes."

"Well, whatever Barry's house sells for will set the bar for other houses on the Bluffs."

"See!" Penelope hopped off the stool to pace around the kitchen, her stiletto heels striking the bricks like pistol shots. "That's what I mean. You're talking millions not a petty six figures." She stopped pacing to stab the air between us with a forefinger. "There was a lot more to Carmen than breast implants and a perpetual tan. Every business deal she ever made turned to gold. Even dead, she still has the touch. It isn't fair, Honey. It isn't fair."

I could have told her she was comparing apples to oranges. But after all that had gone down in the last few days, I was too plumb tired to argue. "See what Winthrop Realty has to say. As you mentioned, a second opinion can't hurt."

She rushed across the kitchen to hug me. "Thanks for understanding. I'm a woman alone in the world and ..." she giggled "... well, not quite. I do have Jesse Raidel."

"The photographer?"

"Yup." She nodded, sending her topknot into a frenzy. "He says his pictures will make a supermodel out of me."

"That would be nice," I said evenly.

"Wouldn't it just?" She shrugged. "Why else would I bother with him? He doesn't have a dime to his name." She squared her shoulders. "I'm not telling him, but as soon as the house is sold, I'm out of Arkansas for good."

"Where will you go?"

She looked at me as if I had flunked kindergarten. "The only place on earth for a girl like me. The Big Apple, even though Carmen thought that was a lousy idea. But what did she know? Look at her now."

Chapter Ten

Though chilled to the toes by Penelope's way of thinking, I gave her my word that if Ridley's handled the sale, we'd do our best to make her happy. As a realtor I meant it, but as a woman I wanted to stomp on her topknot. But like she'd reminded me, I was a working girl. So I smiled (not easy) and gave her one of our sales portfolios. It held photographs of houses we'd sold in the area along with asking and closing figures, tips on how to groom a property for the market and a copy of a boiler-plate contract.

"All this reading," she said, flipping through the pages.

"It's mostly numbers and pictures. And speaking of pictures, my boss, Sam Ridley will personally photograph a virtual tour for the internet. As a sales tool it—"

"Oh, I couldn't allow anyone but Jesse to shoot the interior. He'd be so insulted there'd be no dealing with him."

"Well, that's one solution," I said, smiling to soften my words.

She glanced at me, uncertain of my meaning but nodded anyway. We hugged and air kissed as women who hardly know each other tend to do, though for the life of me, I've never figured out why. Then I drove off not caring for once if I would be asked to handle the sale or not. Penelope expected the moon but … I huffed out a breath that fogged up the windshield … she wasn't the first client who thought her property was worth more than the market could bear. So why was I so irked? Probably the working girl crack, but Lord Almighty, that's what I was.

As I drove, the green hills surrounding the road put on their magic act, soothing away my problems with their beauty. I opened the windows to feel the breeze on my skin and sniff the sweet summer air. After a few miles, I relaxed, and my grip on the wheel eased. It was so calm out here, so quiet, like driving through Eden—except for a black panel truck going the opposite way, its blaring radio loud enough to send birds cawing into the sky.

I peered through the rearview mirror. The truck had disappeared around a bend. Once again, I had the world to myself and all was peaceful. Yet only a few miles away, Carmen had been brutally murdered. I shuddered at the memory of her finger writing a message in her own blood. How—

Super loud rap music shattered the air. I glanced in the rearview mirror. A black panel truck … the same one? … had raced up behind me and was tailgating like mad.

I pressed on the gas then checked the speedometer. *Sixty.* The limit and, on this two-lane windy road, too fast for comfort. Just a few feet behind me now, the truck driver leaned on his horn. *Beep, beep. Beep, beep.*

"Slow down, you fool," I yelled into the wind. A waste of time. He'd never hear me over the din blasting out of his stereo. Fuming, I closed the window and, hands sweating, edged up to sixty-five. Not enough. The horn honked, and in the mirror, a hairy arm waved toward the right.

"Pull over," he hollered. "Pull over!"

That'll be the day. A killer on the loose, and some yahoo wanted me to stop on a lonely road? What kind of fool did he take me for? Revving the Lincoln for all she was worth, I swerved like a crazy woman around one mountain curve after another. Gone was my joy in the birds and the trees and the eternal green beauty. I was so scared, I couldn't think of anything except staying on the road and not flying off into a gully. Or wetting my pants.

Seventy. Seventy-five. Eighty. Way over the limit. Where were the cops when you needed them?

Like some kind of sleek jungle beast, the Lincoln chewed up the miles. At eighty-five I hit a steep curve, slammed on the brakes and screeched around a downward slope to hell. Cursing, sweating, I glanced out the side mirror. Still there. Who was this creep? I didn't dare take a hand off the wheel to grab my cell and call for help. I didn't dare do anything but stare straight ahead and make promises to God.

Somehow, somewhere, in a tiny pocket of my brain, I recalled seeing a country store along this stretch with a hand-lettered sign next to the road. *Bread. Milk. Beer.* The big three. Eyes frantic, sweeping both sides of the road, not wanting to zoom past the store, I inched down to eighty. Then seventy-five. Seventy. The truck was still on me. I could just make out a guy's shadowy figure through his tinted windshield. Sixty-five.

Up ahead, a sandy patch to the left swept out to the road. That could be the store's parking lot, but I couldn't see the sign. And I couldn't keep up this race with death either. Hands shaking, whole body trembling … *Now!*

I pulled onto the rutted lot of Crissy's Country Store and hit the brakes. A shower of pebbles bounced off the car and then more as the black truck, screeching to a halt, pulled up alongside me.

Worn to a nub, ready to weep, I leaned into the backrest, my pulse drumming in my ears, and stared out the side window at the panel truck's big white letters: Jesse Raidel Creative Photography.

I yanked open my door and stormed out of the car.

"What's the matter with you?" I yelled as Jesse hopped out of his truck. "Are you insane?"

"What?" He stepped back a pace, confusion written all over his face.

"Why in hell did you chase me like that?" I pointed a wobbly finger at the road. "We could've died out there. All those hairpin turns."

"No." A big shake of his red pony tail. "There's not a hairpin on that whole stretch. You didn't slow down, so I thought you were enjoying the ride. You know, pitting yourself against the laws of physics." Legs apart, shorts again—didn't the man own a pair of pants?—he shoved his hands in his pockets. "Sorry." His grin said he wasn't. "Didn't it get your heart pumping, your blood racing—"

Blood. "Only two days ago, I found Carmen murdered. Now I'm supposed to stop on a deserted road to chat it up with a total stranger?"

"We're not strangers. We met the other day. Jesse Raidel, remember?"

"You jerk. How was I supposed to know what you drive? And even if I did, I don't know you. We only met once."

"Yeah, I should have remembered you were scared that day too."

"Of *what*? You?" Shouting now.

"Nah, of stripping. Too bad. With the right lighting and makeup you could be a supermodel."

"Oh really?" Hands on hips like a crabby ol' grandma, I scoffed. "A supermodel?"

"Yeah, you've got what it takes. That long, curvy bod. Sweet blond hair and those cheek bones. The camera will eat 'em up. Has anyone ever—"

I showed him a palm. "Enough."

"I mean it. You could be on the cover of *Vogue*."

"Along with Penelope?"

"Why not? I can multitask."

"So can I. That's why I'm flipping you the bird when I drive off." I stomped toward the car, then thought better of it and whirled around to face him. "I'm punching 911 into my cell which I'm keeping on my lap. Follow me and I'll hit send."

His lips twisted, not a pretty sight.

"No need to get your knickers in a twist, Ma'am. I'm not plannin' on followin' you a-tall." He eyeballed the sign. "I'm just fixin' to get me some milk and bread from this here Crissy."

"Oh? Getting all country on me, are you? Well, just so's you'll know, I grew up on a dirt road, so I don't pay no never mind to such mouthy carryin's on."

"Well, I'll be hornswoggled."

"That's a great line. Stick to it." This time I did stomp off.

Chapter Eleven

BEING RED HOT mad had given me an appetite so fierce I could eat two cows. The nerve of Jesse scaring me like that. Putting us both in danger. Anyway, before seeing Saxby, who was on my original master plan for the day, I swung by Josie's Diner for a burger and fries.

In her usual brown and orange uniform with a crocheted hanky peeking out of the breast pocket, Josie greeted me with a big smile and a cup of scalding coffee. Black. No sugar or cream. Just the way I liked it.

"Haven't seen you all week," she said. "But I've been reading about you." She leaned over the counter to whisper. "Was there a lot of blood?"

"Lots, but do you mind if we don't talk about blood right now, I was thinking of having a burger."

"Oh sure." She straightened, looking a little hurt, and yelled my order to Tommy Lee at the grill.

I reached for her hand. "I'll tell you everything as soon as the sheriff says it's okay."

"Oh, I get it. You can't talk about it, huh?"

"No. Not while the case is ongoing."

She looked right, then left, then back at me. "My lips are sealed."

"Good. Mine too."

Tommy Lee must have put the burger on the minute I walked in, for Josie served it up pronto. I'd about finished eating and was digging in my purse for lipgloss when someone ran a finger along my spine.

Startled, I looked over a shoulder into a pair of dark, bloodshot eyes.

"Saxby, of all people. I was just on my way to see you."

"And here I am. Anticipatin' your every move." He patted his briefcase. "Come join me for lunch. I've got something here to show you."

"I've eaten, but I'll sit for a while."

We took the last booth in the corner. "Just like old times," Saxby said, settling in on his side of the table.

"Not quite."

"Sadly so."

When I didn't say anything, he picked up a menu, though I doubted he needed to. The diner's food never changed, and we both knew the choices by heart. After hardly giving the menu a glance, he said, "A western omelet" to Josie who never wasted time getting to a booth. "And a black coffee. For you, Honey?"

I shook my head. "I'm fine."

When Josie walked away, he said, "Though I'd like nothin' better than to linger, I'll get right to the point."

"Excellent."

"That's what I supposed would be pleasin' to you." He sighed. "I know you mighty well, Honey …" a quick glance to see if I caught his double meaning "… so I went ahead and had a document prepared for your perusal." He unsnapped his briefcase and handed me some legal looking papers. Set down in writing was everything he'd offered the day before.

"You're serious then?" I asked, resting the papers on the table between us.

"Course. You're not plannin' on turnin' me down are you?"

"Your offer's very generous, Saxby, and I'm thinking seriously about it. But first I need to speak with Sam." I pointed to the agreement, "and have a lawyer take a look at this."

"You should. That's the smart thing to do. Now here's my *caveat*. Sam gives you half the sales commission on the sale of the McHale house or the deal's off."

"But suppose—"

Josie plunked his lunch down in front of him. "No buts about it. You'll need that commission as seed money." He cut into his omelet. "I'm not settin' you up in a business my granddaddy started to have you fail."

"I see." And I did. That possibility existed, of course, and was one of the reasons I hardly slept last night. That and what Sam's reaction would be when I told him the news.

"Should Mr. Ridley protest, you can tell him I'm choosin' to pay him fair market value despite the ghastly murder of his next door neighbor." He eyed me over the rim of his coffee cup. "A circumstance not every buyer is apt to overlook. A fact I'm sure he's aware of, bein' an astute businessman and all."

He took a hefty swig of his coffee. Not that he had much choice, Josie didn't serve anything stronger.

Chapter Twelve

LOAFERS ON HIS desktop, sleeves rolled to his elbows. Sam was on the phone when I got back to the office. I guess he couldn't see my heart thumping in my chest, for he waved me in with a smile, said goodbye and hung up. "The hospital just called. Dad's being discharged in the morning. Going to a rehab for a while, then home."

"Oh that's mighty good news."

"Yeah. A big relief." He lowered his feet and sat upright. "Now that dad's out of the woods, I can concentrate on business. Snagging this McHale property is a fantastic boon for Ridley's. Even at three percent, the commission will make up for a few months of shaky numbers. As your contract specifies, for anything over a million, you earn one half of one percent." He picked up his iPad and made some quick calculations. "That adds up to over five thousand for you. Not bad for a few hours work."

I needed to sit down and kind of fell onto the chair across from his desk.

There hadn't yet been time to get to a lawyer and check out Saxby's offer, so I could have—should have—kept quiet about it, but I didn't. Couldn't, for some reason. This had been eating at me for a whole day and was clawing to get out into the open. Besides, my daddy was a gambling man, taking chances ran in the blood. Anyway, I gulped and blurted, "Saxby Winthrop's made me an offer."

He nodded, slowly, as if digesting the info. "Saxby? What kind of offer?"

I got it out fast before my throat dried up. "He wants me to take over his agency."

"Wow. That's a good one. You turned him down, right?

"Not quite."

I watched Sam's every move. Not that there were very many. A frown, a tossed pen, a heavy sigh, then eyeball contact and, "Why not?"

"He's gifting the agency to me, Sam."

"Well," he leaned back in his swivel and set it in motion, "I guess you've earned it."

"Whatever do you mean?" Although I knew. *I knew.*

He didn't answer me but stared straight ahead at an imaginary spot on the wall. My spine stiffened. "There is one condition though."

"There always is." Sarcastic now.

I suppose I should have been happy Sam didn't want to lose me, but his attitude was so cold, so lacking in good will, everything I had once felt for him shriveled. "I get the agency if I get fifty percent of your commission on the McHale property. Otherwise the deal's off."

"Ha! Why the ol' coyote, what a gold-plated nerve. Telling me what commissions I should or shouldn't pay. Why—"

"There's more, Sam."

"Well, don't hold back, girl, let it all out. Let it all out."

Girl. Is that all I was to him? All I had ever been? Just a replaceable girl? "Saxby is prepared to buy the McHale house from you at the asking price only if his condition is met."

Sam leaped out of his chair and went over to slam his office door shut. A little late, I thought. Mrs. Otis and anyone else in the outer office had probably heard our every word.

"*He* wants to buy it? Egads why? He has the family homestead now."

I shook my head. "Too many memories. He wants to live on the Bluffs."

Sam stopped pacing long enough to look down at me, a frown creasing his brow. "I don't get it. You know how much money's involved here? At one and a half percent, your cut would be about fifty thousand dollars."

"Closer to fifty-two."

I had told myself I was over Sam, and I was, but after loving him so hopelessly for so long, little tendrils of feeling, like habits that refused to die, kept popping up and curling around my heart. In that moment, if he had said the money wasn't important, he didn't want me to leave, couldn't live without me, I would have caved, fallen into his arms and let my former love for him overwhelm me once more. But he did none of those things.

And I didn't cave.

I stood.

"Earlier today, Sam, someone told me I'm a working girl. And since I truly am, maybe it's better if I work for myself than for someone … else. It's what *you* do, Sam, and it's a good feeling, isn't it?"

Without waiting for an answer, I left and, lower than a snake's hips, strode into my cubicle and typed out a resignation.

Chapter Thirteen

A S MY GRANDDADDY, a religious-minded man, used to say, "Sufficient unto the day is the evil thereof." And I sure had had more than enough stress—if not downright evil—for one day.

Not feeling up to telling Mrs. Otis my news just then, I escaped out the front entrance with a goodbye wave and beat a coward's retreat around the building to our rear parking lot. I didn't want to tromp across the whole office to get to the back door. My heels clicking across the hardwood floor might have brought Sam out of his office to recharge our conversation. I'd had enough for the day. Enough. I wanted to go home to my apartment, kick off the heels, and flop on the couch with a beer.

Well, the best laid plans … a Eureka Falls PD cruiser sat parked beside my Lincoln, a familiar dark-haired officer behind the wheel. He wasn't alone. As I walked over to my car, both Matt and Deputy Zach exited the cruiser.

"We were just coming in," Matt said, the look on his face one I hadn't seen there before. Whatever the reason for it, I knew it wouldn't be good.

"We have an order to impound your car," he said.

My handbag nearly slipped off my shoulder to the ground. "*Why?*"

"In reading your witness statement, Detective Bradshaw realized your car had been parked at the McHale property the day before Mrs. Carmen DeLuca was killed."

"Yes, of course, it was. For several hours. I was supposed to meet Mr. McHale at his house, but he was delayed. I don't see what … . oh … . Carmen's note. The one she wrote in blood." *Under car.*

"Correct. The state forensics lab wants to go over your vehicle just to be sure nothing's hidden in it like drugs, contraband or a—" He stopped short.

I could feel the blood drain from my face. "Bomb?"

He nodded.

"There couldn't be. My God, Matt, I just got off a high speed race. Some yahoo chased me along route sixty-eight for miles. Nothing exploded."

As my knees suddenly went all wobbly, I leaned against the Linc. Maybe that was why Jesse had chased me so hard, to force an explosion. Make it look like an accident. But on second thought, no, that kind of stuff only happened in movies.

"I doubt we'll find anything," Matt was saying, "but we have to make sure."

"It's been two days since the murder. Aren't y'all a little late with this impounding thing?"

"Yes." His jaw clenched. "We are. But better late than never."

"What if they find drugs or something? Will I be blamed?"

"Of course not." He took my arm. "Come sit in the cruiser. You look faint." He helped me slide into the back seat and leaned in the open door. "I'll drive you home. If you give Zach the keys, he'll have your car towed to the lab."

"Are they going to rip it apart? I need those wheels for work."

"They won't harm it. Whatever is dismantled will be replaced."

"Terrific. How long?"

"As long as it takes." He straightened. "Now if you'll stay put for a few minutes, I'll go in and explain the situation to Sam." He winked. "Don't want you to get in trouble with your soon-to-be former boss."

Ha! For the first time since I'd known him, Matt had lied to me. Twice. Lie number one: he damned well knew if drugs were found I could be incriminated. And lie number two: he'd love it if my rift with Sam was wide enough to drive his cruiser through.

Chapter Fourteen

O N THE DRIVE back to my apartment, Matt kept telling me all would be well, but I put his words down to happy talk. He didn't want me to worry, but how could I not? After the drag race with Jesse, I doubted they'd find a bomb or I wouldn't be here now. But drugs maybe. Yeah, Lord Almighty, maybe crank or pot. And then what? Deep trouble. That wouldn't be the end of the fix I was in, either. I was out of a job, at least until I signed Saxby's contract.

At dawn, not able to lay there stewing any longer, I threw back the covers and climbed out of bed. I'd get dressed, call a taxicab and see a lawyer fast before Sax changed his mind. My rent was due next week.

WITH THE CONTRACT in a slick-looking fake leather binder, I climbed the wooden stairs to the office of Andarius Ballou, Esq. Something told me not to go to Daren Tully, the attorney Ridley's usually used for closings and such. Maybe I was being silly, but I wanted a lawyer who didn't know me and would be … what was the word? I disremember, but, anyway, I figured a person with a name like Andarius came from a high-toned background. I mean, who would name a helpless baby something like that unless they had a successful granddaddy they were honoring? So in my red high-heeled pumps and navy suit, the one Carmen scoffed at and the one I always felt safe in, I pushed open the door to his law office and stepped inside.

The outer room with its reception desk stood as empty as a poor man's kitchen, but the inner office door was open a crack and someone with a deep voice was talking on the telephone. Well, either he was on the phone or plum crazy, for no one else in there was saying a word. I tried not to eavesdrop, but listening in on the conversation didn't do me much good anyway. It was all regulations and statutes and the rule of law. Finally, when I was about to cough or something, he hung up, and I knocked on the partly open door.

"Come in," he shouted, loud as if calling me home to supper or something.

I pushed open the door and stood there, taking him all in, the man who in a few minutes would hold my future in his hands.

Though he sat behind his desk, I could tell he was tall, rangy like, with long arms and a long square jaw and untidy brown hair dipping over his forehead.

He looked up from whatever he'd been writing, blinked and jumped to his feet. He was tall all right, and I judged his age to be about thirty-five or so.

"Well, my, my," he said, smiling in a big white way. "How may I help you?"

Just like that. His exact words. So elegant and what you'd expect from a man who answered to Andarius.

I stepped forward and held out the portfolio. "Mr. Ballou?"

"Andy."

"Yes ... well ..." He kept on smiling for some reason. "I have a contract here I'd like for you to examine."

"Happy to. Do have a seat, Miss ..."

"Oh, sorry. Honey Ingersoll. You can call me Honey.

Everybody does."

"Is it your given name?" he asked, a little disbelieving.

"Yes, sir. When I was born, my daddy said I was a honey of a baby and the name kind of stuck."

"Your father was an astute man."

While that's not a word I ever would have used for Daddy, I didn't fuss about it, but took a seat and gave Andy the portfolio.

As he read the document, I read the framed diplomas on the wall behind his desk. He graduated from U of A then went on to Vanderbilt for his law degree. I nearly asked him what *Summa Cum Laude* meant, but I didn't want him to know how poor my formal schooling had been. I put the words to memory instead, so I could look them up later.

His hands holding Saxby's offer had long tapering fingers. On his right hand, he wore what looked mighty like a school ring; his left hand had no rings on it at all. Not a single one.

As I sat staring at his hands, thinking all kinds of things I couldn't quite put voice to, he lowered the contract and looked up. "Miss Ingersoll, Honey, this document is evidence of the most remarkable business transaction I ever had the pleasure of examining."

"Then you like it?"

"Like it? It's unbelievable. A wily old coot like Saxby Winthrop practically giving away the store ... why—"

Words failing him—I had the feeling they didn't very often—he threw his beautiful, long hands in the air.

"You think I should accept?"

Tenting his fingers, he peered across at me with eyes that held questions.

"On the basis of this document alone, I would give you an unqualified yes. But in any other regard, I can't advise you."

"What all does that mean? Exactly?"

"Simply put, it means I don't know enough about you to offer personal advice. I only know you're with Ridley's Real Estate. And according to the *Star*, you found the unfortunate woman who was murdered up on the Bluffs. But that's all. So

I can only assume ol' Sax has a solid reason for his generosity. One completely hidden to me."

He paused, those eyes staring straight into mine. I guess it was my turn to say something, but how much did I want to say? Did I tell this fine, tall man the story of my life or not? I did a mental shrug. Why not? After all, a lawyer was used to hearing secrets. Still I hesitated. I would hate to see a film of disappointment cloud his eyes when he learned the truth about me. On the other hand, my life with Saxby couldn't rightly be called a secret around town. So I lifted my chin and plunged in, right up to my hips.

"First of all, I'd love to run my own business. And second, Mr. Winthrop and I once lived together for two years. This ...." I pointed to the contract ... "is his way of .... uh ... repaying me for services rendered."

"I see." His tented hands dropped to the desk top. "In that case, Miss Ingersoll," no Honey this time, "I suggest you sign this document with all due haste. It's a *bona fide*, blue ribbon offer."

"Just what I hoped you'd say." I reached into my purse for the checkbook. "Now please tell me what I owe you."

"It's been my pleasure, Honey. You owe me nothing."

"In that, sir, I'm afraid you're mistaken. "Is a hundred dollars enough?"

The smile back, he shook his head. No."

"No? Two then?"

"No."

"But—"

"Instead I would consider the pleasure of your company over dinner this evening more than sufficient payment."

I snapped my checkbook closed. "Mr. Ballou, as you surely understand, I'm no virgin. But I'm not for sale either."

"You have the wrong idea, Miss Ingersoll."

"No, Andy." I grabbed my purse and plucked the contract off his desk. "You do."

Chapter Fifteen

DRAT THE STILETTOS, anyway. That's what I got for being so all-fired vain. Had to show off my legs, didn't I? Well, let this be a lesson to you, Honey Ingersoll. When you don't have wheels, you don't wear heels. Never again would I be so …

Toot, toot. Toot, toot.

"Hey, good looking."

Some country boy wanting to be heard. I'd pay him no mind. Andy or Andarius or whatever he called himself had used up all my good will for the day. I didn't need no flirting … any flirting … just a pair of flat-heeled shoes.

Toot, toot.

"You still holding a grudge. Still mad at me or something?"

Now *that* caught my attention. I glanced out to the road. *Oh, no.* Jesse Raidel in the flesh, cruising along behind me in his big ol' van. I flung my hair over my back and kept on strutting along. Or *tried* to strut. Not easy with my feet kicking up a storm.

"Honey, those shoes look like killers. Let me give you a lift."

Not a word escaped my lips.

"Where's your car? In Herbie's garage?"

As he crawled along the edge of the road, I ignored him. Problem was, I ignored where I was stepping too and, before you knew it, my heel caught in a break in the sidewalk and down I went. *Boom.* Right on my tush in the middle of town.

Brakes squealed and, faster than a lightning strike, Jesse ran around the front of his van, helping me up and dusting off my tote bag like it was some kind of precious object.

"No arguing now," he said, handing me the bag and hustling me toward the van.

While I hadn't gotten over my vexation, truth be told, I was only too glad to get a ride and sank onto the passenger seat with a sigh of relief.

"Where you headed?" he asked.

"Ridley's."

He got in behind the wheel and pointed at my shoes. "Kick off those killers if you want to."

I surely did want to, but had no intention of riding around with Mr. Raidel in any condition except fully clothed. And five miles under the speed limit.

"No racing," I warned.

He grinned like I'd said something funny. "Absolutely not. How about five under all the way."

"That would be just about perfect, Mr. Raidel."

"Jesse."

When I didn't answer him, a silence fell, one of those long, quiet times that make a body uneasy.

After we'd driven halfway down Main Street and gone through two or three lights and a couple of busy intersections, he said, "You know, life is too full of sorrow to go out looking for it. Take what happened to Carmen. But for the grace of God, her bloody corpse could have been me or you, or who knows, even Penelope."

"The grace of God?" I glanced across the seat. "You on an inside track with the Almighty?"

"No. You?"

I shook my head. "Hardly think so after all that's gone

down in my life. But I hear tell He's forgiving."

"Aha! Gotcha!" He eyeballed me across the seat with one of those lip-splitting grins there was no ignoring.

"All right. You win. Point made fair and square." I held out a hand. "You're forgiven, and I thank you kindly for the ride. This one. Not yesterday's."

"No problem. One woman's gone out of my life. I'd sure hate to lose another."

"Whoa, back up, Jesse. I'm not in your life."

"Yeah, you are. Fate's thrown us together. Fate and my work. How do you think I ever got close to a knockout like Carmen?"

He took his attention off the road to stare across at me.

"Your picture taking?"

"Exactly. We were kind of getting into something … you know … like a relationship, and …"

"The road, Jesse, the road."

"Not to worry. I'm on it … at first everything was great between us. I'm not suggesting anything heavy here like the M word. We were just cozying up to each other, but then she changed. Didn't want to party so much, didn't want to pose. One time I was there, the McHale guy called."

"Red light!"

He stomped on the brake. "So after his call, she hangs up acting real low. I remember asking her why. 'Nothing to do with you,' she said. 'It's Barry, is all.' You ask me …" taking a corner on two wheels "… I think she had something on him."

"You should tell this to the police, not to me."

"They got most of it, except for my hunch about McHale. Because it's only a hunch, no more. Remember those old TV reruns? 'Just the facts, Ma'am. Just the facts.' That's what the cops want—facts. And when it comes to McHale, I haven't got any." He shrugged and swerved around a pedestrian. "Look at him! He gave me the finger."

"You scared him is why."

"Yeah, well, as I was saying, I think Carmen had something serious on the guy, something to do with money. And judging from a few hints she dropped, she wasn't as well off as people thought. You know something else? I don't think the phony next door to her is either. You ask me, he's all hat and no cattle."

Nobody *had* asked him, which I didn't bother to mention. Jesse was so full of himself, he wouldn't have listened anyway. Besides, I was trying to make sense out of what he'd just blabbed. Was it possible Carmen could have had money problems? It wasn't what Penelope believed. But then, what did Penelope know about Carmen's business doings?

And what did Jesse know? True, if he and Carmen were as close as he claimed, he might have heard something. Or seen something—like a document. Just a hunch he said. *Hmm.* I had a feeling Sheriff Matt had a fondness for hunches like that.

Chapter Sixteen

DOING A FIRST-RATE imitation of a NASCAR driver, Jesse
screeched to a halt in front of Ridley's office. How he
managed to do so five miles under the speed limit, I didn't
know. Didn't care. I waved good-bye, shaking my head at his
offer to make me a supermodel, and hobbled inside, right past
Mrs. Otis who was busy on the phone, and straight on to my
cubicle.

I had to get off those open-toed ankle snappers—not that
those little bitty openings had helped my poor feet any. Too
bad. The pumps did perk up the navy suit nicely, even if they
were sassy, go-to-hell shoes not fit for a serious-minded real
estate lady. But I'll say this much for them, they were the best
sitting down shoes I ever did own.

Anyway, I'd given Sam two weeks' notice, so I had time
to reschedule a condo showing for later in the week. As for
my fresh leads, I'd send them to Sam and clean up some desk
work. Even more important, I needed to sit down with Mrs.
Otis and tell her my news. I was about to do so when a familiar
form blocked the cubicle doorway. I tossed down my pen.

"Matt, just the man I want to see."

"That's music to my ears, Honey," he said, setting the keys to the Lincoln on my desk. "Your car's in the back lot. No problems. It's clean as a whistle."

"Did you really think there was a bomb on it? Or drugs or something?"

The big smile he'd walked in with disappeared. "Didn't know and didn't want to take a chance. The victim's last words, spelled out in blood that way, weren't anything to be ignored."

Under car. "I wonder what she meant? What she was trying to say?"

"When we find out … *if* we find out … we'll likely find the killer. In the meantime be careful." He half turned to go. "Gotta run. Zach's outside waiting for me."

"Can Zach wait up a bit? There's something I need to tell you. Something Jesse Raidel said about Carmen." I pointed to the open doorway.

He closed the door and turned back to me. "Shoot."

"Jesse thinks Carmen had financial troubles. Maybe she wasn't as well off as everybody supposed." I leaned across the desk. "Barry McHale might have the same problem. Jesse called him a phony."

"All this is based on?"

"Hints Carmen dropped. Barry used to call when Jesse was with her. After they hung up, she got kind of sad and moody like."

"And?" An eyebrow arching into a question.

"And that's it."

Matt laughed. Out loud. "Did it occur to Jesse or to you that a lover's quarrel may have caused her mood change?"

"Don't you go pooh-poohing my information, Matt Rameros. Jesse knew Carmen very well. Why the day before she died, he was photographing the Velveteen Vixens at her special request and—"

"The *what*?"

After I told Matt the Velveteen Vixens was a pilot show Jesse had shot for TV, he assured me Carmen's financial status was being examined by the state police. And despite his laugh, he had a serious interest in my information and appreciated my concern. At any rate, that's about what I understood him to say. Every once in a while, Matt went professional crime buster on me and hauled out words he learned when he got that psychology degree of his.

While it was downright interesting that Carmen's affairs were being investigated, I hoped the police would take a look at Barry's affairs too. Not to be crass about the situation or anything, but selling a house owned free and clear or even with a bank mortgage was one thing. But a house with liens against it, or multiple legal claims raised a whole raft of problems. And if Barry did have financial troubles, that might well be the case. Then selling his Bluffs house would be no simple matter—not even to a ready buyer like Saxby.

Though the cubicle was cool, beads of sweat trickled down my spine. Fear, pure and simple, gripped me tight and, from the pounding of my heart, had no intention of easing up. Now what? Ambition and greed, yes greed, had caused me to quit a good, solid job for a chance at the brass ring. I'd been hasty and, and ... *stupid*. I wiped my moist palms on my skirt. I'd trusted Saxby, a man who had always been untrustworthy. Except ... I jumped to my feet and regretted it ... except when it came to business. In business dealings, he had always been straight as an arrow and clever, very clever. As he'd told me more than once, he had his family's honor to uphold. No, Saxby was too much a wily ol' fox to offer a fortune for a house without a clear title. And I had a good idea who could ease my mind of any doubt by leading me to the truth of the matter.

I fumbled under the desk for my shoes, dropped them in the tote and picked up my keys. I'd pad barefoot out to the Lincoln and go home for some comfortable flats. But I didn't get far just then.

A teenaged boy, something a real estate office seldom saw, knocked on my open door. He held the handles of a big, white bag with Eureka Falls Inn printed on its side in dark green letters.

What in the world?

"I'm looking for a Miss Honey Ingersoll."

"That would be me."

He held out the bag with a big grin plastered all over his face. I was too flustered to give a thought to tipping him, so I'm afraid he left with no more than a "thank you."

I set the bag on my desk and reached inside. An envelope sat on top of a white restaurant box. Actually, when I counted them, on top of two, three, four restaurant boxes, all too neat and pretty-looking to be doggy bags filled with leftovers.

I slit open the envelope.

> Dear Ms. Ingersoll,
> Dinner for one. Alas, not for two.
> With my apologies,
> —Andarius Ballou

Well, my, my. What a surprise. I guess Mr. Ballou was the kind of lawyer who took pride in never losing a case, or a date. If so, he was in for a surprise too.

Chapter Seventeen

A T HOME, I changed my shoes and popped the Inn's take-home bag in the fridge. But not before checking out the contents of those little white boxes—beef filet, some creamy potatoes, a lettuce salad and a darling chocolate tart slathered with whipped cream. I don't much cotton to uncooked greens, but the rest was a mouth-watering sight.

As good as it looked, a thank you—but no apology—to Mr. Ballou would have to wait. I needed to get to the Eureka Falls First Federal Savings & Loan Bank before closing time.

"Why Miss Honey, what a pleasure," Cletus Dwyer said as I stepped into the bank. Some things never change, including Cletus who took over as president after his granddaddy passed. Today, as usual, he wore one of those lavender shirts with the white collars he favored and elastic arm garters. But more important, he wore his usual glad-to-see you smile.

"Cletus darling, I need to speak to you privately," I said when he hurried over to me.

"Of course, you do." Smooth as silk, he took my elbow and escorted me into his office. Holding his lavender tie to his belly, he eased onto his swivel chair. I took a seat across the desk from him.

A few months ago, he married my best friend, Amelia Swope, and adopted her two little boys. Boy number three was now on the way, much to his delight. We chatted about the family and how happy he was and then, ever the gentleman, he asked, "How may I help you, Honey?"

"Well, truth be told, I'm in need of some research information."

"Oh?"

"From your files."

At my request, he sat back, kind of stiff like. "Don't know if I can help you there. Our client information is—"

"Confidential," I finished for him. "I know, but you have my future in your hands, Cletus. So please hear me out before you start in refusing." I leaned over his desk and upped the ante. "My asking isn't for the sake of personal interest alone, but …" I looked over my shoulders, left, right, then behind my chair at the closed door " … what you tell me may help with a murder investigation."

Then I sat up straight and let my words sink in.

His eyes widened, and staring at me all dilated, he said, "You mean the killing up on the Bluffs?"

"The very one." Good grief, how many killings did we have around town?

"The *Star* said you found the body of the dead woman."

"Carmen DeLuca. Yes, sad to say, I did. The property I'm inquiring about is situated right next door." I let my glance fall to my lap as if too shy to do otherwise. "I can't reveal my sources, but …" I sent another darting glance around the office before lowering my voice " … it's my understanding there may have been a connection between the two owners."

He laid his hands on his desk blotter. In the five years since I'd known him, it had never had the slightest ink stain. Still didn't, which told me he was fussy enough to keep a perfect set of records.

"I confess you have my curiosity by the tail," he said. "So

what information do you require?" He held up a warning finger. "That's not to say I can help you, but I will if I can."

"The estate next door to the DeLuca property, the one belonging to a Mr. Barry McHale, is about to go on the market. I may have a buyer for it. But before making any commitment, I need to know if there's a cloud on the property. Something Multiple Listing may have overlooked."

"Everything's in the record. You know what I know." Cletus's forehead tensed up and wrinkled, not a good sign, but I pressed on.

"True, but since First Federal handled the previous transaction, if there's anything amiss, any small thing at all, you'd surely have noticed."

He didn't answer, so I upped what my daddy would have called the ante. "This sale's very important to me, Cletus, or I wouldn't ask."

He nodded, his tension lines eased a bit, and he said, "There's a mortgage on the property, but otherwise the parcel is clean as a whistle."

"You're sure?"

"Without a doubt. When McHale purchased the place a year or so ago, our title guarantee gave it a clear deed. Funny you should ask. Why Saxby Winthrop was in here just last week asking the same question. But the DeLuca property now, that's a different story."

I straightened up in my seat, ears as alert as a bunny's in an open meadow. "How do you mean, different?"

"Mrs. DeLuca, you know, the—"

"Murder victim," I finished for him. Seems like Cletus just couldn't bring himself to use the words.

"Yes, exactly. She over-improved the estate to a radical degree. I warned her she'd never get a return on her money, but she wouldn't listen. Said it didn't matter. She wanted what she wanted. Did it all for the view, she said. It's lovely, of course, but my Lord, she sank a fortune into building there, and that was foolhardy as all get out. Now she's gone, and I can't imagine who'll buy the place—not for what it cost to build."

"You gave her a mortgage on the property anyway?" My question came out kind of squeaky.

"Not on your life. I have a fiduciary responsibility to uphold. She paid cash for the whole shebang. Liked living dangerously, she said." Cletus shook his head. "Those were her exact words. A self-fulfilling prophesy, wouldn't you say?"

Chapter Eighteen

THE GOOD NEWS about Barry's house had given me a wood chopper's appetite. At supper that night, I took a bottle of Mexican beer out of the fridge and set myself down to enjoy Andy's dinner. In no time flat I'd downed the steak, the potatoes and the darling little chocolate tart, even the two soft rolls with the cute pats of butter shaped like roses and snugged in a tiny plastic container. I tossed the salad, though.

Later, full as a tick, I stretched out on the living room couch to digest and to think. Since Barry's house had no legal entanglements which might cause Saxby to shimmy out of the deal, I'd go ahead and sign his contract. Then the house sale would go through, I'd be in business for myself, and my future would shine like a new set of hubcaps. Or was that too comfortable? Too tempting to fate? I mentally crossed my fingers. From what life had shown me so far, nothing ever ran as smooth as a brand new factory engine. Things were always sputtering and lurching and breaking down before coming to a complete halt.

But not this time. My jaw tightened. This time, all would be well. I knew it in my bones. Mortgage doctor Cletus had given

Barry's property a clean bill of health, and I put full stock in what he'd said. After all, he hadn't hesitated to state the truth about Carmen's place, and he'd handled enough transactions over the years to know if a deal was sweet or not … come to think of it so did ol' Sax. *Hmm.* A short while ago, he'd been in to see Cletus too and had asked a lot of the same questions I did.

As I lay there all stretched out and at my ease, an idea leaped into my head and, like a roused barking dog, refused to quiet down. Maybe the steak had started my juices flowing, but whatever the cause, I couldn't shake the notion that Saxby knew all about Carmen's property. But why would he even bother to learn about it?

Ah, of course. A wild notion drew me off the couch to pace around my living room. With Carmen gone now, most likely her house would soon be up for sale. A clever ol' coot, Sax might have it in mind to acquire the property for a song and resell it—for millions. Wouldn't put it past him to have already set the wheels in motion. Say he'd found Carmen's heirs … whoever they might be … and said he was ready to take the place off their hands. For a modest price, of course. I could see him now, talking up far-fetched legal entanglements, offering to buy the place anyway, to keep his home next door nice and private … and on and on. Then he'd flip the property.

Nothing illegal about doing so, but nothing nice about it either. If he did have something similar in mind, why buy Barry's estate for almost the asking price? Why not wait and acquire Carmen's on the cheap? Only one reason made a Saxby kind of sense: I'd put money down that he had looked into the possibility and his offer had been refused.

If I'd hit on the truth, and the chill running down my spine told me I had, then maybe I'd hit on something else too. Maybe Saxby wasn't turning his business over to me because he loved me, or any such flowery feelings. He was just doing what Saxby did best—wheeling himself a deal.

Chapter Nineteen

WELL, IF SAXBY's momma hadn't raised no stupid ... any stupid ... children, I hoped my momma hadn't either. Which meant in dealing with Saxby I'd better be as crafty as he was. Or try to be.

At least in the morning my heartbeat was calm and my palms weren't sweaty as I signed his contract. I'd hand deliver it to him, get his signature and an earnest money check. Then I'd call on Barry to say I had a buyer for his house. The sight of one of those checks had a way of convincing owners to accept an offer like nothing else I'd come across.

There had been no need to panic after all. As soon as Barry agreed to the sale—and why would he not?—I'd be the proud new owner of a proud ol' business.

Filled with good feeling, I stopped in at Ridley's before driving out to the Bluffs. Mornings, Sam worked his phone from home and usually didn't get to the office till after ten or so. I'd check the mail, answer calls and be gone before he got there. I swung onto the back lot and went in as usual through the rear door.

Mrs. Otis was already at her desk by the front windows,

and the minute I stepped inside she came hurrying over to me, worry creasing her forehead, her eyes suspiciously damp.

"Is something wrong?" I asked.

"Oh Honey." That's as far as she got before bursting into tears.

"What is it?" I asked, alarmed, but she was crying too hard to answer.

Always cheerful, always calm, Mrs. Otis never cried, never let on she had a single sorrow in life. And now this. Had someone she loved died? With an arm around her shoulders, I led her back to her desk. She slumped into the chair and dabbed at her eyes with a tissue.

"Tell me," I murmured when her sobs eased into sniffles.

"Sam called earlier and—"

I gasped. "Did his father pass?"

"No, nothing like that." She blew her nose and sniffed for a while before forcing herself to say, "He wants you out of here before he comes in today. 'Lock, stock and barrel,' he said. I'm to help you get your personal things out of your office and then lock it. He ordered me to make sure ..." She broke down again.

"Make sure of what?"

"That you don't touch any files. In fact, in fact ..."

"It's okay. You can tell me."

"I had to lock every file cabinet in the place. I need your keys, too. All of them—for the door, the filing cabinets, the P.O. box. You're being thrown out, Honey. Out!" And with that she laid her head on the desk and lost it completely.

I patted her back, but what good did a little pat ever do for a body? "Please don't take on so, Mrs. O. I was leaving in a week anyway. And you know something ..." I waited until she looked up "... it's just as well this is happening. It erases any regretful feelings I might have had, if you know what I mean. I'll surely miss you, more than I can say, but we'll stay in touch, won't we? Have lunch together some days, or dinner after work. This isn't the end of our friendship. Not by a long shot, as my daddy used to say."

With my promise to meet again, her head came up to stay, and she gave me a lopsided smile that nearly tore my heart in two.

"So let's get my things out of the cubicle, and I'll be long gone before Sam gets here. Will you help me?"

She nodded, dried her eyes one more time and heaved to her feet. "I found a couple of cartons in the store room. We can use those."

A half hour later, the trunk of my Lincoln was about to be stuffed with a three year collection: laptop, emergency makeup kit, umbrella, old raincoat, a cardigan sweater, a monthly planner, a desk calendar, pens, pencils, stapler, stick-em notes, and boxes of greeting cards for clients' birthdays, anniversaries and house sales. My supply of power bars, I dropped in the tote. The way the day was shaping up, I figured I might need to munch on them before long.

With the raincoat tossed over one arm, juggling the tote and a carton, I opened the back door and stepped outside.

"Be with you in a minute, Honey," Mrs. Otis called before answering the ringing phone.

Behind the Lincoln, I eased the carton to the tarmac, dropped the raincoat on top and reached for the trunk release.

"Hold it right there, real estate lady."

Startled, I shot a quick glance over a shoulder. A gun, small, black and snub-nosed was pointed my way, and none other than Frankie Serrito was doing the pointing.

I stood up straight and slowly turned to face him. "What's this all about, Frankie?"

"Oh it's Frankie now. No Mr. Serrito any more."

Making believe I was calm, I asked, "What do you want from me? Money? I don't have much, but if you need it, take it." I held out the tote. "It's in here."

His eyes followed my every move and lingered on the tote. He wanted money, needed it no doubt, but Frankie had pride.

"I don't want your filthy money."

"It isn't—"

"Shut up. You called the cops on me. Got me jailed again. I didn't break into that house, I tell you. The man asked me to stay there. As a personal favor, he said. And look at how he's treated me. Well, I set him straight, and now it's your turn."

My armpits were damp and getting damper. The man was crazy as a loon, waving a gun around like it was a toy. Hey, wait a minute. Squinting in the sun, I peered hard at it. *Was* that a play toy in Frankie's fist? Gripped in his hand and aimed at my innards, it sure looked real enough. The finish, though, was dull not shiny. Didn't real guns have a shine to the metal? For the life of me, I couldn't remember, or I'd knock this one out of his hand, a skinny little guy like him … but I wasn't sure. And the cold beads running down my spine told me I was too scared to risk learning the truth the hard way.

The back door to Ridley's opened and out came Mrs. Otis, loaded down with a carton full of my office things. *Go for it, Honey. It's now or never.*

"Hey, Mrs. Otis! Call the cops!" I yelled loud enough to bring a razorback on the run.

Bingo.

Frankie swiveled around to see who I was yelling to and, in that split second, I slugged him with the tote, knocking him off his pins and sending his gun flying across the parking lot.

"Get the gun, Mrs. O!"

Without a second's hesitation, she dumped the carton to the ground where it fell with a crash of broken glass—*so long picture frames*—and dove for the weapon. I hopped on top of Frankie who was on the ground flat on his back. The same position he was laying in the first time I clapped eyes on him. But this time, praise the Lord, he was wearing pants.

Chapter Twenty

THE GUN TURNED out to be a toy after all. But it earned Frankie more than a brief stay in the town jail. This time, he was taken to the Yarborough County Hospital for what Matt called a psychiatric evaluation, even though, in my opinion, Frankie was just a harmless drifter. Those picture frames and Mrs. Otis's skinned knees were his only victims. Or so I thought anyway. So we all thought: Mrs. Otis, me, Matt and Zach, but we were wrong, every last one of us.

Since the morning was hustling on toward noon, I decided I'd better get over to Saxby's and have him turn his offer into an honest-to-God reality. After hugging Mrs. Otis goodbye and promising to keep in touch, I drove off with the sight of her standing in Ridley's parking lot, her two skinned knees kind of looking like stop lights.

As soon as I got to Winthrop's, Saxby ushered me into his lair and closed the door in Mindy's face. Very unmannerly. I stood by the door with my hand on the knob until he took a seat behind his desk. Once he was safely swiveling, I handed him the contract, and he signed it without a bit of regret on his face. In fact, he looked downright happy at the transaction and about ready to celebrate. At least I think that's what those longing glances at his bourbon drawer were all about. Anyway, we shook on the deal—the first time I'd touched him in over two years—and while he clung to my fingers, I said, "I'm on my way to give Barry McHale your offer on the house. To make it stick, I'll need a check."

"Earnest money?"

I nodded. Slowly, as if he didn't want to, Saxby let go of my hand. He reached into his top desk drawer and removed a check already filled in and endorsed. Giving it to me along with one of his sly ol' dog looks, he said, "You were doubtin' me, Miss Honey. Shame on you."

"I didn't have the slightest doubt you'd come through, Saxby. I signed the contract first, didn't I?"

"Yes, you did, indeed. We're tied together now. For good." He pointed a finger at my nose. "A tie as bindin' in its own way as matrimony. Don't you go forgettin' that."

All on its own, my mouth opened to speak, as it has a way of doing, but my brain caught up with it in the nick of time. So I just smiled sweetly, tucked the check in the manila envelope with my copy of the contract and said, "I'll be in touch as soon as I meet with Mr. McHale."

"Lookin' forward to it, Honey. Lookin' forward to it."

On my way out, I stopped to ask Mindy a question. "You want to work for me?"

She stared up at me, surprised. "I already have a job."

"Not for long. Didn't Mr. Winthrop tell you he's retiring?"

She hesitated, struggling to remember. "Now that you mention it, a while back he did say something about retiring. I thought he wanted to go to bed." A blush rose to her face, the heat of it bringing her carnation perfume on real strong.

"A natural way of thinking," I said. "But I believe he meant stopping his real estate work. And you know what that means?"

"What?" Her mouth a round O.

"Why he'll be home keeping you company all day long and all night too."

The O collapsed.

"But not to worry, my offer's for real. I'm taking over for Mr. Winthrop. You know how things operate around here, and I'll need someone to help me run the office. So how about it?"

She jumped up and gripped my hand. "Yes. Double yes. You won't be sorry."

Lord Almighty, I hoped she was right.

And she almost was.

Chapter Twenty-One

WITH THE CAR windows down and Blake Shelton strumming out *Footloose*, I drove to the Bluffs, hair whipping around in the breeze, humming along happy as a puppy with a fresh, new bone.

At last my troubles were over. Winthrop's was an established business with a long history in town. Folks knew the name, remembered it—along with Ridley's of course—when they wanted to buy or sell a piece of property. And if I put my mind to it, which I had every intention of doing, there was no reason, none in the world, why I couldn't be a success too. Despite some bitter memories of my Saxby days, when I went back with Barry's contract, I'd make a point of saying thank you. I'd been a bit sluggish in doing so, and I wasn't raised to behave that way.

Closer to the river, the breeze grew stronger. No wonder the Bluffs were so prized. The view of the water shining in the sun, carrying sweet cooling air along with it, rolling on past, never stopping, always moving, always—

A sudden burst of dense fog swept into the car. I inhaled and coughed. Phew. What *was* that? Not the sweet river air

I expected. I sniffed, cautiously, not good, and raised the car windows. As I left the highway for the rise leading up to Bluffs Boulevard, a haze filled the sky, and the sharp odor set my eyes to watering.

Somebody must be burning old tires, or plastic tarps or something. It sure wasn't a barbeque. No mouth-watering aromas were rising out of that smoke, and the nearer I got to the top of the Bluffs, the stronger the nasty odor became. I rounded the crest of the hill and wished I hadn't.

As I peered through the windshield, the haze cleared for a little bit. And then there was no denying the horror. Flames red as hell fire were shooting through Barry's roof. Frozen in fear, I sat still for a second—no more—while my mind struggled to believe what my eyes were seeing. A window exploded, shooting glass into the air., Scared into action, I dumped the contents of my bag on the front seat, grabbed the cell and punched in 911.

With help on the way, I blew out a breath of relief. Still, there was no telling how long the first responders would take to get here. Until they did, someone could be trapped inside the house desperate to get out. *Barry.* Oh God, if only I'd phoned ahead, I'd know if he was home or not. I should have called, but eager to bring him the sales agreement, I'd just jumped in the car and headed out of town.

Maybe I could try now. Why not? I snatched up the phone and pressed in his cell number. It rang and rang but no answer. I flung the cell on the car seat. Wasn't there anybody who could help—neighbors, a passerby—*someone*? But the street with its acre-wide lots was quiet as a tomb. Not a soul had spotted the fire and come running.

No wonder. Barry's house was the last one on the rim of the Bluffs. Carmen's manse stood empty, and Lord only knew if the mansion on the other side of her estate was unoccupied too. Though it had to be. Nobody could ignore that haze and smog, the crackling heat.

A crash loud as thunder split the air. I screamed as a

chimney toppled to the ground. How long had it been since I called 911? One minute? Two? I'd better move off the driveway. I'd be in the way when the fire fighters got there. If they ever did. Hands shaking, stomach in a knot, I put the car in reverse, backed out to the road and pulled onto Carmen's drive.

I couldn't leave, and I couldn't just sit there doing nothing. I jumped out of the car and raced across the lawn, cut through the opening in the boxwood hedge and dashed over to Barry's front entrance. This close, the heat was stifling, strong enough to suck the oxygen out of the air. But I couldn't let that stop me. Barry might be inside, unconscious, needing help. Sweat running down my spine, my face wet with it, I punched in the security code, praying for a response.

Yes! I yanked open the door and stepped into the smoke-clogged foyer. My heart pumping overtime, I held a hand over my mouth and nose, pushed open the inner door and stumbled into the great room. Into hell. Flames, leaping like live creatures, were devouring the room. As I stood there, shaking, the wine-stained chair burst into a shower of sparks.

"Barry!" I hollered. "Barry! Are you in here? Answer me!"

Sparks feeding on the chair flew through the air and landed on the silk couches. In seconds, they erupted into flames. I shouted Barry's name over and over, but it did no good, no good at all. He never answered me, and then, loud as a freight train racing down the tracks, a rear wall collapsed. Terrified, shrieking my head off, I fled out the front door and into a pair of strong arms.

"I got you, lady. You all right?" the fire fighter asked.

Gasping for breath, trembling all over, I couldn't answer. He gave me a shake that brought me back to my senses and I blurted, "The owner. He might be inside."

"If he is, we'll find him. One way or the other. Now get out of here. Fast."

Not waiting to be told again, I ran past the fire trucks crowding the drive. Another firefighter in boots, parka and helmet, waved me away—as if he had to—hollering words I couldn't hear, didn't want to hear, and couldn't have understood anyway.

I cut through the shrubbery and went back to the car where I sat for a spell, my head on the steering wheel, my mind in turmoil. No way could I drive just then, and no way could I leave without knowing for certain what had happened to Barry. Though I didn't know him well, I knew he was a good man who deserved a better fate than death by hellfire.

I'd never forget the way he'd made excuses for Frankie, saying how he put him in mind of his brother Tommy, the one who'd gone missing. The one he feared might be homeless and needy too. Poor Barry. I hoped to heaven he was alive and unharmed, though there was no hope for his house. It was gone. *Pouf.* Just like that, in a cloud of smoke, a multi-million dollar mansion turned into a pile of rubble.

That's when my own reality hit, snapping my head up in shock. Stunned by the weight of it, I stared out the windshield into my future. Without Barry's house, I had no sale, without the sale, I had no contract. And without the contract, I had no job.

Worst of all, without the job, I had no future. At least none I could look forward to. None that could lift my heart like a bright, sunny day. All I could see were clouds ahead. My apartment rent was due in a week, about the same time as my last paycheck. After that, I'd have to dip into what savings I had … making that dream of a house of my own some day less and less real … and when those savings were gone, what then? Back to waitressing at Josie's Diner? If she'd have me back, because Sam Ridley sure wouldn't, and besides, I'd starve before I'd step foot in there again. After the way he treated me, locking the files like I was about to steal them from under his nose and ordering me to get out of that tiny cubicle. It wasn't even a corner office or anything. Why—*whoa, hold on gal. You're heading down the wrong path.*

Oh my, I remembered that voice. Grandma Ingersoll, a bred-in-the-bone mountain woman with grit in her craw.

She passed ten years ago, but I could hear her now, *You got a backbone? Then stiffen it up and stop your whining. Make me proud of you, gal, like I always been.*

I took a deep breath and was sorry for it. Most likely the air outside wasn't any better, but needing to get out of the stuffy car, I took a chance and stepped onto Carmen's driveway. Over at the McHale site, flames no longer reached for the sky, and the clouds of smoke had lightened a bit. No sound of trucks revving up either. Only shouted orders shattered the quiet. The men were still there then, wetting down the embers, dousing every spark.

I glanced at Carmen's front entrance. Curtains drawn across the windows and fallen leaves scattered on the stone stairs gave the place a forlorn, deserted look. The wind had picked up, and little flecks of gray ash floated through the air like dirty snowflakes. I brushed them off my suit and tried not to take deep breaths. I could get back in the car, but why bother? No relief to be had there. Maybe out by the terrace the river breezes would make breathing easier. A wind blowing downstream might carry some of the smoky haze along with it.

Wait, what *was* that? A movement inside the windows? Yes, I was sure of it. It was only a quick twitch at the curtains, but in a deserted, locked house, curtains don't move. Not without a reason. I forgot all about the forlorn look of the dead leaves and the neglected lawn and the nasty air. My attention was riveted on those windows, waiting for another sign of life, no matter how slight.

There. It happened again. A hand stroking the drapes, the heavy cloth swaying a little then easing back over the glass.

Who could that be? While the McHale house burned to the ground, no one in here had raced out to offer help or to see what was happening? Unbelievable. The only car in the driveway was mine. And after the murder, the police had locked Carmen's three bay garage.

Strange and stranger.

No further movement at the window, no hand brushing the drapes. All had become still once more. Though too curious to let the mystery go unsolved, I hesitated. Carmen's killer could be inside, armed and dangerous, and I was alone. As I stood there, torn and uncertain, a shout echoed across the lawn. One of the firemen. No, I wasn't alone. Help would be just a scream away. Besides, who ever proved a killer always returned to the scene of the crime?

Without waiting another second, I mounted the stone stairs to the front entrance and rang the bell. Deep inside the house, chimes rang musical and soft but plenty loud enough to be heard from where I stood. Though I rang and rang, no one answered. Using my fist, I pounded on the door.

Bang, bang, bang. Nothing.

Scorched, hot, panting for a breath of clean air, I wanted to kick the door—my shoes were wrecked anyway—but I resisted the urge. Instead I hollered, "Open up or I'll call the police!"

That did it. A moment later, the door parted an inch or two, all the chain across it would allow, and the scared face of Sophie, the housekeeper, peeked out at me.

My whole body sagged in relief. Of course. I should have known. The fire must have rattled my mind. "It's me, Honey Ingersoll," I said. "Carmen's … ah … friend. Do you remember me?"

"*Si, Senorita.*"

"I thought the house was deserted, but then I saw the curtains move and, well, a squatter did break in next door. You never know."

Saying not a word, she just peered through the narrow opening.

I had to be sure. "Did you hear the fire trucks? Do you know the house next door has burned to the ground?"

"*Si.* I called 911. I saw the flames."

"Oh. But you didn't come out or … or anything."

"No. I see fires before."

Half-turning to go, I pointed to the driveway. "There's no

car here."

No answer. Unmannerly as it might be, I had to ask. "So how did you get here? How did you get in?"

"My Juan, my *hombre*, he drive me. I have house key."

"Sophie, if you don't want to tell me why you're here, you don't have to, but the police will want to know."

Her eyes, dark as ink, flared wide. "I clean for Mrs. DeLuca."

"She's dead, Sophie."

"*Si.* I mean for the *patron*, Mr. Ballou. He say house will be sold. He pay me if I clean. So I clean."

"I see. Well, sorry I bothered you. I was looking for Mr. McHale, but I'm afraid he died in the fire, so—"

"Mr. McHale? He's not *morte*. He's out in back by the pool."

In the rear garden, the scent of gardenias greeted me like a welcome home, and I risked inhaling their perfume. Better, but sadly, the blossoms were dotted with gray ash. Even the pool had a gray scum on its surface. Not like the day of the photo shoot when the water lay all blue and pretty in the sun.

On the other side of the pool, a man with his head in his hands sat slumped on one of the lounge chairs.

"Barry?"

He glanced up, kind of startled like.

"What are you doing here?" he asked.

I didn't see fit to answer. Why say I had a six figure check in my purse that I no longer had reason to give him.

Looking plumb wore out ... worn out ... he crouched down the way he'd been, head lowered, eyes staring at the ground.

Eyes smarting, and not from the smoke, I hurried over to him. It was all I could do to keep from throwing my arms around him and hugging him. "I'm so glad you're alive, Barry. I thought you had died in the fire."

"I should have," he said, not raising his head, still staring at his feet or the ground or whatever was down there that he found so worthwhile.

"Please don't say such a thing. You're alive. That's what matters."

Eyes bleak, he glanced up. "How would you know?"

"Bricks and stones can be replaced. You can rebuild ... as long as you're alive." Lord Almighty, I sounded just like Grandma Ingersoll.

He shook his head. "Everything's gone. Everything." He gave out a short bark of a laugh, one with no humor in it, and pointed to the spark holes in his clothes. "Look at this. I don't even have a pair of pants to my name."

"Not true." I wanted to give him the kindly words I could tell he craved, but something told me agreeing with him, saying how awful the situation was, wouldn't help a bit. What Barry needed was spine stiffening. "You're a strong, healthy man in the prime of life. You can rebuild a house. It's been done before. You didn't lose anyone you loved in the fire. Not even a, a canary."

Uh-oh. Too late I remembered only a few days ago he *had* suffered a loss—Carmen. I should have bitten my tongue before saying such a hurtful thing. But truth is, he didn't seem to take offense.

"You don't understand," is what he said. "I'm a stupid man. Everything's gone. Everything." To make his point, he peered up at me for a moment. "You'll be reading about it in the paper soon enough."

No doubt. *The Star* always put house fires on page one. But I couldn't let Barry wallow in his grief.

"Your property insurance will take care of rebuilding costs."

He shook his head. "I need the money *now*. Why do you think I was selling the house? Because I wanted to?" That laugh again. "No, I'll never recoup the loss. At best, I'm underinsured. And let arson rear its ugly head, the property'll be a total loss. I won't collect a dime."

"Arson?" I could feel the blood drain from my face. *Frankie.*

"Barry, there's something you need to know."

Chapter Twenty-Two

THOUGH I TOLD Barry about Frankie's threats and the toy gun and all, he just shook his head. "I think the guy's harmless, but even if he isn't, it's too late. Losing the house is only one more nail in the coffin."

What that was supposed to mean, I had no idea. Worried about him sitting there alone while his house crashed to the ground, I offered him a ride into town, but he waved me off with, "No need. I've still got a car and a credit card. At least for now."

At least for now. "If you're sure."

"I am. Run along, Honey. It's been nice knowing you."

What he said had a final kind of sound to it, like the tolling of a church bell. I hated to leave with him all moody blue and despairing, but I couldn't insist he let me stay. Or mention what I was fearing—in his present state of mind he might do harm to himself. All I could do was leave as he'd asked me to and hope for the best.

Out in front of the house, a familiar PD cruiser sat behind the Lincoln, blocking me in. Matt and Deputy Zach were striding down the drive. When I called to them, Matt whirled around and came rushing back to me, with that pale look he got whenever something worried him.

"Good God, Honey," he said, gripping me by the arms. "I saw your car there and thought—"

"I got trapped in the fire."

He nodded. "Yes."

"I know the feeling. I thought Barry McHale was dead, but he isn't, he—"

"Not the same feeling at all. Unless," Matt stopped, a stricken look crossing his face, "you're in love with the guy."

While I knew what Matt was really saying, I had to pretend otherwise. I had feelings, fond feelings, for him, but was he the man I wanted to spend the rest of my life with? I didn't know, not for sure. Doubt kept creeping in like a mangy cat. And how could I tell him about such a doubt? Especially since, in a time of weakness, I'd spent a night in his arms? A night he hadn't been able to forget and, to be blunt about it, neither had I. Except for that one night, though, I'd pretty much been living like a nun. Still, was. But as any Bible-reading person would say, that was no excuse for giving Matt ideas when I wasn't ready to commit to him. Or to anyone.

"Well?" Hands on hips, one cradling his holster, he waited for an answer.

"Oh," I said, coming back into the moment, "you're asking about Barry? He's a client. Or used to be. Right now, he's sitting out by the pool all by himself, and I'm worried for him."

"Why, does he need medical help?"

"I don't know. He's bluer than a new pair of jeans."

"Despondent?"

"Could be. Didn't even listen when I told him about Frankie Serrito's threats."

"You mean with the toy gun?"

"Not just that, he boasted he'd get even with me like he did with Barry." I pointed in the direction of the McHale property. "And now this."

"I'll make sure the fire chief hears about Serrito." Matt turned to Zach. "Why don't you spend some quality time with Mr. McHale? See he gets back to town okay. Has a place to stay. I'll drive Honey home."

"No need to, Matt," I said.

"Yes there is, and no argument. You look done in." His glance swept me head to foot. "I've never seen you in such a sorry state. You've got soot on your face and spark holes all over that nice blue suit."

"Carmen never liked it anyway."

"What?"

I shook my head. "Not important."

"Pick me up at Honey's place in, say, an hour," Matt told Zach.

"No, not at my place. At the Winthrop Agency."

Chapter Twenty-Three

"No need askin' where you've been," Saxby said when I walked into his office with my sooty face and pock-marked clothes. "Fire's been all over the news, 'long with pictures of the house goin' up like a torch."

If I didn't know better, I'd say Saxby looked ready to bust out crying, but at least his eyeballs weren't bloodshot. Yet.

"Lord Almighty," he said, "I set my heart on havin' that house."

"Like I set mine on being my own boss, coming in here and working for—"

He held up an interrupting palm. "No reason why we can't proceed accordin' to our original plan."

"But—"

"Some alterations will be required, of course." He leaned back in the swivel and spread his hands over his belly. "Before gettin' into the particulars, you have my check, Missy?"

I fished it out of my purse and laid it on his desk. Without bothering to reach for it, he said, "So we can discuss the situation in a leisurely fashion, why don't you take a seat and rest that pretty little ass of yours?"

I folded my arms and stood exactly where my feet had planted me.

Seeing as I wasn't about to move, he said, "You objectin' to me using that there French word?"

"Ass isn't French, Saxby. But as I recall hearing some place, *couchon* is. And that's what you are. In case you're wondering, it means pig."

He grinned, the devil, from ear to ear. "I'll interpret your words as a badge of honor, seein' as our state university has a razorback for a mascot."

He was quick-witted, no doubt about it, but hard to like. No doubt about that either. I dearly wanted to stomp out and slam the door, but my problem was too serious for such a luxury, so I parked my fanny in the chair across from him and, gritting my teeth, waited for the preaching to begin. It didn't take long.

"My momma left me all her worldly possessions for one main reason." He paused, and I knew he was going to ask one of those irritating questions. His favorite kind. The ones you couldn't possibly answer because you had no idea under the sun what he was getting at. "You know what the reason might be, Missy?"

Not trusting myself to speak in a civil tone, I shook my head.

"She wanted me to be happy. And damn it all to hell," he pounded the desk top, his flabby fist making a surprisingly loud thump, "I wanted McHale's property."

"A pity," I said, trying to sound sorrowful. "But what's a body to do? God had his eyes on it."

"That so? You got a direct link to the Almighty?"

"Why don't you get to the point, Saxby?"

"What's the rush? You're not giving me a chance to develop my thoughts."

I tapped a finger on my temple. "Your thoughts spring out of your head all ready to go. So pretend you're a Yankee for once and tell it to me straightforward like. I've had a wearisome day."

He leaned as far over his desk as he could. "Very well, since you insist. Here's what I'm proposin.' The DeLuca estate? The one next to the McHale property?"

"I know the one."

"I have a notion to buy it."

"Well, I'll be hornswoggled," I said, the surprise setting me back in my chair.

"Exactly. And as far as transferin' the agency over to you, nothing will change. We'll just ink out the McHale name on our contract and ink in DeLuca. How's that sound?" he asked, knowing full well it was glorious.

"Excellent but—"

"Ah, the 'buts.' And there are some, indeed. A murder, a cold-blooded killin' took place on DeLuca land, and the killer is still at large." His eyes narrowed as he peered across at me. "You know full well how such events affect property values. Why most folks wouldn't …"

"No need to go on, I understand your drift."

He held up a finger for silence. "I have more to say. Not only was there a murder …" he seemed to enjoy repeating the word " … the house next door has been burned to the very ground. The TV showed there's nothin' left but ashes. Scorched earth they call it. Bad as what happened hereabouts during The War."

"Your point?"

"When it comes to price, the DeLuca estate has two strikes against it."

"It's still a beautiful piece of property."

"Yes and no. The Bluffs are a yes, but that darn fool pool is an embarrassin' addition."

I sighed.

"However,"

"Yes?"

"I'll be willin' to overlook all the deficits if—"

"The price is right."

He leaned back. 'You know something, Honey, my agency's

going to be in good hands when you take over."

"*If* I take over. First off, the property you're seeking isn't yet on the market. Second, even if it does go up for sale, the price may not be dropped low enough to suit you. Three, if neither of these hurdles can be overcome, our contract is null and void. Correct?"

"You're taking too much on your pretty little shoulders all at once. Let's concentrate our efforts on securin' the DeLuca piece, which involves contactin' the attorney who's handling the estate. A Mr. Andarius Ballou, Esquire.

Andy. Wouldn't you know? Out of the half dozen or so lawyers in town, it had to be him.

"One of us needs to pay a personal call on Mr. Ballou and inquire about the property in question. I have no hesitation in doing so, but ..." he reached for the lower desk drawer "... my manly instincts tell me you'll get much further in dealin' with the gentleman than I would." He pulled out a half empty fifth of Maker's Mark and set it on the desk top with a thump. "Hair of the dog?"

"No thanks. When do you think this meeting should take place?"

"First thing in the mornin', Honey. First thing in the mornin'."

Chapter Twenty-Four

Too nerved up to sleep, I stayed awake most of the night, the sheets all twisted and my mind at fever pitch. What would I wear? What would I say? What would I do when I walked in on Andy with Saxby's proposition?

More than a house sale was at stake. My whole life hung in the balance. At least that's how it seemed at two A.M. By three-thirty or thereabouts, my mind settled down, and I fell into a fitful sort of sleep. When the alarm went off at seven, I slapped the ringer with a groan and sat on the edge of the bed for a while, studying the interesting way the morning sun struck the bedroom wall.

After three hours of sleep I was facing what could be the most important day of my life. It called for coffee, grits and a plan.

First the coffee.

I leaped up and got to work in the kitchen. Later, after drinking the coffee and waiting on the grits, I took out a pad and pen and wrote down my plan:

A) Call on Andy. (Look as good as I can.)

B) Thank Andy for the doggie bag. (Be sure to call it a

carry-out dinner.)

C) Apologize for stomping out of his office the last time we met. (I was justified in doing so, but use sweet words anyway.)

D) Ask if he's planning to put the DeLuca estate on the market. If so, say I might have a client for it. (Ease into this without seeming to hurry, so he won't think I'm eager.)

E) If the estate is for sale, convince him Saxby's low-ball price is the best he can expect for a house tainted with the blood of its former owner.

E was the toughie, the boulder in the road. Or maybe not. Due to its history, selling the property might be well nigh impossible. For sure, it would fetch a lower price than before the murder. So Saxby's offer might be the best solution for Carmen's heirs after all.

Still, letting him practically steal a show stopper of a place stuck in my craw. On the other hand, no sale on the house, no contract on the Winthrop Agency.

The lid on the grits pot started rattling away. I got up and shut off the stove. Who could eat grits at a time like this?

ALL DECKED OUT in a cornflower blue sundress, I covered my shoulders with a skimpy little blue sweater I'd picked up on sale at Belinda's Boutique. She called it a bolero and swore it was the latest fashion craze. Privately I thought it looked a little dumb, but I wore it anyway. And since I had my car back, I didn't hesitate to slide into the killer red spikes. So with Plan A in place—hair shining, lips glossed and fingers mentally crossed—I once again climbed the stairs to the law office of Andarius Ballou, Esquire.

As soon as I stepped foot into his empty reception area—still no assistant or paralegal at the front desk—he came out of the inner office as if he'd been waiting all morning to see me. Not that I put much stock in such fanciful notions. After all, his office window overlooked Main Street, so he'd probably spotted me on my way in. Whatever the reason, he stood leaning against his office door jamb kind of loose and easy, waiting for me to say something.

Rattled, I blurted out Plan B. "Thank you kindly for the doggie bag. I mean—"

"You're most welcome. Was the steak done to your preference?"

"The steak? I like it every which way."

He laughed, not the reaction I expected which rattled me even more. "So that's a yes?"

"It certainly is. The meat and all those little potatoes and the butter pats and everything were wonderful." Instead of stopping there, under his blue-eyed gaze, I blushed for some reason and yammered on, leaving Plan C and the need to apologize in the lurch. "It was so different from the specials at Josie's Diner. Don't get me wrong, the diner's fine, but … ." He waited until I ran out of steam and still he didn't say, "Come in" or "What can I do for you?" or anything. He just kept on staring, and I finally launched into Plan C.

"You're probably wondering why I'm here on your doorstep, Mr. Ballou—"

"Andy."

I nodded. "Well, the hasty way I left here last time wasn't mannerly, and I wanted to say—why haven't you cashed my check?"

Where that came from I couldn't honestly tell, but drat it, instead of sounding sweet and sugary, I'd out and out nagged him.

"I have no intention of cashing it, Miss Ingersoll."

"Honey."

His turn to nod. "The fee for my … ah … services, was your company at dinner. Sad to say, I haven't yet had the pleasure."

Something in his tone caused my face to turn the same cherry red as my shoes. I know it did. You don't get that hot otherwise. No doubt about it, Lawyer Ballou was a wizard with words, something I'd better not forget. Men like him were too dangerous to trust—even if they were attractive. To cover my confusion, I dumped Plan C for D.

"I also have another purpose for this call, if you care to hear it."

"By all means. Do come in, Honey."

With a half bow, he allowed me to enter his office first. So I could only guess which part of me those blue eyes took in as I strolled over to a visitor's chair.

When we were both seated comfortably, he leaned back in the seat behind his desk and smiled. That's all. The air conditioning needed to be turned down, but not wanting to sound troublesome, I didn't mention it and went ahead with the business at hand.

"It is my understanding, Mr... Andy ... that you're managing the estate of the late Carmen DeLuca."

"My, my, news travels fast."

"So that's a yes?" I asked, echoing his question of a few moments ago.

His eyes sparked. "It is," he said, "and?"

"As trustee, you would know if that particular house is on the market now or soon will be."

"Ah." The spark in his eyes faded a bit. "So I owe this delightful surprise visit to your real estate interests?"

Uh-oh, a hitch in the Plan D clothes line. "Not entirely," I quickly said. "I do want to thank you for the ..." I caught myself in time "... the take-out dinner and to apologize."

"Also to be first in line for the DeLuca house?"

At the abruptness of his question, I sat up ram-rod straight. Fast as a lightning strike, his tone had switched from warm to icy cold. "You think there'll be a line? You must be wearing your rose-colored glasses today."

"How so?" he asked, one eyebrow arching. He was so cool, so sure, so full of himself I wanted to lean across the desk and slap the know-it-all smile off his face. The feeling didn't last long, but while it gripped me, I pointed a finger at his nose and brought out my big guns.

"You'll be happy to know I'm prepared to answer you, Mr.... . Andy. First, a murder took place on that very property. Second, the house next door has burned to the ground, under what is looking like questionable circumstances and is now an unsightly patch of scorched earth. Three, we're a small town in, let me be frank, the middle of nowhere. Not too many folks hereabouts are clamoring for mansion-sized properties. And four, I know for a fact the land on which said house stands has encumbrances going back to The War. All of which means there will be no line."

His eyes took on a shiny quality, and he said, "You know something, Honey? Something I figured out the last time you came to call?"

"All I know is your questions are a lot like those of my former employer, Mr. Saxby Winthrop."

He grinned, ear to ear. "I'm familiar with Mr. Winthrop's rhetorical style. I can assure you, mine is vastly different."

"That's mighty gratifying to hear. Now—"

He held up a hand, palm out. "Not so fast. I haven't expressed my observation yet which is, not only are you beautiful, you're smart. Very smart. An unbeatable combination of which I'm sure you're aware."

He paused like he was in a courtroom or something, waiting for the other party to respond to his prodding. While I loved what he said, I had no intention of turning into a simpering fool just because an attractive man sweet-talked me.

But I did allow myself to believe a bit of truth clung to his words. Maybe I *was* brighter than the story my school grades always told. It was a comforting notion.

So I paused to thank him, briefly, and plunged back into Plan D. "If the DeLuca property should be for sale, my client is prepared to make an offer."

"All cards on the table then, Honey?"

"I've never been good at playing cards." A lie. A white one, well, a shade of gray.

When I was no bigger than a tadpole, my daddy showed

me how to play stud poker like a pro. Nowadays I never played cards at all; I hated gambling. It had destroyed Daddy and my momma, and … *whoa, wait a minute*. My breath caught in my throat. What on earth was I doing here in this law office today if not gambling? Talking to a man with a winning hand who held all the cards to my future? And what did I hold? A fist full of nothing. But no doubt about it, this was a form of stud poker, so I held myself firm and kept my thoughts from surfacing.

"What's your client's offer?" Andy asked. "In dollars and cents?"

A clever move on his part, one that would force me to negotiate up. A far better move was negotiating down. For that I needed an asking price. "My client can't plunge into the unknown. He needs a figure."

"The price is three million, five hundred and fifty thousand dollars."

I burst out laughing and rose from my chair.

I'd hardly lifted my purse when he said, "Please be seated, Honey."

"Why?" I slung the tote over a shoulder. "The figure you just quoted is the same as the original asking price for the McHale property. You're joshing with me, Andy, but I'm not in a funning mood today."

"Sorry. A lame attempt at humor." He indicated my seat with a graceful sweep of his long, elegant hand. "Please."

"If you'll be serious."

He nodded. "I'm glad you came in this morning. I was about to contact you."

"You *were*? Why?" Curious, I sank onto the chair.

"Yes. Yesterday, I met with Cletus Dwyer over at the bank. Among other things, he gave me his opinion as to what the DeLuca property might be worth on the open market. His figure pretty much matched mine. Also, he advised that I contact you to handle the sale. Said you were the sharpest gal in town and the best thing to ever hit Ridley's Real Estate."

"I'm no longer with Ridley's. I'm acting as an independent agent and can assure you my client is prepared to pay an honest price ..." I paused "... considering the circumstances."

"And I can assure *you* my client will accept two million even."

I shook my head. "You weren't listening up, Andy. Those circumstances, remember."

"Then name your price."

"One million seven hundred and seventy-five thousand. In cash."

"Exactly half."

"Of your humorous figure, yes."

"May I ask who your client is?"

"I'm not free to say until a deal is struck."

An out and out lie. Saxby had given me no such orders, but I guess I was trying to prove to Andy Ballou, Esquire, that a girl in a sundress and a stupid sweater could play hard ball.

I'm not sure my message got across though. He smiled and said, "Your offer will be given serious consideration, but it does require further discussion." He glanced at his watch. "I'm due at the Yarborough County Courthouse in one hour. Therefore"... clearing his throat before continuing "... would you consider having a discussion over dinner? Let's say on Saturday evening? Two days, two nights and seven hours from now?"

Chapter Twenty-Five

I F I WAS one to use fancy words, I'd say I was mighty conflicted leaving Andy's office. Another way of saying all mixed up. Happy Saxby's offer hadn't been refused, worried it might be yet and excited over the possibility of success.

Of the three feelings, excitement topped the list. As soon as I strapped on my seat belt, I started right in humming *Slip On By*. No music, no Austin Webb, no nothing, just me and my song. I was grooving along so good I didn't welcome the interruption, but the moment the cell rang, I grabbed it, thinking it might be a client. Old habits die hard.

Then with a rush, I realized I didn't have any clients.

"Is this Honey?" she asked.

Not recognizing the voice right off, I said, "Yes, this is Honey Ingersoll."

"It's Penelope, Honey. Isn't the news about Barry's house awful? Burning to the ground like that? What a shame."

"No question, it is a downright shame."

"First Carmen's killed and now Barry's house goes up in flames. When stuff like this happens to your friends, it makes you nervous. Very nervous."

"That's under—"

"You know the Winthrop man, the other realtor I contacted?"

"Yes, indeed."

"He said he's retiring and to call you. So it looks like you're the one. I want to unload my house fast, never mind holding out for the highest bidder."

Before I could squeeze in a single word, she lowered her voice. "I'm still dying to get to New York. My career'll go nowhere around here. How can it? Nothing's happening in Eureka Falls except murder and fire."

"Then you want me to handle the sale?"

"Of course." Her voice dropping again, "I've got to get out of here."

"Why are you whispering, Penelope?"

"Someone's in the next room. Can you come out to the house tomorrow? Ten A.M.?"

"Yes, no problem."

"See you then." *Click.* The phone went dead.

I tossed the cell on the passenger seat. Penelope's call reminded me that the predicament I found myself in wasn't an out and out disaster. True, I didn't have a job, but I did have a State of Arkansas Realtor's license and could legally list houses and sell them. That meant I didn't need Sam or Saxby or anyone else to earn a living. I had everything I needed. My sigh fogged up the windshield. Everything except deep pockets.

Halfway down Main Street, I perked up a bit. Costs for a one-woman operation wouldn't be awful steep. I could work out of my house for a while. I had a phone and a computer with Wi-Fi. Business cards and some stationery with my company name were all I'd need for starters. Plus some ads in the *Eureka Falls Star*. The Honey Ingersoll Real Estate Agency made for a nice-sounding name.

A woman jay-walked against the light. Why do people take chances like that just to save a minute or two?

No, on second thought, I'd leave off Honey. Ingersoll

Real Estate. Now that had a dignified ring to it. But how to get listings? Searching for them took time. To gain folks' confidence in a brand new agency wouldn't be easy, and I'd have to earn a living in the meantime.

But first things first. Most mornings, Saxby didn't arrive at the office any too early, but he should be in by now and wondering if he was about to become the proud new owner of an estate on the Bluffs. I ought to let him know an answer wouldn't be winging his way until Saturday evening at the earliest.

Saturday. What to wear? Always a vexing problem. What to say? What to do? For some reason, the idea of being with Andy in the darkened Hickory Lounge with just those little bitty oil lamps on the tables for light made me uncertain. I couldn't forget how in his office his voice had switched from warm to cold without any warning ... and without much reason to speak of. A tendency to be wary of. Or was I simply being fearful?

My mind was boiling over with bothersome thoughts. I needed something different to think about for a spell and snapped on the radio. The familiar voice of Lenny Purvis came floating out of station KIKK. A good ol' boy, Lenny served up local news along with his notion of clever patter. He knew everyone in town and everything that went on. He also featured a mystery guest every day. Tuning in was fun, for he might be interviewing someone you knew.

Even better, no matter if he was bald as an apple and skinny as a sapling, Lenny's speaking voice poured over you like warm molasses. Bad news oozed out of his mouth so nice and easy you tended not to grasp what he said until he stopped talking.

But not today.

Today, I listened up real hard the moment he announced, "We have a special treat for y'all this mornin'. An art—eeest, a picture-taker the likes of which you won't come across again any time soon—Mr. Jesse Raidel, photographer to the stars." Lenny chuckled over his own lame joke. "Well folks, Jesse's right here beside me, and he'll agree I got carried away a little just then. What I meant to say is Jesse Raidel takes pictures of the stars of *tomorrow*. Isn't that right, Jesse?"

I'd about reached Saxby's office at the corner of Main and Elm when Lenny asked his question. Feeling wary, I parked by the curb and listened.

Jesse came purring over the air waves, spouting about how he specialized in wedding videos and high school graduation pictures and such. While he still offered his usual full service, oh Lord, yes, he now had something new on the fire.

"I'm proud to say a reality show I shot for TV will be airing next week on Channel 8, and it features some gorgeous local beauties. Trophy wives and such who call themselves the Velveteen Vixens."

Oh my. Oh no.

"The pilot was shot at a pool up on the Bluffs. A heart-shaped pool, believe it or not, folks."

"Wow, you don't say!" That would be Lenny.

"Yeah." A chuckle. "And let me tell you, those trophy wives sure know how to strut a bikini."

"I'll bet." Lenny again.

"Every red-blooded male in Yarborough County should tune in. For sure, they'll get an eyeful. And that's not all. There's something in the show for the ladies, too."

"My, my. Are you listening up, folks?"

"The hostess, the late Carmen DeLuca ..." Jesse let his voice go low and kind of reverent "... allowed the camera inside her house. A house the likes of which I've never seen before. Why, her clothes closet alone is the size of a small apartment. Unfortunately, the poor woman was shot to death the morning after my crew photographed the show."

His crew?

Lenny's silky voice said, "So I heard, Jesse. So I heard. What a tragedy. Folks, Carmen DeLuca was an outstanding woman if ever there was one, and a fascinating guest on this very show many times. Many times. A brilliant woman, too.

On her final visit here, she spoke about how she was turning rundown properties in Central America into luxury resorts. Sounded like a world-class operation to me. No doubt about it, her death is a loss to a lot of people."

"Sad. Sad." Why didn't Jesse sound more remorseful?

Lenny piped in. "Though I'm sure the po-lice are working on the case twenty four seven, so far her murder is still unsolved."

"Yes, a terrible situation. It breaks my heart to think of her alive and well, splashing in the pool with her beautiful friends, not knowing she would be dead a few hours later."

"Jesse Raidel's a modest man, folks. He's not telling you what I'm thinking. Without his reality show we'd never get to see Carmen DeLuca ever again. What's happened can't be changed. But you *can* see her one last time on the Velveteen Vixens Show. This is one you won't want to miss. Bathing beauties, a murder victim, a heart-shaped pool, and an inside look at a mega mansion. This show has it all. As soon as Channel 8 announces a scheduling date, I'll keep you informed. Right here at station KIKK."

Playing his voice like a fiddle, Lenny dropped it several tones but picked up the beat, "Now how about telling the listening audience your future plans, Jesse? Where do you see—"

I snapped off the radio, steam coming out of my ears. The nerve of Jesse Raidel! Using Carmen's death to publicize his dumb show. That was the worst of it, but not all. Those bikini shots would cause me a pile of grief. I cringed thinking back on it. Coming out of the pool soaking wet in those skimpy little scraps of blue cloth. Sipping from a champagne flute. Posing on the pool stairs, my hair streaming wet. Oh Lord, what a message that would send. It could be the kiss of death for a serious-minded real estate woman. A woman who was about to go into business for herself—one way or the other.

I had to stop the show. Or at least my part in it. And Jesse needed to respect Carmen's memory and to pay heed to my say in the matter.

Uh-oh. What of Penelope's say? Hell bent on a big modeling career, she'd never agree to my wishes. So if I insisted, there went my chance to sell her house. There went my only client.

I huffed out a sigh and, forgetting the car was in idle, I stomped on the gas, revving the engine but not going anywhere. Up ahead at the intersection, drivers were lurching to a halt on red then surging ahead on green. An omen. Keeping on moving. Don't let anything stop you. At least not for more than a minute or two.

To my right, lights gleamed in the Winthrop Real Estate office. I should call on Saxby before doing anything else, but the news he wanted would keep awhile. Jesse wouldn't.

Housed in a concrete block building on the edge of the highway, Station KIKK was about a twenty-minute ride out of town. Without running any lights and pausing—not exactly waiting—at a couple of stop signs, I made it out there in eighteen minutes. Just in time.

In the gravel lot fronting the station, Jesse was about to climb into his truck. Saying good-bye to him was a little, apple-headed guy. Lenny Purvis in the flesh. I yanked open the car door and, telling myself sugar worked better on men than vinegar, I hurried over to them.

"Jesse!" I yelled. Both men glanced up, a bit startled. I held out a hand to the little guy. "You must be Lenny Purvis. I just caught your show."

"And you drove all the way out here to tell me so? Enjoyed it, huh?"

"Well—"

"One of the best interviews I ever did have. Jesse here knows what to do with a microphone. No need to pry every word out of his mouth like it was a gold filling. Glad you liked it, Miss."

"This is Honey Ingersoll," Jesse said. "She's one of the Velveteen Vixens."

"I am not."

He shrugged. "My tape says otherwise."

"Your tape is a lie. I don't want you doing that TV show." *Uh-oh, no sugar there.*

"You have nothing to say about it."

"What's the matter?" Lenny ran his gaze over me. "You don't look good in a bikini? Hard to believe."

"She looks fabulous," Jesse said. "They all do. You girls will capture the attention of everybody who sees you, and I'm not talking dirt farmers and good ol' boys. I'm talking film producers, booking agents, talent scouts."

Sugar, remember the sugar. "You're such a good photographer, Jesse, why not create a new pilot with other models. Girls like Penelope who are dying to be filmed."

"It isn't just the girls. It's the story concept, the setting, the idea of some of the sexiest women in the world living in the middle of nowhere. Why should I dream up a new concept when I have this one all ready to go?"

"You're mistaken. It's not ready to go." *Forget the sugar.* "You have no contract with me. I never gave you permission to flaunt my body in front of the public."

"You certainly did."

"Absolutely not." *This was war.*

"You signed a release. I have your signature on the dotted line."

Chapter Twenty-Six

HE LIED. DURING the bikini afternoon at Carmen's, I hadn't signed any documents. All I'd done was leave a business card on the marble countertop in the kitchen where Carmen would be sure to see it. No, Jesse didn't have my John Hancock on any release form whatsoever. Which meant I could go to the police and stop the pilot film from airing.

All the way back to town, I stewed over the situation. What about Penelope? No doubt she'd be counting on the show to help her boost her modeling career when she hit New York City. And Jesse was hell bent on using it to boost his own career. If I insisted on having things my way, I'd be the spoiler. Something you hate to be. You want to go along and get along, play the game other folks enjoyed playing, not go home with all the marbles and leave your friends in the dirt.

But did it have to be either or? A whole show or no show at all? Why couldn't Jesse erase the parts I was in and use the rest of his footage? They were splashing about in the pool before I got there and maybe afterwards too. If I remember rightly, I was the first to leave. He must have plenty of bikini shots, not to mention Penelope's topless act.

Back on Main Street, I slowed down and drove toward Saxby's office. But the Lincoln had a mind of its own. Without making a single stop, it headed its snooty chrome nose straight for the Eureka Falls police station and Matt Rameros.

Ellie at the switchboard waved me on through, and I banged on Matt's cubicle door. He'd hardly said, "Come in," when I yanked it open and, without so much as a by-your-leave, started right in spilling my grievance. Finally, running out of breath, I said, "He has to be stopped, Matt."

"Not so fast, Honey." Smiling like he was entertained or something. "Why don't you have a seat and calm down?"

"I *hate* being told to calm down." I stabbed the air with a finger. "And you know it."

He held up both hands, palms out. "If you believe your privacy is being violated, you have the legal right to protest."

"Good. I'm in a protesting mood."

"You've made your position clear. Now if you'll have a seat, I'll tell you what I can do, and what I can't do."

I didn't want to, but to keep him talking, I perched on the edge of the only other chair in his cubicle.

"What I can do is pay a friendly call on Mr. Raidel," he said.

"What good—"

"Not *too* friendly. Semi official is what I have in mind. Uniform. Hat. Hand on holster. No smile. I'll ask him friendly-like to cease and desist. I can't force him to, only hint strongly that I will be mighty displeased if he doesn't comply. Should he refuse either to answer me or to agree, then you have only one recourse."

"Which is?"

"Hire an attorney and sue him."

"Oh Lord, I don't have the money for that. Or the time. The show's due on TV next week."

He grinned, ear to ear. "Then chances are the citizens of Eureka Falls, if not all of Yarborough County, will be treated to the sight of a Honey Ingersoll some have only dreamed about."

Squawking like a wet hen, I leaped out of my seat. "This is

no time for joshing, Matt Rameros. After that darn show airs, nobody will ever trust me to sell a house again. My career's on the line here."

Lord Almighty, I sound like Penelope. Worse. Like Jesse.

"Sorry, no offense meant. Got swept up in the story. In my humble opinion, you're over-reacting, but I'll make a point of getting to Raidel today." He cleared his throat, the way a person does before he's about to change the subject. "When you stormed in just now, I thought you were Detective Bradshaw. But he doesn't make so much noise."

He risked a small smile, but I wasn't about to smile back, especially not after I learned what his throat clearing was all about.

"You were at the Bluffs yesterday," he said. "Same time as the fire."

"You know I was."

He nodded and lost the little hint of a smile. "Problem is the First Responders' Report states that when they arrived on the scene you were apprehended coming out of the burning building."

"Apprehended? What's that mean in plain English?"

He didn't respond directly, but after some hesitating and wall staring, he answered me. "The fire marshal believes the house was deliberately torched. If he's correct and arson was the cause, the fire becomes a police issue. As a Realtor, you had access to the house before the fire, and you were seen on the premises during the fire. Long story short, if you hadn't come in, I would have gone looking for you. Bradshaw's orders."

Perching on a chair edge wasn't a good idea right now. I slumped as far back as the hard seat allowed. "I was afraid Barry McHale had been trapped inside. I was on an errand of mercy."

"Tell Bradshaw exactly what happened. And when he asks a question several times over, don't deviate one word from your original story."

"It won't be a story. It'll be the truth."

"You know that and I know that but bear this in mind: McHale's insurance company does not. They'll be looking for a reason to wiggle out of paying damages on the claim. And Bradshaw will be looking to break your story … ah, statement. So be careful what you say." He checked his watch. "Since you're here, you might as well stay put. He's due in any minute."

"Not wasting time, is he?"

"No." Matt huffed out a breath. "There's more. I shouldn't tell you this, but I will."

Fighting the sudden urge to upchuck all over my shoes, I sat tall while Matt got out his big guns, so to speak, and aimed them at me. "You see, Honey, whoever set the fire may also have killed Carmen DeLuca."

Chapter Twenty-Seven

NEVER ONE TO shirk his duty, ten minutes later, Detective Bradshaw hot-footed into Matt's office and took over. Grim-faced, he started right in poking at me with question after question: When did I first notice the fire? Where was I at the time? How long did it take me to get there? Why had I entered the burning building? How long was I inside? And on and on.

While I didn't appreciate being badgered, I took Matt's advice to heart and answered each question the same way every time. After about an hour of tramping over the same ol' ground, though, I was about to set aside all common sense and tell Bradshaw either to arrest me or to button up. But before I got pressed to that point, he eased off the edge of Matt's desk where he'd sat peering down at me and said, "When we need to question you again, Miss Ingersoll, we'll be in touch."

What! His tone, so cold, so high in the sky, infuriated me. Or maybe I was smarting from an hour's worth of being looked at like I was a bug in his grits. Anyway, I stood, too, and faced him, eyeball to eyeball.

"Did you just have yourself a real good time, Detective?"

Startled, he stared at me without saying a word.

"Yes," I said, "That's a question for *you*. Now here's another one."

"Honey," Matt warned.

I ignored him and kept my sights on Bradshaw. "Last year, I risked my life to help solve a murder. Remember? I wore a wire so the police could hear the killer confess. Now ... now ..." I was sputtering "...you're treating me like an *arsonist*?"

I threw my hands on my hips, elbows out, shrew style. "Well, I've got news for you. I don't play with matches. Never did. I'm insulted by your questioning, you hear me?" I waved a finger under his nose. "*Insulted.*"

I grabbed my tote, tossed it over a shoulder and, waving the same finger, I pointed at the rickety door. "You see that? I'm going through it. You want to stop me?"

No answer.

I flung the door wide, enjoyed the bang it made crashing against the wall, and stormed out. The thrill didn't last long, though. I sure as hell hadn't burned down any houses, but for certain, I'd burned my bridges.

I HADN'T FINISHED stomping to my car when Matt hollered, "Honey, wait up."

I didn't. No siree. I was on a roll. Indignity had me in its grip. And then so did Matt.

He grabbed my arm and whirled me around. His eyes sparked brown fire, and he wore a big ear-to-ear. "God, you were wonderful in there."

"Really?" My jaw sagged. "You're not mad?"

"Mad? I ought to pin a medal on you. Bradshaw's a good man, a fine detective, but he's stiff as hell." If anything, Matt's grin widened. "I don't think anyone's ever told him off before." He shrugged, "I know I haven't."

I leaned on the Linc, plumb wore ... worn ... out. My temper tantrum had drained me. "Now what? I made an enemy out of the top fuzz. How smart was that?"

"No need to worry. Bradshaw may be stiff but he's fair. He just told me he went too far with his questioning."

"I'll say."

"He's doing his job, Honey. What the taxpayers hired him to do. Nothing personal against you."

Feeling sheepish, I hung my head. I could make an excuse and say the strain of the past few days caused me to snap, but truth be told, I had a fierce temper and, like a wild dog, it got loose sometimes.

"I'm sorry about what happened, but I sell houses, not burn them down."

"No need to explain. Bradshaw's worried about you. Can I tell him you're okay? Really okay?"

Fresh out of words, I nodded. He ran his hands up and down my bare arms. "You are so smooth," he murmured.

"So are you, Sheriff," I said.

He laughed. "That's more like it."

His hands dropped to his sides. "Any chance you'll be free later? We haven't had dinner together in a long time."

Feeling sorry for doing so, but not wanting to give out a false message, I shook my head. Dinner wasn't the only thing he had in mind, and we both knew it.

Chapter Twenty-Eight

ON MY WAY home, I stopped by Saxby's to tell him I'd have a decision on the DeLuca property by late Saturday. He wasn't overly happy with the delay, but as I pointed out, he'd come in with a low ball figure and at least it hadn't been thrown out of the game.

He snorted at me. "Course not, Miss Honey. My offer's the best one they're going to get, and you know it. If that Ballou fella is smart as I've heard tell, he knows it too."

He sat back at his ease and swiveled a little. "No, I ain't worried a bit." He smiled, kind of sly like. "It's after five. You want—"

"No thanks, Sax. Have to run. I'll be in touch as soon as Mr. Ballou makes a decision."

He eyed me up and down, as he'd always done, the sly smile still in place. "I know, Honey. I know."

Of course he did. Right now, I was a loose canon, no job, no income, no anchor in my life. I was adrift in a rough sea. The only safe harbor in sight was the one Saxby, of all people, offered. But instead of selling me the business straight out, he'd set up this wearisome game, tying my future to his real estate holdings. Making me sweat, in other words. No wonder a trail of Yellow Diamond Cologne followed me wherever I went.

At supper time, I ordered in Chinese, watched a Sissy Spacek rerun and, in the morning, drove out to Penelope's with a copy of a boilerplate contract. I'd scanned it through my computer after using White Out on Sam Ridley's name. Strictly speaking, since I worked for Sam when Penelope contacted me, any sale of her property belonged to him. So in fairness, and also because the last thing I needed was more entanglement with the law, once the house sold, I'd only keep my usual commission. Sam would get the rest. For the very last time. If he had any objection to the arrangement, he'd call me soon enough.

On the ride out, I rolled down the windows. Cool mountain air, crisp as an apple, blew through the car mingling with Katy Perry shouting out *Roar*. By the time I reached Penelope's, Katy had me as fired up as a brand new diesel engine, smoking hot and ready to sell igloos to Eskimos.

Look at that house. The minute my eyes lit on it, I was charmed all over again. Sitting on a green rise with a big ol' oak on either side of the front veranda, all comfortable and at ease, it put me in mind of a person without airs, sizable and welcoming.

Since my last visit, someone had filled the planters by the front stairs. Bright orange day lilies spiking out of them added an extra homey touch. The only things missing were a couple of beagles sniffing down the steps to say hello.

I should have no trouble selling this property, especially now that Penelope wouldn't hold out for an unrealistic price.

Her red Boxter, the prettiest little car I ever did see, sat in the driveway. Before climbing the stairs, I peeked inside at the black leather upholstery and the cool dashboard. A stick shift stuck up between the two front seats jaunty as can be, just waiting for a girl to grab it and *go*. I guess I never did get Billy Tubbs's Harley out of my blood. I'll bet a ride in that Boxter would be just as much fun and not nearly as scary. Well, maybe someday.

I hustled up the wide verandah stairs and rang the front door bell. No answer.

I glanced at my watch, five past ten. *Come on, Penelope.* Yesterday she seemed hell bent on having this meeting, so where was she? I leaned on the bell again, sending the chimes into a tizzy then banged on the door. Even shouted out her name. But that didn't do no good … any good … either.

Now what? I hoped she hadn't dragged me all the way out here on a wild goose chase. Vexed at the likelihood, I tried the door knob. It turned under my hand. I opened the door, poked my head inside and hollered, "Penelope, it's Honey. Where are you?"

Only silence for an answer.

"Anybody home?"

Nothing. For heaven's sake. Was she in the shower or something? I shut the door, closing myself in with the quiet and the shadowed light. Had no one seen fit to open the curtains this morning?

At the parlor windows, I fumbled in the half dark for the curtain cord, found it, gave it a strong yank and let the morning sun stream in. What a pleasing sight. Penelope's ex sure had a way of making a house pretty. He'd done up the room in pale yellow with deep blue and white touches. For the life of me, I couldn't understand why Penelope hated the place. Oh well, not a bothersome thing, just one person's preference.

I went back into the hall and yelled up the stairs. "Hello, girl!"

Between my hollering and my high heels clicking on the hardwood floor, I made enough noise to raise the dead, or at least to let someone know company had come to call. But nobody hurried out to check. *Hmm.* Maybe Penelope had gone off without locking up. A lot of country folks were in the habit of doing so. I don't recall my momma and daddy ever locking the trailer. They trusted their neighbors like they were kin. Penelope might share their way of thinking.

Not wanting to stomp through the house without an invite, I decided to leave and forget all about doing business with a butterfly named Penelope. My hand reached for the front door handle but stopped in midair. *What was that?*

There. That. A kitten's mewling, soft and high-pitched. I stood stock still, head tilted back, straining to listen. Had I really heard something or had the silence spooked me? A silent moment passed and another. My imagination then. *Wrong.* The kitten cry came drifting toward me again, light as a whisper, not a bit louder. But a sound had a cause, a sound always had a cause.

Cold beads slid down my spine, and my palms went all damp and icy. Why? Over a kitten's cry? That shouldn't send me into a panic. Yet my heart had taken to pounding, telling me to flee, run out of the house, jump in the car and race away. But something stayed me. Stubbornness, more than likely, and curiosity. As far as I could tell, the house hadn't been disturbed, and no stranger had parked a car or truck anywhere in sight. So why should I race off in a panic? Because Carmen's death had me all nerved up? True, her killer hadn't been caught yet which was worrisome. But she died miles from here and, besides, Eureka Falls was a peace-loving town, no need to think the worst right away.

Maybe a kitten *had* stolen into the house. Or Penelope had taken in a stray. Or ... she'd met with an accident and needed help. That meant I should search the house without delay. Still I hesitated, frightened, my mind spinning in circles. I could call Matt at the station and have him drive out here to check around. But his job didn't include keeping nerved-up women calmed down. Even if it did, what would I say? Penelope's not here, and there's a kitten in the house?

Fretting, scared, but ashamed to walk away without knowing if all was well, I dropped the cell phone and keys in my pants pocket and eased the tote to the hallway floor. Then I opened the front door wide and left it that way. Should I have to leave fast, there'd be no fumbling with a door handle.

Now if only I had a weapon of some kind … just in case … my glance fell on a blue and white umbrella stand circled with little Chinese figures. It held a collection of walking sticks, including the twin of one my granddaddy once had. A shillelagh he'd called it. Stout as a club and hefty in the hand, it would do nicely.

Fighting trip-hammer panic and telling myself Momma might have raised a stupid child after all, I eased my way, one step at a time through the four downstairs rooms. I even opened the closets, stick raised. Not a thing looked out of place.

At the foot of the staircase, I paused, wondering if the mewling would begin again. As I started up, only creaks on the stair treads and jays jabbering in the trees made a noise. Inside, the house had returned to silence. My imagination had played tricks on me after all … there was no kitten and no problem. Penelope had gone off with a friend, and while I searched her house, she was racing along Route 68 in a sporty convertible, her hair blowing in the wind.

By the time I reached the master bedroom, I knew my wishful thinking didn't amount to a hill of beans. Penelope had been home the whole time, in the big, ol' high-posted bed. Tied hand and foot to the four posts, she lay there naked as a jay bird except for her bra. It had been knotted around her throat.

Chapter Twenty-Nine

THE SHILLELAGH HIT the floor and clattered down the stairs. Throwing away every smidgeon of common sense I possessed, I paid no heed to who might have heard the racket and rushed over to the side of the bed. I stroked Penelope's cold cheek and arm and murmured her name, but she didn't respond, not even with the flutter of an eyelash. Was she dead? My glance swept over her. Long and slender and pale as snow, her body was marked with purple bruises. With the bra cinched so tight under her chin, how could she breathe?

Fingers trembling, I undid the knots and flung the bra aside. "Can you hear me, Penelope? It's Honey. You're okay now. You're okay."

Not sure that was true, not sure at all, I grabbed a phone that had been knocked to the floor, dialed 911, and screamed for help. Then I dropped the phone on the bed, hurried over to the bedroom door and locked it—a sure sign I'd gone plumb out of my head. Whoever hurt Penelope had fled a long time ago, or I'd be as good as dead by now.

Desperate to free her, I rushed into the master bath for something to use as a tool. Scissors, a nail file, anything. I found a pair of manicure scissors in a drawer and ran back to the bed. As I bent over to cut the cords binding Penelope's wrists and ankles, the sharp, acrid odor of urine rose up from the mattress. She had soiled herself, poor thing, but didn't moan or make a sound as I severed the bindings. I closed her thighs and lowered her arms to her sides, her skin icy cold to the touch. A quilt had been folded over a stand in a corner; I yanked it off and covered her with it. Could she feel the quilt's warmth, its weight? Not able to tell and hoping to get a pulse beat, I pressed two fingers to the inside of her wrist. No throb, no nothing. I moved my search an inch higher on her wrist. *Ah.* Delicate as the flutter of a moth's wing, a faint throb met my fingertips. *She was alive.*

Weak with relief, I knelt by the bed and kept her hand in mine, not letting go, talking nonstop, telling her she wasn't alone, to hang on, not to give up, she'd be a super model yet, she'd go to New York, she'd take the city by ...

A siren raged in the distance, came closer and closer and suddenly stopped—just like that. I let go of Penelope's hand, unlocked the bedroom door and screamed, "Up here. She's up here."

"WE WANT YOU to step out of the room, Miss," the paramedic said.

"Will she be—"

He shook his head. "Looks like her trachea's been damaged. It's a wonder she's alive at all. Now please ..."

I nodded and went downstairs to the pretty blue and yellow parlor. Alone and still scared, but not for myself this time, I sat listening to the movements overhead and the chatter of the birds, my mind flooded with questions. Who could have hurt Penelope so savagely? Beat her, bound her, nearly strangled her? Maybe hurt her in other ways too? But *why?* I had no answers for any of it, but one thing was clear, Eureka Falls wasn't the quiet, peaceful place it appeared to be. I could no longer deny that evil stalked her green hills.

A car motor purring to a stop caught my attention. Through the open doorway, I spied Matt and Zach jumping out of their cruiser and hurrying toward the verandah. A few long strides and they were in the parlor with me.

"Where are the paramedics?" Matt asked, not bothering with any social niceties.

"Upstairs."

"See if they need anything, Zach," Matt said. "And take a look around while you're up there. I'll check down here." Swiveling his attention to me, "Are you all right?"

I nodded.

"Sit tight, I'll be back."

I could have told him he wouldn't find anyone lurking about, but I sat there numb and wordless.

A few minutes only, and he returned. We were alone. For that reason, I guess, he sat beside me on the sofa and held my hand. "Tell me what you found."

A good listener, he let me stumble through the sad tale without interrupting.

Then, "Do you know if Penelope has any men in her life?"

"All I know is she was recently divorced and planned to move in with Jesse Raidel, the guy who shot the reality show. Only for a while though. As soon as the house is sold, she's leaving for New York." *Or was.*

"Anyone else."

I shook my head. "No one, except maybe Barry McHale. He used to watch some of the Velveteen Vixen photo shoots."

"What can you tell me about her ex-husband?"

"I never met him. She said she despised him." I didn't bother to add that whoever he was, he had a gift for making a house beautiful. But what did that have to do with Penelope's assault?

Zach thumped down the stairs and strode into the parlor.

I leaped up. "How is she?"

He shrugged. "Can't say. They're taking her to County Hospital."

"You photograph the scene?" Matt asked.

"From all angles."

"Want to take a look around outside?"

Zach nodded, gave his pants a hitch and left.

The medic with the name Brad stitched on his shirt pocket stomped down the stairs and hurried into the parlor. "We performed an emergency tracheotomy, but she needs to get to the ER. Will you contact her family, Sheriff?"

"Yes. As soon as I locate them."

"Fine." Brad ran back up, and in a matter of minutes the two men came down the stairs carrying Penelope on a gurney. As Matt called the station for information on her next of kin's address and phone number, I followed the medics outside to the waiting ambulance.

Ashen and lifeless, Penelope lay still as death under a gray blanket, the tube jutting out of her windpipe a sick reminder of the jaunty Boxter stick shift I'd admired such a short time ago. Brad climbed into the back of the ambulance with Penelope. The other medic closed the rear doors, got behind the wheel and wasted no time driving off. I watched them retreat down the country lane until all that remained behind was a wisp of dust blowing in the breeze.

A hand grasped my elbow. "Honey, you look done in," Matt said. "Why don't you go home? Zach and I'll stay on for a while. Check the place over thoroughly and see that it's locked up."

"Did you reach Penelope's family?"

"Yes, her mother, a Mrs. Joyce Welles. She'll meet them at the hospital. Then Zach and I will pay a few calls on the men in Penelope's life."

"You think whoever hurt her is someone she knows?"

Frowning, clearly not wanting to answer what he saw as a trick question, all he said was, "If she rallies, she may be able to tell us. In the meantime, we'll make some inquiries around town. Without a sign of forced entry, it's possible the victim knew her attacker and willingly let him in."

The victim. Not the supermodel. Poor Penelope.

Chapter Thirty

Six P.M. Yarborough County Hospital's Patient Information: "You're asking about who?"

"Miss Penelope Richie."

"Are you next of kin?"

"No, Ma'am, just a friend."

"I'm sorry we have no information for you on a Miss Richie."

Midnight. Patient Information: "I'm sorry I can't help you."

Seven A.M. Saturday morning: "We have no one here by that name."

I gave up and hung up. No way would the hospital staff tell me a single thing about Penelope's condition. Not family, not even a close friend, only what folks call an acquaintance, I didn't qualify, but all the same, I worried about Penelope like we were kin.

At two o'clock the phone rang, and I dove for it. Matt wanted me to know Penelope's mother was with her. He didn't mention anything else about what had happened or who might have attacked her and left her for dead. But I knew he was checking out all possible leads and working hard to find the creep—he just didn't want to vent about it.

Before hanging up, he hemmed and hawed a little before asking if I'd like to grab a bite at Tony's Bistro later on.

"Sorry, Matt, I have a business meeting tonight," I said. "For a sale I can't afford to lose."

Not having to lie helped me deal with the disappointment in his voice when he said he understood. After I hung up, I sat staring at the phone in my hand, telling myself that despite everything, the excitement I felt was tension over tonight's outcome. But in case there was more to it than just tension, I slammed down the phone and took a cold shower.

Actually my hair looks better after a cold rinse. Smoother, with more shine. My skin glows more too. Anyway, clean as a clothesline of fresh-washed sheets, I sashed a robe around my waist and tried to figure out what I should wear to the Hickory Lounge. This was the part I hated. No good at fashion, more often than not I picked the wrong outfit—the too short skirt, the too trashy heels, the too bright colors. Or else I went all drab—navy suit, plaid shirt and chunky heels. And I depended too much on Belinda at the boutique and all those style magazines I picked up at the drug store every month.

Instead of listening to other people, I should be my own woman and do my own thing. If I could cut a deal in business, hold my own in a man's world, spar with a shark like Saxby, I could pick out a reasonable, acceptable, classy outfit, couldn't I?

No.

So I called Amelia. We've been friends since the day after I rode into town on the back of Billy Tubbs's Harley. We met waitressing at Josie's Diner. I left waiting tables first to go to work for Saxby Winthrop, and Amelia left shortly thereafter to marry Joe Swope. My job with Saxby—if you could call it that—lasted about two years, the same length of time Amelia put up with Joe's abuse. Now she was happily remarried to banker Cletus Dwyer and expecting his baby. If anyone would give me good, honest advice about what to wear, it would be

Amelia.

"Black," she said when I called and laid out my problem.

"I was afraid you'd say that." Still in the robe, I slumped at the kitchen table. "How about the blue flowered dress with the cute little—"

"No. Black sets off your hair like nothing else. Especially at night. In candlelight. Over wine." Her voice had taken on a teasing warmth.

"Okay, Mrs. Dwyer, that's enough. Besides, it's not like that. This is strictly a business meeting."

"Even so, you want to look your best. So wear that black halter dress and high heels. Very little jewelry. Some dangly silver earrings maybe and a silver bracelet. Keep the look big city smooth.

"But I'm small town klutzy."

"And wear your hair down."

"Well, that's easy enough."

"The trouble with you, Honey, is that you're beautiful and you don't even know it."

"You really mean it?"

"Don't ask me, ask Sheriff Rameros."

"Matt? I'll do no such thing."

"No, I suppose not." She sighed into the line.

"My but you've changed since you married Cletus," I said. "Where's that shy gal I used to know?"

"I'm the same, just fatter and happier. I'm glad you called. When I heard your voice, which I haven't much lately—"

"I know, life's been—"

"No need to explain. I've been reading the *Star*, and Cletus has filled me in a bit about what's been going on with you and all, but I do have to ask …"

"Go ahead."

"Are you all right, Honey? I mean really all right. Like happy."

"No, not happy." I crossed my fingers. "But that condition is subject to change."

HE WAS WAITING for me in a corner booth in the dimly lit lounge, his fingers drumming on the tabletop. Even from the doorway, I could tell right off he had dressed up special in a dark suit, a white shirt and a gold-colored tie. All for me, I guess. As I followed the hostess across the room, he leaped to his feet and smiled.

I slid into the seat across from him and smiled back.

"At last," he said. "I was beginning to think you'd stood me up."

"No, I … . ah … . the traffic."

A lie. The cold feet that attacked me as soon as I slipped into the black halter dress had caused the delay: What if Andy refused Saxby's bid? Then more than likely Saxby would withdraw his offer. If so, was I really prepared to start an agency of my own? Had I gone over the start-up costs carefully enough? Not only that, what about those stories in the *Star* lately, saying I'd been mixed up in a murder, a fire and now a sexual assault? Who could trust such a person with the sale of a house—for most folks, the biggest sale of a lifetime? And that wasn't counting the damage the Velveteen Vixens Show would cause if Jesse refused to keep it off TV.

All these disasters had stared me in the face and seriously slowed down my makeup application. Andy deserved an apology, but what could I say? Not the truth. Flustered, I felt my cheeks go hot of a sudden and was glad that in the lounge's dim light, he couldn't tell. At least, I didn't think he could.

Anyway, I clutched my fingers together, somehow finding the presence of mind to say, "So sorry I'm late. It's not a bit like me, but the traffic on 68 was fierce for some reason. Actually, I'm known for always being on time. Goodness, when folks invite me to a party, they tell me to come a half hour later than everybody else because I'm always so early. You know, ringing the bell when the hosts are still running around in their underwear trying to get ready and all."

What was the matter with me, anyway, nattering on like this? I glanced across at Andy. He was smiling, a smile that looked suspiciously like it was at my expense.

"Don't distress yourself, Honey," he said. "Anything good is well worth waiting for."

"Welcome to the Hickory Lounge." I'd kind of forgotten Andy and I weren't alone. Startled by the sudden deep voice at my elbow, I glanced up.

The waiter handed Andy a leather folder that looked stiff enough to be somebody's last will and testament. "The wine list, sir."

"What would you like, Honey?" Andy asked, peering at the folder.

What I would've liked is to calm down, to flee from the Hickory Lounge and from Andarius Ballou, Esquire, with his all-knowing smile. But I was here for a reason, what might be the deal of a lifetime. Escape wasn't a possibility.

So right then and there, I made a decision. It was show time. Time to prove I had some backbone and, come hell or high water, just be the real me. Maybe I'd destroy the evening… the sale … the future … but so be it. He might as well know the truth about me. I was tired of pretending to be what I wasn't, classy and well bred, a girl who knew all the right words and how to dress and who drank nothing but wine from little crystal glasses.

"I'd like a beer," I said. "Bud Light. In a bottle."

Andy tossed down the leather folder. Grinning from ear to ear, he said to the waiter, "You heard the lady. Make that two."

"Very good, sir."

"Very good, indeed, Honey," Andy said when the waiter left. "Are you always so direct about what you like?"

I nodded. "You can take the girl out of the trailer, but you can't take the trailer out of the girl."

"Oh? I don't see you that way. My interpretation is far different. By its very nature, honesty contains an innate elegance."

Listen to him talk—my, my. Elegance I understood, but innate? I wondered what it meant and how to spell it, but I didn't ask. I wasn't *that* honest.

We chugged our beers, after clinking, of course.

As I sipped, I did calm down, and my fingers slid around the neck of the bottle easy as anything. I even ate my dinner, every bit, though I can't remember what it tasted like. Chicken, maybe.

And then came dessert—two pieces of coconut cream pie—and my question.

"About the DeLuca property, Andy? Have you reached a decision on my buyer's bid?"

He looked up from his plate and across the table real quick as if surprised by my question. "Business as usual, Honey?"

"Isn't that why we're here?"

"Partly." He set his fork down without having so much as made a dent in his pie. "But not entirely."

The waiter came back and poured our coffee from a little silvery pot. Andy added cream to his cup, stirred it a half a dozen times, and picking up his fork, he dug into his pie.

I cleared my throat a little, waiting, waiting.

"The pie is delicious," he said. He cut himself another forkful and glanced across at my untouched piece, my unsipped coffee. "What's the matter? You don't like it?"

That did it. I was sick and tired of playing head games with men, catering to them, awaiting their wishes, trying to please.

"Andy, dammit all to hell, forget about the pie. What's the verdict on the DeLuca house?"

He cut into the creamy stuff on top and, cool as a drink of well water, said. "It's a yes, Honey. Of course, I accept the offer. What else? Did you think for one minute I'd refuse?"

Chapter Thirty-One

A T HIS WORDS, my future opened up like a flower, a great big sunflower. Thrilled at the prospect, I jumped up without thinking and scooted over to his side of the table, threw my arms around his neck and hugged him.

He dropped his fork and reaching up, pulled me into the booth beside him and hugged me right back. I didn't know where to turn for the embarrassment. Not to the waiter who stood a foot away, his jaw slack. Not to the couple at a nearby table who were staring at us round-eyed and, for sure, not at Andy. I guess he felt the same, for he released me and I hustled back to my side of the booth.

"Well that settled it," he said.

"Settled what?" Kind of quavery like.

"You *do* go after what you want. Directly. Without letting anything stop you. And I'll tell you something else, Honey Ingersoll … I don't for one minute believe you react that way over every house you sell."

"True, but you don't understand."

"Oh, yes, I do," he said, smiling like he had the first day we met.

Uh-oh. I'd gone too far, given him the very idea that a week ago had caused me to storm out of his office all indignant with my feathers ruffled up.

Vexed with him, but mostly with myself for giving in to the first notion that popped into my head, I said, "No, I don't believe you do. All I want is to eat my pie."

He laughed. "No comment."

I pushed the dessert plate out of the way. "Please, Andy, I'm serious, so let me explain why I jumped all over you just now."

He threw his hands up, palms out. "It was a golden moment, Honey. Don't explain it away by saying it wasn't like you, or you were delayed in traffic or something."

So he'd seen through my late excuse, had he? No doubt about it, he was as smart as Saxby had said. He was attractive too. Tall and firm-jawed with hands I'd swear had never touched a shovel or a plow. But he reminded me of my daddy, a man who had been fast with words and slow with support. The kind of man a woman couldn't really trust. Something I'd have to keep in mind going forward.

Leaning in over the table, I said, "Here's the thing, Andy, the DeLuca property means more than a single sale to me. My whole future's hanging on it." I looked him straight in the eye. "Don't you want to know who the buyer is?"

"I haven't had time to ask, but was about to." He glanced over at me, a question in his eyes.

"Saxby Hunter Winthrop the Third."

"Well, I'll be damned." Flat out flabbergasted, Andy slumped back against the booth. "The author of the blue ribbon contract you showed me last week?"

"The same. There's more, too. If you had refused his bid, that very same contract would be null and void."

Null and void sounded so slick I enjoyed voicing the words though they were just a fancy way of saying dead as a doornail.

Andy frowned and mulled over my surprise. "Something puzzles me more than the contract itself which, as you know, is pretty extraordinary. Why is your assumption of the Winthrop agency contingent on selling the DeLuca property? What's his reason?"

I shrugged. "Only the good Lord knows for sure, but Saxby did say I'll need the commission to run the agency."

"That still doesn't compute. He's the one paying the commission on the sale." Andy's eyes narrowed. "It's a way of controlling you, of keeping the upper hand. Of letting you know he's a force to be reckoned with. Be careful in your dealings with him, Honey. Should he want you to sign any further documents, show them to me first so I can check the fine print. I'm speaking as your ... ah ... friend and as your attorney." He cocked an eyebrow. "Assuming I *am* your attorney."

My attorney. "Well, goodness, of course you are." I never had one of those before. Daddy would be so proud, and he'd like Andy right off ... oh, well. "I can't fathom Saxby's reasons for doing a blessed thing, but I do know he's set on having a house on the Bluffs. So he'll be mighty pleased to hear you accepted his offer."

Andy chuckled. "For half of what the house is worth, he should be pleased. However, with the fire next door and Carmen's murder, I think it's prudent to sell the place as quickly as possible. So if he's serious, I need to see some earnest money."

"First thing Monday morning, I'll be knocking on Saxby's door and will come by your office right afterwards with a check. I suspect he'll want to know how fast he can move in."

"Immediately upon a transfer of funds."

"Good. He'll be paying cash for the house, so there shouldn't be a delay."

His coffee cup half way to his lips, Andy glanced up fast. "Excellent. Carmen's heirs will be happy to hear that. Some issues are emerging with her estate, so a cash influx will be welcomed. On Monday, why don't we celebrate your sale over lunch?"

"I'd like that, Andy," I said, hoping he'd understand our meeting would be strictly business.

"Ok. Sounds good." He signaled to the waiter. "Now I'm

afraid I have to call it a night. I left my roommate in the middle of a heated discussion and need to get back."

His roommate? Oh my, what a surprise. He'd never let on that he was in a relationship.

"We're old college pals, and the poor guy's staying with me for a while until he gets his affairs back in order. You know him. He owned the house next to Carmen's, the one that burned to the ground. His name's McHale. Barry McHale."

Chapter Thirty-Two

AFTER I GOT home and shed the black dress and heels for my old chenille robe, I curled up in a corner of the sofa and pondered what Andy had said.

First off, he had been Carmen's attorney and was Barry's close friend. All three knew each other well. So chances were Andy also knew Penelope. Or at least had heard of her. If so, how strange that he didn't mention her name all evening. Yesterday's *Star* had the story of her attack on the front page along with her high school graduation picture and some snaps of the outside of her house. For Pete's sake, one even showed the Porsche sitting in the driveway. How could he not know what happened to her? In a town like Eureka Falls, news traveled fast, bad news with the speed of light. Whatever *that* was, it sure sounded fast.

Still, I told myself Andy might not have wanted to bring up such a distressful topic. Besides, he wasn't the only one around here who knew all three crime victims, a lot of folks did. True though that might be, I found the notion that he'd been secretive disturbing and spent a restless night worrying about it. By morning, with the covers all in a tangle, I figured out what was really bothering me. I'd lost all trust in Andy Ballou.

Penelope had been weighing on my mind too, and first thing, as soon as my feet hit the floor, I decided to give County Hospital's Patient Information another try. A tired-sounding woman finally answered on the fourth or fifth ring.

"Good morning, Ma'am," I said. "Can you tell me how Penelope Richie is doing today?"

"Just a moment, please." After that, a pause stretched on so long my hand holding the cell grew cramped and sweaty. I'd about decided the phone had gone dead when her voice came back on. "Sorry, but we have no patient by the name of Richie."

"You must have. She was too sick to be sent home so soon." My breath caught in my throat. "Oh, Lordy, did she die?"

"Sorry, I have no further information."

"Oh. Who does?"

"I have no idea, Ma'am."

"No, of course not. Thank you kindly." I hung up and scrolled down to Matt Rameros's home number. Why had I asked a perfect stranger about Penelope? If anyone knew anything, it would be Matt.

Sleepy-voiced, he picked right up.

"Are you in bed?" I asked.

"Not any more. You okay?" His voice tightening.

"I'm fine."

"That's great. So what's up? You calling to tell me how your meeting went last night?"

"Oh. That. Good. I got the sale."

"Congratulations." He cleared his throat. "I don't usually have the pleasure of a phone call from you at … ah … seven-fifteen A.M., so why today? What's going on?"

"I just called Yarborough County Hospital. They said Penelope's not a patient there, but they wouldn't tell me another darn thing. I'm scared she died." Silence on the line, nothing but silence. "Did she?"

I held my breath.

"No, at least not the last I heard."

"Then where is she?"

"She was stabilized then helicoptered out for reconstructive surgery. Her larynx and trachea were badly damaged."

"Where did they take her?"

"For her own safety, I can't say. The fewer people who know the better. Also what I just told you is strictly confidential."

"I understand, but will you let me know what happens? Good or bad?"

"As soon as I have any news, I'll give you a ring."

"Thanks. Now go back to bed."

"Good idea."

"Hey, are you alone?" I suddenly had to know. But this wasn't my day for gathering information. All he did was laugh and hang up.

The next few hours I kept busy doing laundry and baking cookies—Aunt Sadie's secret recipe for molasses drops—trying not to dwell on whether Penelope was dead or alive, or why Andy hadn't mentioned her all evening. But I didn't have any luck doing either one.

By noon I figured Saxby would be up and pretty much recovered from his usual Saturday night fling. When I called, he surprised me by answering real fast, sounding like he'd been sitting near the phone, wide awake and sober.

"Good news, Saxby," is as far as I got.

"Ha! So Ballou bit, did he? I knew he would. That means only one thing, my offer was too generous. So how about you go back there and tell him I changed my mind? Ask him to knock off fifty thou or so."

"That would be a big mistake. Mr. Ballou said at under two million, the place is a steal. He's only agreeing for the sake of a quick sale. Go any lower and he's liable to put the property on the open market. So if you want the house, I honestly believe it's a take it or lose it proposition." A lie and not exactly a snow-white one either.

Andy hadn't said a thing about the market. But Saxby's bid *was* way under the house's true value, and *that* was no word of a lie. My heart in my mouth, I clutched the phone, waiting for the axe to fall. But it never did.

Saxby blew a breath into the receiver, making me grateful I wasn't standing close to him. "Stop by the office in the morning and I'll give you a five percent binder. I want the place, no question about it, but I don't buy no pigs in pokes. So get a set of keys from Ballou, and you and me'll go out to the Bluffs and look around before I pay in full. Just to make sure I'm gettin' what I'm payin' for."

"That'll be fine, Sax. I'll stop by in the morning for your check."

"Not too early, Missy, okay?"

Some things never change.

Chapter Thirty-Three

THE NEXT MORNING, I was up, dressed and ready far too early for Saxby's liking, so before calling on him I headed over to Josie's Diner. Grits and eggs and maybe some home fries on the side wouldn't do me no harm … any harm. About all I ate yesterday were molasses drops, and I could do with a little reinforcement.

Like I'm fond of saying, some things never change, and I'm sure glad the diner's one of them. Bright orange on the outside with shiny stainless steel trim, inside it had a stainless steel counter running the length of one wall. Orange vinyl covered the countertop and the tables, and all the seats were brown leatherette. Even the heavy crockery had orange and brown stripes circling the edges of the plates.

Today, like most days, the place was hopping, the windows steamed up from the heat off the deep fryer and not a seat left in the house. But I lucked out. Right in front of me, on a stool next to the cash register, a good ol' boy in coveralls plunked down some change on the counter and stood.

He spotted me hovering and said, "I'm leavin', Ma'am. Take my seat. It's all warmed up for you."

"Much obliged."

He touched a finger to his John Deere cap and grinned, showing off gaps where some teeth had gone missing. A true gentleman.

My tush had no sooner settled on the cozy stool when Josie approached, carrying a steaming pot of coffee that gave off a beautiful aroma. As she had most every day for the past twenty-five years or so, she was wearing a brown uniform, a crocheted hanky with orange trim spilling out of the breast pocket and a great big sunburst of a smile.

"Well, look at you first thing Monday morning," I said, "grinning to beat the band. Don't you ever have blue moods?"

"Not lately." She filled a mug and set it in front of me.

"So what's happened lately to make you so happy?"

Josie put down the coffee pot and leaned in over the counter to talk kind of intimate like. "I'm getting married."

"*What!*"

"Yup, just like I said."

"To who … to whom?" I blew out a breath and gave up. I'd never get that straight. "Who's the lucky guy?"

Her brown eyes flared. "Who else? Tommy Lee, a course."

The tall, balding drink of water who'd been flipping burgers and frying eggs in here forever? "*Your* Tommy Lee?"

"He's the only one," Josie said, a woman clearly smitten by the love bug.

"Well, you took my breath away, Josie. I never expected any such thing. It's a, it's a—"

"Shock," she finished. "I reckon most folks'll feel the same way. Nobody understands that T.L. and me, well, we've been bumpin' fannies behind this here counter for many a year. It's high time I made an honest man outta him."

"Amen." I winked at her and picked up my coffee mug before all the heat went out of it.

"Will you stand up for me," she asked. "Be my maid of honor?"

"Am I hearing you right, Josie?" a male voice behind me

asked. "You getting married or something?"

She looked up, her smile curling down into a frown.

Jesse Raidel, red hair flowing over his shoulders, stood beside the cash register with a 'gotcha' gleam in his eye. "Who would've thunk it?" he said, clearly pleased he had.

"You keep my news under your hat, you hear?" Josie ordered.

"Yes, Ma'am," he promised, though his devilish smile said something different.

"Anyway, Honey, I don't have a sister to ask," Josie said. "So I'm askin' you." She leaned in even closer. "That way all my cousins—and I've got nineteen of 'em—won't go getting' their britches in a twist because I singled out one for the job. Know what I mean?"

"I surely do, and I'll be honored to stand up, Josie."

"In case you're wondering, the service will be in the Baptist Church on Elm Street. The reception'll be right here in the diner where me and Tommy Lee—"

"Fell in love?"

She turned bright pink in the cheeks. "Something like that. T.L.'s brother Darren'll be the best man. He's a whiz with a barbeque. Already picked out the porker and is digging a pit out back so he can slow cook him whole. Tommy Lee'll take care of the sides. Baked beans and potato salad, mac and cheese. The works."

"Wedding cake?"

"Naturally. Four tiers. I mean, my kin can *eat*."

"Sounds wonderful, Josie. You have a date in mind?"

"I surely do. Preacher inked it in his book, too, but …" she pointed a finger at Jesse "… he's not to be told."

"Oh, come on, Josie," Jesse said. "Invite me, and I'll photograph your wedding free of charge."

"Well, that's mighty nice of you, Jesse. I'll speak to T.L. about it and let you know."

"Hey, Josie," a man called, "got any of that there peach pie left?"

"Comin' up." And taking the coffee pot with her, she hustled down to the other end of the counter.

"Now don't that beat all?" Jesse said as I sipped my coffee.

"What do you mean?" I asked, knowing right well what he meant and trying not to show how irked I was to have him standing at my elbow, crowding in real close.

"Those two old coots getting hitched. What a hoot."

"That's not nice. They have a right. And Josie's the best-loved woman in town. I'm happy for her. For T. L. too."

"Yeah, I guess they deserve each other."

To my complete vexation, the stool to my right opened up. Jesse slid onto it, ready to keep on talking.

"My offer still stands," he said.

Oh heavens, not the super model stuff again. "What offer?"

Play acting like he was stunned, he flung back his crop of red curls and flat slapped a hand on his chest. "I can't believe any woman in the US of A would forget that my camera can turn her into a goddess."

"Oh, stuff it, Jesse." *Good Lord, I needed grits bad.*

I swiveled so's to stare straight into his eyes—pale blue—and spoke slow so there'd be no mistaking my meaning. "I don't want to hear no more … any more … super model nonsense. Save your magic for Penelope. Looks like the poor thing's going to need it."

"What's that supposed to mean?"

If I was reading his puzzled expression right, he really didn't know.

"She's in a hospital fighting for her life."

The blood drained from his face. "What happened?" he whispered as if too scared to ask out loud.

"She was attacked. In her own house."

"Oh God. Not Penelope. Tell me everything."

"I don't know everything. The hospital only gives information to next of kin."

But I told him what I'd found that awful day, and as I related the grim tale, he got paler and paler till I thought he'd keel off his stool and land on the diner floor.

"I can't believe you didn't know about this," I said.

He shook his head, sending his hair tumbling every which way. "I've been out of town. Went to Branson for a few days. A friend of mine works at the park. Said Brad Pitt was coming in. I thought there might be a chance for some photo ops, but it was a bust." He shrugged. "That's how it goes in the arts. But Penelope, wow, what awful news." He propped his elbows on the counter and rested his head in his hands. In a voice muffled by his fingers, he asked, "Do the police have any idea who attacked her?"

"I don't know." With Matt's warning ringing in my ears, I knew I'd already said more than enough.

Josie spotted me looking her way and saved the day. She hurried over to give Jesse a mug of coffee. Fingers trembling, he raised it to his mouth and kept sipping nonstop. A good thing. The color came back to his face and then he said something that made me wish he *had* fallen off the stool.

"If she's as bad off as you say, there goes her modeling career." He sucked up the last of his coffee. "And there goes my chance of selling the Velveteen Vixens Show. One woman's dead, one's been assaulted ..." he glanced over at me and frowned "... and one's not willing to seize the gold ring. So, maybe the Good Lord is telling me something."

"Such as drop the Vixens film or you'll be sued?"

"Naw, not quite. He's telling me to move on, Honey, to move on. Without you girls I've got nothing to sell, but this wedding thing with Josie's given me an idea." He raised his mug in the air for a refill and said, "How about a series featuring Everyman? You know, working stiffs struggling to make it day by day, show their problems, their good times, their ups and downs. Start off with Josie's wedding. Interview the guests, get a shot of the pig out back, the cake, the bride, the groom working the griddle." He swiveled around to face me. "I think a show like that would have a lot of appeal. What do you think?"

"I think you're a horse's ass."

Once again, he struck a palm to his chest like he was in shock or something. "I can't believe such a nasty thought came out of your sweet mouth."

"Believe, Jesse. Believe."

"You've got no call saying such a thing to me. A man has to look to his future."

"True," I said, slipping my purse over a shoulder and grabbing my mug. "A man also has to quit using his friends as Guinea pigs in his hair-brained schemes."

"Hey, wait a New York minute."

"That any longer than an Arkansas minute?" I shook my head. "Either way, it sure puts me in mind of Penelope. Remember her? Sounds like now she's in trouble and no use to you, she's getting dumped mighty fast."

"I didn't dump her. She dumped me."

"Smart little gal, Think I'll take a page out of her book and dump you too. Let me say it again so's you'll understand—if you ever release the Vixens Show with me in it, I'll sue the pants off you. If you think I'm fooling, try it." Then I stomped off to sit in a booth that had just opened up.

So Penelope had broken off with him, had she? Good for her and a good thing he'd been out of town lately or I'd be thinking evil thoughts about him right now. Anyway, I'd have my breakfast then high-tail it over to Saxby's office where I'd make a point of being accommodating and mannerly. With the day hardly begun, I'd already made one enemy. I didn't need another one.

Chapter Thirty-Four

A PLUMP SIX-FIGURED CHECK sat in the center of Saxby's desk. I eyed it like a toddler eyes a Christmas tree—it was too beautiful to be real. And by far, the biggest amount I'd ever been given as a binder on a property.

Wasting no time, I tucked the check in my purse along with the contract and lit out for Andy's office. He offered me a seat when I strolled in and smiled too, but he didn't put a lot of teeth into it. Shadows ringed his eyes and stubble shadowed his jaw. Saturday night's party mood had plainly disappeared.

As I reached into the purse for the documents, I noticed his fingers playing with a paperclip. He flipped it across his desk and caught it up again and again. I remembered Floyd Jones in fifth grade doing the same thing just before a big math test.

Anyway, Andy's smile got broader when I gave him the check and dimmed a bit as he read the contract. But he signed it willingly enough and gave it back to me without getting testy over the sale price. Even so, he acted like a man with a heavy weight on his mind.

"You look worried, Andy," I said. "Something bothering you?"

He gave the paperclip another toss. "Client woes, Honey. Nothing I can talk about." He pointed to the check. "This will help. Mr. Winthrop has seventy-two hours to change his mind. As you know, after three days if he decides against the sale, he forfeits his deposit. Otherwise, I'll see you here on Thursday." He reached for the paperclip again. "Should Mr. Winthrop wish to complete the deal before then, I'll be happy to oblige … let me put it that way."

Sounded like Andy's client, or maybe Andy himself, was caught in a financial bind and needed the cash as soon as possible. "I'll see what I can do," I said.

"Excellent. The quicker we settle the better all around." He cleared his throat. "As for lunch, I don't have time this noon for a restaurant meal."

Well, he was sure being blunt today, not a bit like the smooth, elegant Andy I'd come to know. Whether he had problems on his mind, or was tied up with other appointments, I couldn't tell, but something sure had him in a funk.

Though a bit irritated by his attitude, I hauled out my best business language and said, "I'm busy too so, yes, let's cancel lunch. A good idea. Later, when we have more business to discuss, we can reschedule."

"Of course," he said, rising to his feet. "I'll be in touch."

"Excellent," I said, excellent being one of my new favorite words. I picked up my purse and stood. "I must run along. Saxby wants to tour the house before the final signing. I'm hoping you have a key to loan me."

"Here it is." From his desktop, he lifted a furry lump with a key dangling off it. He held it out.

"What's that?" I asked, a little leery about touching it.

"A monkey paw. Carmen's personal key."

"From a jungle in Guatemala?"

He shrugged. "Could be. Go ahead, take it. It won't bite."

I reached for the key and took it. His usual sassy smile had fled for the hills. Likewise the spark in his eyes. I felt like I was looking at a whole new person, someone overwhelmed by whatever devil plagued him.

Torn between going and staying, I stood there, the monkey paw in my hand and with no warning, right out of the blue, I blurted, "Is Barry McHale the problem?"

"You're close." Shaking his head, smiling despite himself. "You're going to do just fine running your own realty business. You've got insight, Honey, insight. A right, rare commodity."

Insight, a college word for being able to figure out what folks was … were thinking. If that's what I had, how come I couldn't figure out my own thoughts?

Whatever the reason, my business with Andy was through for now, so I turned to leave. Before I reached the door, he said, "Don't forget our rain check. I'll hold you to it."

Forget? Fat chance. I hurried out to the stairs. How could I forget? I was doing business with a man I didn't trust and off to do business with another one.

Life sucked. Little did I know.

Before I reached the bottom of the stairs, two men started up, stepping politely to one side to let me pass on by. They were serious types in grey suits, white shirts and dark ties. I watched as they continued on up, disappeared into Andy's office and closed the door.

Hmm. I'd swear on a stack of Bibles they were strangers to Eureka Falls. Not that I knew everybody in town, but men in business suits and starched white shirts tend to stand out in these parts. Curiosity seized me in its grip. Easing my toes out of the red heels, I crept back up the stairs. Silent as smoke, I cracked open Andy's outer door a sliver and put an ear up against the opening.

"Andarius Ballou?" one deep voice asked.

"Yes," Andy answered. "Can I help you?"

"Could be. I'm Agent Kennedy. This is my partner Agent Mianelli."

A pause, then Andy's shocked voice. "FBI?"

"Yes, sir. Is there a place where we can sit down? We have a few questions for you."

"What's this about?"

"Your associate, a Mr. Barry McHale."

"Why don't you come into my inner office," Andy said. "We'll be more comfortable there."

Heavy footsteps crossed the creaky wooden floorboards, and then the inner office door slammed shut.

I eased away and tiptoed down the stairs, shoes in hand.

Oh my, wait till Matt heard about this.

"HERE'S MY CELL phone number," I said to Mindy, handing her one of my Ridley cards. "I'm taking Saxby to the DeLuca house on the Bluffs out by Moon Mountain. Call me in one hour, no matter what. Okay?"

Her eyes got big. "Why?"

"Mr. Ballou, Saxby's attorney, may try to get in touch with me. If he calls, get a number where I can reach him." Then I gave her the other reason, the real one. "Even if Mr. Ballou doesn't call, you ring me, hear? If I don't answer, contact Sheriff Rameros and tell him where I am. His cell number's on the back of my card."

"Omigod." Mindy shot a quick, startled glance at Saxby's closed office door. "You think Saxby's going to kill you?"

"Good heavens, no."

She shivered. "But you're going into the DeLuca house with him? Where a woman was shot to death?"

"Can't be helped. Part of the job."

"They haven't found her killer yet, have they?"

"Not yet. I'm probably silly to be worried about going out there, but will you check in with me anyway?"

"You can count on it. I don't blame you for being careful. These days a girl has to look out for herself." She dropped her voice to a whisper. "Saxby thinks I'm moving into the DeLuca house with him. Way out on the Bluffs with nobody close by. Only him." She shook her head. "I'm not going. I can't take it no more."

"You can't take it any more."

"That's what I said. I can't take it no more."

I must have been all nerved up to mess with Mindy's way of talking when my own was plenty shaky at times. So I dropped playing teacher. "What can't you take any more?" Though I knew.

"I can't take Saxby no more. And now he expects me to move into a creepy house on top of everything else. He don't—"

"Doesn't."

"Right. He don't know it, but I've got my eye on a cute little apartment here in town. So I'll need this job real bad. That's why I'm axing."

"Asking."

"Yes." Looking puzzled. "You having trouble understanding me, Ms. Ingersoll?"

"No, not at all. Call me Honey. Everybody does."

"So what about the job?"

"As soon as today's sale goes through, it's yours," I said, sounding like it was a sure thing, though my heart was as low as a garage sale rug. If Saxby thought she'd leave him over the DeLuca house, he might not go through with the deal. Then what? Back to Plan B, start an agency from scratch? In fairness to Saxby, I probably should snitch on Mindy, but it was in my own best interest not to. I satisfied my conscience by telling myself Saxby's so-called love life was none of my business. Not any more, praise the Lord.

"Well, well, look at you two beauties," he said, suddenly flinging open his door and popping out like a Jack-in-the-box.

We both jumped a little. Guilt, I guess.

"Look at *you*," I said.

He had gone all out for our meeting, in a double-breasted navy blue suit buttoned tight across his chest, a stiff, starched shirt and a bright red tie. He'd even folded a red silk handkerchief in his jacket pocket and slicked back what was left of his hair. As he came closer, a perfumy cologne wafted across the room with him.

Oh boy.

"Ready?" he asked.

"I think so," I replied and winked at Mindy as Saxby took my arm and escorted me out of the building.

We were both buckled up and the Lincoln was purring away ready to roll. "You want my client music playing?" I asked him, reaching for a smile.

"What would that be? A little Willy Nelson?"

"No, siree. I've got classical CDs here. One's for somebody named Vivaldi. Another one's Beethoven." I arched an eyebrow. "I only play this stuff for a special type of client."

"I like that." He stretched across the seat and squeezed my right knee." "It's classy. Just like you."

I should have known better than to try and swap friendly banter with him or, worse, raise an eyebrow in his direction. But this was the first time I'd ever been called classy, and it sounded kind of good—for a second or so. I'd been bought before, but never again. I grabbed his thumb. "You want me to bend this back?"

He yanked his hand away. "Certainly not."

"Then please remember this is a business trip. And business has rules."

He heaved a sigh that fogged up the air and didn't help the windshield much either. "I'm trying to do something fine for you. Is this the thanks I get?"

I put the car in gear and headed out of the parking lot. "I thank you kindly for the compliment, but no whining allowed, Saxby. You're about to get the house of your dreams for a bargain basement price, and you know I'll run the agency almost as good as you do." *Or better.* But there was no need to go out of my way to give offense. So semi-bought, I drove through town to the cut-off that led up to Bluffs Boulevard.

At the top of the ridge, standing proud and tall like a beauty queen sure of her powers, Carmen's house shone in the noonday sun. Big, boxy and white it caught the eye and held it.

Though for all its size and glittering whiteness, the building's plain lines put me in mind of ol' country barns. A notion I didn't intend to share with Saxby.

That's when he surprised me. "I love this post-modern architecture, Missy. It takes the look of ol' timey buildings and, in a manner of speakin', puts a new spin on it. I admit talkin' evil of the dead's a bad practice, but the DeLuca woman had a gem here and came close to wreckin' it with that darn-fool pool out back." He shrugged. "But a little expenditure will take care of the pool. Now let's see what's awaitin' me inside."

I pulled onto Carmen's circular drive and had hardly turned off the engine before he opened the passenger door and set a foot on the pavers. A good sign, eagerness.

I stepped out too and sniffed air rich with pine and new-mown grass. To my relief, the odor of smoke and soot from Barry's burned-out house had disappeared. And from here, the boxwood hedge hid what was left of the blackened remains.

We strolled up the walk to Carmen's front entrance, Saxby smiling all the way. I turned the monkey paw key in the lock, and in we went.

The lofty rooms looked much as I remembered, dark tiled floors and high, beamed ceilings, the outsized paintings casting splashes of hot color against the cool walls. I loved it all. Every single thing about it sang to me. And everything was a reminder of Carmen—the alive Carmen, fun-loving and sassy in her sexy red bikini—not the woman whose dead finger pointed at a bloody message. "*Under car.*"

I shivered in the warm air. Though I knew Detective Bradshaw, Matt and the entire police department of Yarborough County were working day and night to solve the crime, so far no one had been arrested, no one declared a suspect. I wondered … no, I hoped to God … an arrest would take place soon. Very, very soon.

"This place has good bones," Saxby was saying as he slowly toured through the downstairs rooms, his realtor's eagle eye taking in every detail. "Kitchen's mighty fine, mighty fine, indeed." He opened the SubZero refrigerator and peered inside. Before he slammed it shut, I caught a quick glimpse of a taco and a bottle of sparkling water.

"Some Mexicali food left in the fridge needs to be thrown out," he said, moving over to the Wolfe stove, trying all the burners and fiddling with the oven controls. Finally, as he turned off the stove, a little half smile lifted the corners of his mouth. "Just as well Mindy had to keep the office open today. It wouldn't do her any good to see this place. She'd fall in love with it, and that would make it harder."

"What all do you mean?"

"Breakin' up with her's what I mean." He paused. "I've got no intention of keepin' our … ah … acquaintance goin'. Made up my mind. New house, new life. No baggage comin' along."

I must have looked stunned or something, for he went on explaining. "Why my momma would turn in her grave if she thought an unsuitable female was usin' her Kentucky pieces. Sittin' on her parlor chairs. Sleepin' in her tester bed." He paused. "Not that I want Mindy thrown out on the street, you understand. So I'm hopin' you'll keep her on at the agency."

"Rest your little heart on that score. I'll need her help."

"Good. That's a load off my mind. Course I'll be a mite lonesome out here all by myself." He waved his arms around, at least as much as he could in his tight suit. "It's a gorgeous house … you'd fit it somethin' fierce. And it's not too late …"

"I'm afraid it is, Saxby." I didn't bother to mention that when Miss Eloise, his beloved mother, was alive, he never let on to her that I existed. Nor did I mention he would never touch me, not ever again. All I said was, "Doesn't a new life require a brand new woman?" Taking a chance, I arched a brow at him.

He laughed. "You could be right. And the world's full of women, ain't it?" He glanced around the spacious kitchen, gave a satisfied nod and said, "So far so good, now I think I'll stroll on upstairs and check out the bedrooms. Don't suppose you want to come along."

He never gave up. I'll hand him that.

Somewhere in my tote, the cell rang. *Saved by the bell.* "You go ahead. I'd better get this, Sax."

"Good girl, business first."

As he traipsed up stairs, I took the call.

"You okay?" Mindy whispered.

"Fine and dandy. Any messages?"

"Nope, not a one for you. Just a couple of inquiries about property."

I'd no sooner hung up when a scream tore through the air. A high-pitched scream of pure terror. Followed by another, louder this time.

Thinking fast or more likely not thinking at all, I grabbed a copper fry pan off the stove rack and raced up the stairs.

"Saxby!" I yelled. "Where are you?"

"In here, Honey! Hurry up."

I found him—and Sophie—in the master bedroom. She stood trembling in the center of the room, wringing her hands on a dust cloth, her big brown eyes filled with tears. Like he was being held at gun point, Saxby was leaning against a wall, his hands in the air. As soon as he caught sight of me, he said, "For God's sake, Honey, tell her I mean no harm."

I lowered the fry pan. "Don't be afraid, Sophie. He won't hurt you. This is Mr. Winthrop. He's buying the house."

Trembling, she sank onto a soft little chair by the foot of the bed and mopped her damp face with the dust cloth. "*Si*, I understand. He come in so quiet I no hear him."

I pointed to the duster. "You're still working here?"

"Mrs. DeLuca liked things nice."

"True, but—"

"I get paid. Her lawyer, he says keep up the house. So I come in once a week."

Attempting to recover himself, Saxby collapsed onto the foot of the bed. "You gave me a hell of a scare, lady. What did you do, fall out of the sky? I don't recall seein' a vehicle in the driveway."

Before Sophie could tell him her husband usually dropped her off, my cell rang. Mindy on the line.

"You just got a message," she said. "A Mr. Jesse Raidel

called, claimed you'd want to know the news right away. It's about a Miss Penelope Richie."

"Yes?" I said gripping the phone.

"She passed an hour ago."

Chapter Thirty-Five

A T Mindy's news, the air swooshed out of my lungs, and I slumped on the bed next to Saxby. His fingers hovered above my knee for an instant, ready to swoop down and squeeze, but I guess he thought better of it, for his hand just flopped onto the bedspread.

"What's the matter, Honey?" he asked kind of soft like, reminding me that once in a while when sober, he could be sweet as a praline. "Bad news?"

I nodded, forcing the tears back behind my lids. "A friend of mine just died." I guess that was as close to the truth as a body could get. Penelope and me, well we became friends the day I found her all beaten up and tied to her bed.

"Anybody I know?"

"The girl in the headlines last week."

"I'm sorry to hear she's gone. Losin' a friend is an unfortunate happenin." Saxby hesitated, then patted the back of my hand.

I turned to him. "You know something, Sax? You can be real nice at times."

"I'm nice all the time, Missy. All the time."

That's not how I remembered it. So when his fingers tightened around mine, I got up off the bed and walked over to the window. For the second time in a hand span of minutes, the breath left my body. In the distance, Moon Mountain rose as it always had, waiting and patient, to the sky. Below it, closer in, the Bluffs' rocky ridge peered down at the river sparkling in the sunlight, pretending nothing sad had ever happened.

"I dust in the other rooms now, Senor," Sophie announced.

"That's fine," Saxby told her. "Go right ahead, Sophie."

A moment later he came up behind me, his arm stole around my waist, and he pulled me tight. "You need comfortin'," he murmured in my ear, running his hands along my hips, snugging himself up against me.

I sighed and wriggled free. "It won't work, Saxby."

"What won't?" Reaching for me.

"Taking over your agency. I can't do it." Maybe I was being stupid, but somehow I had to make him understand nothing, not even the agency, was worth getting tangled up in his life again.

"Why … why … why can't you?" he sputtered, out of oily words for once.

"Our contract is for business only. But I'm wondering what else you've got up your sleeve."

"Not a darn thing. You know me better than that."

Hands on hips, facing him eye to blood-shot eye, I said, "You're not planning to be the power behind the throne? Dropping in all the time with advice? Sitting around the office checking up on sales? Trying to get me or maybe Mindy in a corner so you can hit on us? Like you've been trying to do just now?"

"Why you're being downright—"

I waved his words away. "Nope, stop right there. You can keep your agency, Saxby. The price is too high." I turned back to the window. "Deal's off."

I might have sounded like my mind was made up, but in truth I was playing strip poker—in a manner of speaking—

with a wily ol' coot who had aced the game long ago. He'd probably tell me to take my cards and go home. Not even call my bluff. No wonder my heart was beating like a jungle drum.

To put a little distance between us, I moved over to the other window, the one facing the McHale property and peered down at the scorched earth and the blackened remains of what had been a showplace. What a shame, it was …

"Honey," Saxby said, his voice kind of soft like, "I want you to know something."

When I didn't answer, he went on, "First thing in the mornin', I'm buying' this here house, and I'm turnin' my business over to you. The way I see it, you ain't got a choice in the matter. You refuse, I'll sue."

I glanced over a shoulder at him, and this time I arched a brow as high as that sister would go.

"You know why I'll sue the pants off you? No double meanin' there," he hastened to add. "Because takin' over the Winthrop Agency is the best thing that could happen to you." He poked the air with a finger. "And don't you forget it." Out of breath, he stopped for a second, then with a sigh added, "If it'll make you happy, I'll add a no harassment clause to the contract."

I slowly turned from the window to face him. "You'll leave me alone to run the business as I see fit? No dropping in, no phone calls, no playing footsie?"

His sigh deepened. "You drive a hard bargain."

Now *I* stabbed the air with a finger. "I want it in writing. One visit a month. One phone call a week. And fiscal updates once a quarter. No daily accounts."

"A mighty skimpy agenda, but it'll do. Now what say we have a drink on it? Sophie!" he hollered, loud enough to call cows in from the fields. When she came hurrying into the room, he said, "Any bourbon around the house?"

She shook her head. "No senor. Tequila only."

"Well now, that'll do just fine. What don't you show me where you're hidin' it?" His voice had taken on a lilt. "Comin',

Missy?"

"You go ahead. I'll be there in a minute." A movement in the wreckage next door had caught the corner of my eye. Someone or something was pawing through the remains of the McHale house. Ah, there he was, stooped over sifting the ashes, a man in jeans, denim shirt and work boots. He stood, dropped whatever he'd been examining and brushed the soot off his hands. Oh my Lord, it was Barry McHale.

Chapter Thirty-Six

WITH SAXBY IN the kitchen sipping his happy juice and chatting away with Sophie, I snuck down the stairs and out the front door. I cut through the opening in the boxwood hedge, carefully easing my way onto the disaster zone next door. Up close, the odor of soot and ashes and charred wood made me gag. Taking only shallow breaths, I stepped over a pile of bricks.

"Barry, where are you?"

He popped out from behind a crumpled wall. "Honey Ingersoll? What on earth are you doing here?"

"Showing a client the DeLuca property. Thought I'd come over and say hello."

He nodded, glanced briefly at Carmen's house standing white and unharmed in the afternoon sun, and shrugged. Dark shadows ringed his eyes and under a dusting of soot, his face looked pale and drawn. In his soiled work clothes, he'd pass for a hard-scrabble mountain man, old before his time.

"I've been sifting through the ashes," he said, "trying to see if there's anything worth salvaging. Maybe some pictures of my brother Tommy, but they're all gone."

"I don't know about your brother, but I saw some pictures of Carmen next door and one of the two of you together. If you like, I'll ask Andy if you can have them."

Barry snorted. "Why would I want a picture of Carmen?"

Whoa. Hadn't he asked her to marry him? Three times.

He wiped his hands on his shirt front. "So much for having one last look. Let's go."

Skirting a heap of blackened planks and what looked like a broken table leg, we picked our way out to the street. "The site's due to be bulldozed tomorrow then I'm putting it on the market. The view is gorgeous, so the land should bring a pretty good price." He glanced over at me. "I'll need a realtor. You want to handle the sale?"

I nodded. "Very much so."

"Good. I'll be in touch as soon as everything's cleaned up. But I'm warning you now, I'm going for top dollar. I'll need every penny I can lay my hands on. The IRS is all over me for back taxes. And that's just the tip of the iceberg." He stuffed his sooty hands in his jeans pockets. "I'm pretty much tapped out."

The IRS was on his tail, *and* the FBI? While I hadn't the slightest notion of mentioning what I'd overheard on the stairs outside Andy's office, I was mighty worried for Barry as I trudged back to the DeLuca house to pick up Saxby.

Still in the kitchen, he was sitting at the table eating tortillas, a half-empty bottle of tequila in front of him.

"Where you been?" he asked when I walked in. "You're missin' the party." He pointed to his plate. "This Mexicali stuff is great. What do you call them again, Sophie?"

"Tortillas, senor."

"That's it! Right up there with ribs and fries, and I don't say that lightly."

"If you've seen enough, Saxby, I'd like to get back to town."

"Soon's I finish up this here whatchamacallit. Sophie's one great little cook. She's going to stay on and work for me when I move in. Aren't ya, darlin'?"

"Si, senor."

Poor Sophie. A few more days of this and she'd be ready to murder him.

Chapter Thirty-Seven

Saxby slept most of the way back to Main Street, waking when the Lincoln purred to a halt and I switched off the engine.

"Home, sweet home," I said.

"So soon? Well, I'll be hornswoggled. You must have violated every speedin' law in the State of Arkansas."

After two tries, he managed to open the passenger door. "I'll see you first thing in the mornin', Missy."

"I'll be here. Nine A.M."

He stepped out, slammed the car door and lurched in a ragged line more or less toward the agency's back door. I yanked the cell out of my bag and punched in the office number.

"He's coming in, Mindy. Just so you'll know, he's not fit to drive."

Home for real, I kicked off the heels and padded to the fridge for an iced tea. I'd no sooner swallowed a few gulps when the door bell rang. Before answering, I peered between the living room blinds. Matt Rameros's off duty wheels, the Dodge Ram he was so proud of, sat in one of the parking slots.

Pleased as all get out to see him, and a little surprised, too, I hurried to the door.

In a navy polo shirt and khakis with a crease so sharp it could slice your throat, he stood there grinning from ear to ear. He held up a six pack. "For you, only the best."

"Bud Light. My favorite," I said, swinging the door wide. No fancy wines or champagne for me, and Matt knew that. It was good not to have to pretend to be classy, and I followed him out to the kitchen, gratefully taking the can he snapped open for me.

We carried our beers into the living room. Matt glanced around, at the pale blue sofa and the big screen TV on its painted white stand, the blue pot of paperwhites I kept on the coffee table, the photograph of my momma. "Haven't been here in a while. Still looks pretty."

He sat on the couch and patted the cushion beside him, but I took the club chair.

"Okay," he said, "if you prefer life in Siberia."

Though he didn't sound like his feathers were the least bit ruffled, I changed the subject. "So what brings you here today, off duty and all?"

He got serious at that and rested his beer on the coffee table. "Well, I promised to let you know as soon as I learned anything about—"

"Penelope?"

He nodded.

"I heard she passed. Is it true?"

"Yes, sorry to say, it is. She died early this morning. Since you were the first person on the scene of what is now a murder, you can expect a call from Detective Bradshaw. He'll have more questions."

"I'll tell him everything I can recall, but before she died, did she say anything? Tell who hurt her so bad?"

He shook his head. "No. She never regained consciousness."

"Oh God. What's happening to our town, Matt? Two women snuffed out ..." I snapped my fingers "... just like that.

Poof and they're gone."

"Which brings me to my second reason for being here."

"Oh?"

"Be careful, Honey. You found both victims. In some way, you're tied into all this."

I started denying it was so, but he held up a hand. "I'm not saying guilty, I'm saying involved. It's possible ..." he hesitated like he didn't want to go on but felt he had to "... you know the killer. And the killer knows you."

"You think I'm next on the list?"

"No way of telling, not with all the unknowns in the case. Carmen DeLuca's death bed message, for example."

"Under car?" I whispered.

"Yes. Hell we examined every vehicle belonging to every person who had dealings with her, however remote. We found no contraband, no tampering, no GPS tracker, no bomb. No nothing." He shrugged. "Who knows? Maybe the victim didn't write the note. Maybe it was staged."

"But why?"

"If we had the answer, we'd know who did it. And we'd know why you of the three women on the Velveteen Vixens video is the only one left alive."

"Maybe so, but I'm not the only person who's involved, Matt. For one, Jesse Raidel is beside himself. He had such high hopes for his show and now this. I guess he does need a new project after all. As for me, lately I don't trust anybody. I see a killer behind every face, every door. Not only that ..." though we were alone I leaned in closer and dropped my voice "... there's something else going on, too. I don't know what it is, but I've got a creepy feeling it's tied in with the murders."

"What do you mean? Tied in how?" Matt leaned forward, all ears, all interest.

"Earlier today, I ran into Barry McHale out on the Bluffs. He told me he's tapped out, owes the IRS for back taxes. And Andy Ballou? Lawyer Ballou? Well, this morning he had a visit from the FBI. I overheard them say ..." my cheeks heated up a bit "… they wanted to question him about Barry McHale."

"I know."

"You do? Oh. So much for my big scoop."

Matt picked up his beer and took a swig. "I can't discuss an ongoing case, but I can tell you this. Everything you just said is accurate and known to the department."

"Aha!"

"But, and this is a big but. So far, none of it has provided a motive for murder."

"So far."

"Exactly. To get back to my second reason for being here, I want you to be careful. When you're home, make sure the security alarm is on at all times. When you're out and about, park in well lit locations, stay off deserted roads and, better yet, don't go out at night." He frowned, foot tapping like he had a nerve twitch or something. "What bothers me the most is your work. Going into empty buildings alone."

"They're not always empty."

He scoffed. "More times than not. Until this is over make a point of letting me know when you have a showing."

"That's not workable. You can't be at my beck and call."

"Call anyway. Zach and I will work something out."

I felt my eyes tear up. Matt loved me. I know he did. And when someone loves you with a steady, dogged, never give up kind of love, how can you not respond to it? That's exactly what I was asking myself when he smiled and said, "Which brings me to reason number three for being here tonight. How about I treat you to a spaghetti dinner at Tony's?"

Chapter Thirty-Eight

Tony's Bistro never changed, and that's the way folks liked it. The original high-backed booths were still topped with red and white checkered tablecloths and those little oil lamps, the ones that gave off a soft glow and made sitting in a booth feel like you were on a private island. Plus, the food was great. No wonder everybody loved the place.

Best of all, though, when I went there I never had to worry about my outfit. Whether my skirt fit too tight, my top showed too much cleavage or my stilettos were trashy high was never a problem. For dinner at Tony's, I could toss on jeans and a T-shirt and be done with it.

So while Matt watched the last inning of the St. Louis-Cincinnati game, I changed into faded jeans, a black Tee and sandals. I clipped on a pair of dangly silver earrings and, after a fresh dusting of eye shadow, I was good to go, just as the Cardinals whipped the Reds, fourteen to six.

As usual, when we got to Tony's, cars and pick-ups jammed the parking lot, and inside, Musak pumped out an Italian love song.

Tony Junior spotted us as soon as we walked in and rushed

over to shake Matt's hand. "Sheriff. Honey. Always welcome. Always." He leaned in to whisper, "I saved a booth for you. My best one. Over in the corner."

"You knew we were coming?" I asked.

"I called," Matt said and winked at me.

Tony's didn't take reservations, except when they did.

Anyway, we settled in our booth, refused Tony Jr's offer of a free bottle of red and ordered two Bud Lights. Matt might accept an open booth, more for my sake than his own, but nothing that smacked of a bribe.

At our table, the lamp light turned his broad cheekbones and chiseled lips and those dark, hooded eyes of his into a piece of sculpture. The kind you'd likely find on a stone temple somewhere in Central America.

Though I knew he had a lot on his mind, he sat smiling across at me looking relaxed and untroubled. Not wanting to ruin his happy mood with more talk about murder, I said, "Tomorrow's my big day, you know."

"Getting married or something?" he asked, dropping the M word on me all innocent like.

I didn't take the bait. "Sort of. If everything goes according to plan, Saxby and I sign our contract in the morning. Then I guess the agency will be legally mine."

Grinning, Matt high-fived me. "Sounds good. Better than good. You'll do a bang up job, and Winthrop knows it."

"I hope so. As long as he leaves me alone to run things as I see fit, otherwise…"

"You worried about that?"

I nodded. "Somewhat. He's signing something he said is a non-harassment clause, so that should help."

"If it doesn't, let me know. I can always pay a little call on Mr. Winthrop and, let's say, suggest arresting him for non-compliance. If necessary, I'd do it for you in a heartbeat. And just so you'll know, I did get in touch with Jesse about the film. Hinted at a lawsuit. He claims litigation won't be necessary. He's planning on scrapping the show."

"Wonderful." His hand, short and wide with strong, brown fingers, rested on the tabletop. I reached over and held it.

"Two Buds." With a thump, Tony set the bottles in front of us. "And menus. When you're ready, Angelo will take your order."

"He treats you like a king," I said, as Tony hurried off to greet his next guests.

"I kept his brother-in-law out of jail once. Tony remembers. Not that he has to, he just does."

I took a swallow of beer and happened to glance up in time to see Tony escort a couple to a nearby booth.

The man was tall, good looking and dressed to kill in a dark suit, white shirt and tie. His date had squeezed herself into a short red dress and dynamite heels. My bottle hit the tabletop. *Andy Ballou and a date. Well, well.*

Matt noticed me staring and quirked a brow. "Surprised?"

I slugged down some more brew. "Yes. But I shouldn't be. Mr. Ballou is full of surprises.

As we both watched, Andy waited until the woman was seated then took his own seat with his back to us. In no time at all, they were chatting away like old friends who had a lot of catching up to do. *Hmph.*

Angelo suddenly appeared at my elbow. "Another beer?"

"I'm good," Matt said.

"I'm not," I said smiling up at Angelo.

Matt shrugged. "You heard the lady, Angelo. A beer for her. And bring us two house salads and some bread, okay?"

With a nod, Angelo took off, returning almost soon enough with my nice, cold Bud. I hoisted it, and took a swallow. "Cheers!"

"Right," Matt said, tackling his salad.

Though the jelly donut I had for breakfast was a long way off, raw greens didn't turn me on, so I pushed mine aside and sipped the beer, my attention already riveted on the booth across the way. For a fact, what Andy Ballou did in his spare time was none of my business. But seeing him sitting there all loose and chatty didn't fit with the Andy I'd seen at noon. And it didn't fit with a man who'd had a surprise visit from the FBI this very day.

"Spaghetti and meatballs okay?" Matt asked me when he finished his salad.

"Wonderful," I replied, my mind everywhere but on our meal. "You know something, Matt, something that's been gnawing at me? When I saw Andy Ballou earlier today, he never once mentioned Penelope's attack or the fact that she died. He knew I found her and all, so don't you think that's strange?"

"No." His face said yes. "But your denial aside, Ballou does seem to be a distraction. Would you like to leave?"

Andy and his mysterious date didn't have me bothered, not in the kind of jealous way Matt meant, but they sure had roused my curiosity. Still, it was no wonder Matt wanted to leave. Since Andy came in, I'd given his booth more attention than our own. And that *was* unmannerly.

When Andy lifted the wine bottle out of the cooler again and refilled their glasses, Matt's suggestion suddenly made a lot of sense. As long as we stayed here, I'd be fidgeting in my seat, wondering what Andy could be up to.

"Leaving is a good idea. Let's go."

I polished off my beer, plunked down the bottle and stood. I was probably a little too fast with the standing. For a moment there, the room reeled. But I didn't let that stop me. I flung my bag over a shoulder and zigzagged across the floor.

"So," I said, leaning over the back of Andy's booth, "Feeling better than you did at lunch time?"

Startled, he looked up over a shoulder. "*Honey?*" His voice pitched high.

"Yup. That's my daddy-given name, for a fact. Acquired it the day I was born." I glanced over at Andy's date. "The name stuck like glue."

"Mr. Ballou," Matt said, at my side of a sudden, greeting Andy real hearty like they were best hunting buddies or something when I knew for a fact they had never once gone deer shooting together. And to Red Dress, "Excuse us, Ma'am, for interrupting. We were just leaving."

Matt gripped my arm and bent over—though not being real tall, he didn't have far to bend—and whispered in my ear. "Walk out of here with me NOW, or I'll arrest you."

"For what?" I tried to twist free to see if he was joshing or not. No such luck. His grip was too strong. "For *what*?"

"I'll think of something."

Like I was a puppy, Andy reached up to pat my arm. I yanked it away, causing Red Dress to giggle, which riled me no end. Did they all think I was sloshed? "Why don't we continue this conversation in the morning?" I said, lifting off the booth and standing tall. "At the bank. Nine o'clock sharp."

Red Dress was staring at me, smiling up a storm. First a giggle and now a cheeky grin. What was so damn funny, anyway? I was seeing red, and not just her dress alone. I drew myself even taller. "Nine sharp, Andy. Make sure you're on time."

Then with Matt by my side, I strolled toward the door dignified as a preacher's wife after Sunday service. Out in the parking lot, though, the woozy feeling returned, and I leaned on Matt till we got to the Ram.

"Honey, when did you eat last?" he asked, easing me into my seat with his hand stretched across the top of my head and a warning to get my legs inside, like I'd just robbed a 7-Eleven or something. He even buckled my seat belt and laid my handbag on my lap.

"Breakfast maybe."

"That's what I thought."

"You mad at me?" I asked as he got in behind the wheel. "You know, what with me being so distracted tonight and all."

"No. You've been through a lot lately. It's no wonder you had a little meltdown. But bottom line, you shouldn't be skipping meals."

"I'm all right now. And downright ashamed of the way I

acted in there. It was probably because—"

"This is not the time for analysis. It's the time for food."

"I spoiled your dinner," I wailed.

"Only temporarily." He put the car in gear and headed out of Tony's lot onto the highway. "I didn't think you were up for spaghetti and meatballs, so there's been a change in plan. We're going to Josie's. Some scrambled eggs and toast for you. A burger and fries for me." He glanced across the front seat at me. "Sound okay?"

"Yes," I lied. I didn't want to eat anything. I was so mortified, all I wanted to do was go home and hide under the bedcovers. I'd embarrassed Matt. Good, loyal, patient Matt. My friend. I heaved a beery sigh that came close to fogging up the windshield. "There was another reason why I got so upset," I said into the silence, all fight gone out of me.

"Which is?" His eyes straight ahead, his voice cool.

"Mr. Ballou may be handling my first big sale and all, but I really don't trust him."

Andy's head swiveled my way. "Mr. Andarius Ballou? *That* attorney? No way." Smiling for the first time since getting into the Ram, he pulled into an empty slot outside the diner.

Come to find out, Josie and Tommy Lee had the night off, the first time in living memory. I hoped they were having a bang-up evening as I sheepishly ate my eggs and toast while Matt devoured his burger.

"When did *you* eat last?" I asked.

"Breakfast maybe."

"Don't make fun of me. I feel bad enough as it is."

"No need to, Honey. You're the most glorious girl I ever met. Always will be. Now if you're through, what do you say I take you home?"

"Matt," I didn't dare look him straight in the eye which I should have had the guts to do. Anyway, whispering real soft, I said, "Will you stay with me tonight? I'd really love it if you would."

"Why?"

I did look up then—into his frown. "To ease the loneliness I'm feeling."

He sighed. "Not the answer I'd prefer. But a starving man doesn't refuse a feast. Let's go."

Chapter Thirty-Nine

T HE ALARM JARRED me awake at seven A.M. sharp. I raised my head off the pillow with care, no throbbing thank the Lord, and risked slitting open an eye. A note rested on the other pillow.

> Coffee's made. Good luck today.
> Thank you, M.

I flopped back down with a groan. He'd thanked me. How sweet. Truth was, I needed to thank *him*; he got me through the night. If my momma was alive, she'd be standing by the bed right now, waving a finger at me and saying I should marry him. She'd be more right than wrong, but the only decision I could face today had to do with just one man, Saxby Winthrop.

After what happened in Tony's, I couldn't even bring myself to think about the upcoming meeting with Andy Ballou. But be that as it may, I'd have to face him in two hours from now.

Two hours.

I flung back the covers and leaped out of bed. Damage control would be huge, and I needed to get ready. Besides, Matt's coffee was giving off a heavenly aroma.

ALONG WITH MY best black suit—with the skirt that skimmed the top of my knees—black high-heeled pumps and my Kate Spade bag, I wore my hair up in one of those French twists the slick magazines keep showing. No country girl would be caught dead with such a do, and I hadn't taken a shine to it either. But the magazines claimed there was nothing like it for a professional-looking style. And for a lady-like appearance nothing beat pearls. So I slung a rope of fake ones around my neck and clipped on some pearl studs.

The makeup took a while. Getting last night off my face wasn't easy. Those blue shadows under the eyes, those ashy-colored cheeks, the grim set of the mouth. Disguising all that nearly chewed up a half hour and, even then, the person staring out of the mirror looked far from happy.

As I studied my efforts, Jesse Raidel, of all people, popped into my mind. "Emote," he'd said that day by the pool. "Emote."

If ever I needed to heed advice, this was the time. Emote I would and march into Andy Ballou's presence smiling up a storm, the French twist held high. Then after a hand shake, straight into business.

As I spritzed on a little Yellow Diamond Cologne, I knew my plan didn't amount to a pile of sand, but it was the best one I could summon up at the moment.

THE RAIN THAT had pelted the windows off and on during the night left the morning smelling of earth and wet leaves and a hint of fall. I shivered walking into the First Federal, bypassed the teller's cage and headed straight for Cletus Dwyer's office. His heavy walnut door with its brass "President" plaque was closed, but a murmur of voices told me the others were already inside. I gulped in a deep breath of the bank's expensive-smelling air and yanked open the door.

Surprise! I'd expected to see Cletus, Saxby and Andy, but I'd been wrong. Andy wasn't anywhere in sight. But for some reason I couldn't fathom, his Red Dress date from last night—now Purple Dress—sat in a leather armchair with her legs crossed, real as life. Though her cleavage looked the same as I recalled, her expression was different. No smiling or laughing today. I guess nothing struck her funny this morning like my comedy act had last night. But who on earth *was* this woman, and why had she come to this meeting? And where was Andy?

Without him, the meeting wouldn't accomplish anything.

Tearing his attention from the cleavage, Saxby stood— he usually didn't have trouble doing that first thing in the morning—and swept a hand at his seat. "For you, Honey."

"Thank you kindly, Saxby," I said, "but I prefer to stand."

Cletus, behind his big walnut desk looked up, nodded, then went back to the documents he'd been examining. Seated beside him, on folding chairs pulled up to his desk, were the same FBI men in serious suits, the ones I'd passed on Andy's office stairs. Not only was that strange, I had a notion it wasn't good.

My heart beating overtime, I leaned against the office wall for support. Maybe I could use a chair after all. I probably turned pale or looked faint or something, for one of the agents got up from his chair and carried it over to me. "I insist, Ma'am," he said.

"I'm beholden to you," I said, sinking onto the hard seat, telling my heart to stop pumping so fast.

Cletus laid the papers he'd been reading flat on his desktop and cleared his throat, putting me in mind of a pastor about to preach hell fire and brimstone. "Good morning, ladies and gentlemen. We'll begin our meeting as soon as Attorney Ballou joins us. Shouldn't be long. He's putting a last-minute codicil on a contract for Mr. Winthrop here. In the meantime, I don't believe we're all acquainted, so why don't I take care of the amenities while we wait?"

Well, the mystery woman turned out to be none other than Carmen DeLuca's cousin Emilia who had traveled all the way up to Arkansas from Costa Rica and, of course, I already knew the two strangers were FBI men. But Cletus didn't let on why a woman from Costa Rica and two federal agents from Little

Rock were sitting in on this meeting.

Ready to bust wide open with curiosity, I'd about decided to ask that very question when the door swung open and in walked Andy. Like Emilia DeLuca, he had no smile on his face this morning. In fact, he appeared pretty washed out, even had a razor nick on his chin.

I glanced across at Saxby, the only one in the room who seemed cheerful. Either he didn't care what the problem might be, or he didn't have a clue that one existed.

After saying "morning" to the group, Andy fell silent and stood staring straight ahead at Cletus and the feds, not giving me so much as a nod.

"Now that we're all present," Cletus announced, "shall we proceed?" He plucked a sheet of paper off his desk. "This is a contract for the sale of the DeLuca property … ." He dropped the paper back onto the desktop. "Funds in the full amount are in escrow here at First Federal, and both parties involved are prepared to sign the documents …" Another throat clearing, "Until an hour ago, I thought everything was in order. However, something has occurred that needs to be addressed before we move forward." *Uh-oh.* He paused and so did my heartbeat. Nodding at the man on his left, he continued, "For that reason, I'm turning the meeting over to Mr. James Kennedy from the FBI."

Agent Kennedy got up from his folding chair like he was about to give a formal speech or something—which was just what he did.

"Ladies and gentlemen, I'm afraid there will no sale of the DeLuca property today."

"What in hell do you mean?" Saxby said, ready to leap out of his seat. "We're gathered here this mornin' to consummate the deal."

Agent Kennedy sent him an icy stare. A waste of time. Saxby ignored icy stares. "The property in question has been declared a government forfeiture and turned over to the U.S. Marshall's office."

"What the hell? You telling us the house can't be sold?"

"Not at all, Mr… ."

"Winthrop. Saxby Hunter Winthrop the Third."

"You're the potential buyer?"

"You got that right."

"Let me reassure you the property certainly can be sold, and the U.S. Marshall is charged with doing exactly that."

"Well, then, let's proceed without—"

Agent Kennedy held up a warning finger. This time, Saxby was wise enough to hush up and listen. "According to law, a public auction will be held thirty days from now. You're welcome to bid on the house in one month's time."

"I want you to know this is an outrage. I'm a tax payin' United States citizen."

After all his years in the realty business, Saxby knew better than to carry on like he was, but he never did cotton to having his wishes thwarted.

Anyway, why *had* the government seized Carmen's property? With my whole future depending on this sale I needed to know, and raising my hand, said, "Agent Kennedy, sir, I'd surely love to know the reason for this upsetting news."

He nodded. "Understood. In straightforward terms, the deceased owner led what might be termed a double life. In other words, the DeLuca Resort Corporation was a front for a pyramid scheme. You may be more familiar with the term Ponzi scheme. Regardless, both employ the same tactics. For a time, early investors are paid a generous return, not on profits earned, but out of the funds of later investors. Accordingly, the monies the DeLuca Corporation collected from unwary shareholders was not invested in Costa Rican resorts as claimed but went directly into Carmen DeLuca's own coffers.

"At the time of her death, the plan was unraveling and complaints from her clients were mounting. Investigation proved those complaints valid, and we were about to make an arrest in the case, but … ." he shrugged "… her death occurred." Emilia dabbed at her eyes with a handkerchief, as he continued, "Whatever funds can be salvaged from the DeLuca estate legally belong to the innocent stockholders of this Costa Rican scheme. Including the Bluffs property."

Hearing that, Emilia broke down in sobs, and I nearly did too. A good thing I was sitting or I'd have slumped to the floor.

"What Agent Mianelli and I want to make clear to all present is that the monies from the sale will not go to the DeLuca estate as expected and, according to Attorney Ballou, as the will directs, but will be held in reserve by the United States Government for distribution to the claimants."

"The ones who got screwed over by that woman?" Saxby said.

"Exactly."

"Well, hell, I don't care who gets the money as long as I get the house and a clear title along with it."

At that Andy pulled away from the wall and said, "If I may interrupt?"

"You go right ahead, Andy, interrupt away," Saxby said. "But it won't do you no good. Never does with these government fellers."

"This won't take long," Andy said with more than a touch of steel in his voice. "I just want to tell Ms. DeLuca, that there's no need for her to remain for the rest of our meeting." Shifting from one foot to the other, "Emilia, I trust you understand that though I was your cousin's counsel and would be happy to be retained as yours, I can't help you in this matter. The United States government is the final authority. Since there will be nothing left for Carmen DeLuca's heirs, her will is as good as null and void. Now if you would excuse us, please." He opened the door and held it, a silent invitation for her to exit.

As upset as I was over the way all this had turned out, still I had to hand it to Andy. Never before had I seen anyone thrown out with so much style. The slick magazines ought to publish a few pages on how to do that instead of always talking about mascara and pearls and stuff.

Anyway, if I hadn't seen Emilia laughing up a storm last

night, I would've said the woman had never learned how to smile. Frowning like she invented how to do it, she grabbed a bag off the floor next to her chair, wiggled her clothes into place and marched out, slamming the door behind her.

Saxby looked sorry to see her take her cleavage and go, but he got over it fast and upped his chin at Agent Kennedy. "FBI man, when the auction you're talkin' about takes place, I want you to be sure and tell the U.S. Marshall not to start the biddin' too high. A murder was committed on that property, and a fire bug burnt the house next door down to the ground. According to my estimate, those two evil deeds reduce the value of a property by at least half. Maybe more. So can I count on you to make those facts known to the auctioneer?"

Smiling ear to ear, the agent replied, "Rest assured, I'll do my best, Mr. Winthrop. Now if there are no further questions, my partner and I will take our leave." After shaking hands all around, that's exactly what they did. Once they were gone, Saxby quieted down, but in true Saxby fashion, he'd made himself clear: he'd want the house for a song. If he didn't bid up at the auction—and I doubted he would—he'd lose. And so would I.

In fact, sitting there on a rickety chair in Cletus's stuffy office, I felt like I'd already lost. No sale, no agency. No agency, no job. No job, no money. And suddenly, I didn't even care. Fed up with all the meetings, all the talk, all the set-tos with Saxby, I grabbed my bag and stood.

"Thank you for your time, Cletus," I said. "There's no need for me to stay any longer, either." Then making a bee line for the door, I escaped into the bank with my heels clicking on the marble floor, down the stone steps and out to the street.

I'd almost made it to the Lincoln, when Andy shouted, "Hey, Honey, hold up."

With no intention of stopping, I stomped right on, even had my finger hovering over the door lock before he caught up to me.

"What's your hurry?" he asked.

I whirled around to face him. "I've had my fill of being asked questions. How about an answer instead?"

"Very well." Reasonable, arms by his sides, he waited.

"You must have known about the property seizure. Why didn't you call off the meeting?" The look I shot him wasn't exactly snarly, but it wasn't sweet, either. "What were you doing, setting me up for a fall?"

"No," he said, stony calm. "First of all, this wasn't just about you. Second, Carmen DeLuca's heir had to be brought face-to-face with the truth. And third, there's a contract in there waiting for you to sign."

"Without the house, the contract is just a piece of useless paper. Saxby's made that very clear."

"You're wrong. He sent me out here to bring you back. He's hell bent on retiring, he said, house or no house."

FIVE MINUTES LATER, in the armchair Emilia had recently filled to purple perfection, I listened while Andy said, "Miss Ingersoll, will you please take a look at the change in this contract between you and Mr. Winthrop? At his insistence I added what, in my opinion, is a fine built-in protection for you as you assume ownership of his realty agency." He flipped to the last page of "insofars," "in whichs" and "hereafters," and there it was, all printed out neat and pretty, Saxby's promise to leave me in peace while I ran the company.

While Andy waited, with a shaky hand I signed both copies of the contract and Saxby did the same.

It was a done deal.

"That's the best bit of business I ever did conduct," Saxby declared, and heaving himself out of his chair, he came over to give me a big, wet kiss that landed on my cheek. Actually, it only ended up under my ear like that because I turned my head in the nick of time. To make up for it, I reached out to give him a hug in return.

"Thank you, Saxby, you won't be disappointed."

"No need to tell me somethin' I already know." He

straightened up, adjusted his necktie. "Now how about we all go out to lunch and celebrate? My treat."

Before I could answer, Cletus handed me my documents in a no-nonsense manila envelope.

"Congratulations, Honey. Wait till Amelia hears about this. She'll be thrilled for you."

"Tell her I'll drop by to see her soon."

"Better hurry up. The baby's about due, and I'm getting nervous, I can tell you that."

"I'm pretty nervous too, Cletus," Andy said, "if for an entirely different reason. Honey hasn't said she'll join us for lunch."

"Sorry," I said, "but I don't have time for lunch. My brand new company needs me."

Then with my French twist high in the air, I marched out of Cletus's office and went back to work.

Chapter Forty

Though I wouldn't make the same mistake two days in a row and skip eating, it wouldn't be with Andy. I suspected he'd known about Carmen's shady dealings all along, just as he'd known what would happen at the meeting today. I had no proof for being so suspicious, but I couldn't shake the feeling. Besides, I'd been given a right rare opportunity and needed to run with it. I owed it to Saxby, yes Saxby. And to myself.

For lunch, I'd stop by the Main Street Coffee Shop and pick up a couple of ham and cheese on rye to share with Mindy, my new employee. Yes!

Then I'd call the *Eureka Falls Star* and have them write up a piece about the agency's new ownership. I'd contact a sign painter too. Have him paint my name on the front window—Ingersoll Realty. It had a nice ring to it.

But first, the sandwiches and diet sodas. Filled with new energy, I parked in front of the coffee shop and hurried inside. The lunch crowd had beaten me to it and formed a line at the take-out counter. I took my place behind a man who looked familiar. Something about his hair and the set of his shoulders … if he'd turn around, maybe … . He ordered roast beef on a Kaiser roll and a black coffee. *That voice.*

"Barry McHale?"

At the sound of his name, he swiveled around, wearing the same big Hollywood–type sunglasses he had on the day I first met him out by Carmen's pool.

"Well, if it isn't you again, Honey. And just in time. I've been meaning to contact you. A contractor's bulldozing the lot tomorrow. Cleaning it up before it goes on the market. Shouldn't take more than a day or two. I'll let you know when he's through."

"Your order, sir."

As he turned back to the counter, the teenager next in line jostled me. My car keys slipped from my fingers and fell, clattering, to the shop floor. Barry bent over to pick them up and, when he did, his sunglasses slipped down his face. He quickly shoved them back on, but too late. I'd already seen what he was trying to hide—the mother of all black eyes.

"Thank you," I said, taking the keys from his hand. "I'm so clumsy."

"Not at all." Said kind of brisk like, the way a person does when he's embarrassed. As for me, I was stunned. Had smooth, worldly Barry McHale been in a fist fight?

He paid for his order, and while he waited for his change, I acted on a hunch. "Soon as I have an offer on the lot, I'll give you a phone call. Or I can leave a message with Andy Ballou, if you prefer."

"No, No, I'll be sure to return your call." He dropped his change in the tip jar and bolted for the door. "Nice seeing you. I'll be in touch."

"Miss, you want to order something?" the counter boy asked.

I did and, after paying for the sandwiches and a couple of cokes, I sat in the car to think for a while. If Barry'd had an accident, he would have explained the shiner. The fact that he didn't and tried to hide it told me he'd been in a fight. Interesting that he didn't want Andy involved in his business.

Andy who had been pale as death this morning. Maybe the cut on his chin wasn't a razor nick after all.

Hmm. While I couldn't be sure, I'd still lay odds Barry was no longer Andy's guest, and I'd put serious money on the notion that they'd had a major blow-up. The question was why? Over what? Strange and stranger. And truthfully none of my business—or was it? After all, I had found the dead body of a woman they both knew. That made it my business, didn't it? And what about Penelope? I found her too. Had they known her as well? I gave a mental shrug. Even if they had, and though Lord knows I wanted to help, solving murders was police work. I had my own work to do, and I'd better get started or I'd lose it.

I fired up the Lincoln and leaned over to snap on the radio. Perfect timing: Lenny Purvis came rip roaring through the KIKK airwaves as full of hot sauce and vinegar as always.

"Hello all you ladies and germs out there in la-la land. Ha, ha. That's a golden oldie, folks, a golden oldie. But here's something with a touch of gold too, and it's brand new.

"Ever heard of the Annual Hot Springs Documentary Film Festival? Opens this year on October ninth at the Arlington Resort & Spa. Yup, thought you had. Well, this year something special's going on over there in Hot Springs. One of our very own Eureka Falls boys, Jesse Raidel by name, is showing the film I told y'all about a while back. The one set right here on Moon Mountain Bluffs. You may recall the name—the Velveteen Vixens."

Oh, no, not again. What a two-timing, double-dealing rat Jesse was. He had to be stopped. I pulled a U-ee right on Main Street and headed for his studio. The sandwiches could wait. First, I had to put a rat back in his hole. This time, no pleading. This time, I'd threaten him with a law suit.

I screeched to a halt in front of Raidel, Photographer to Tomorrow's Stars—Tomorrow raised up over the other words like an after-thought. Or a mistake.

I yanked open his door and marched in, setting off a jangle of bells. The walls of the reception area in front of a glass display case were covered with pictures of pretty girls and brides and a few important-looking men, but there was no sign of Jesse.

Muffled voices filtered out from behind the velvet curtain that divided the shop in two. Aha! Ignoring the call bell on top of the glass case, I stomped over to the curtain, yanked it aside and nearly dropped dead.

"Hey," Jesse shouted. "You ruined my take."

"Omigod." I clutched the curtain for support.

In front of me, in a push-up bra and panties, her hose held up with sky blue garters, was none other than Josie. My friend Josie. The diner's Josie. The Josie who had lived in a brown and orange uniform for the last twenty five years. That Josie.

"You were supposed to ring." Jesse had the nerve to sound vexed.

"That right?" I ignored him, let go of the curtain and stepped inside. "Josie," I said, trying not to stare. "What's he doing to you?"

"He's putting me in a film." She reached for a robe thrown across a chair. "You kind of spoiled the mood, Honey, barging in like this."

"Do you really want everyone in town to see you in your underwear?"

"It's art, not underwear. Jesse's making a film about my wedding. I've been play acting like I was getting dressed for the ceremony. I mean, Jesse said everybody wears underwear, so where's the shame?" Her voice wavered and I pounced.

"Get your clothes on, Josie, and let's get out of here."

"You can't do that," Jesse said.

"I already have."

Josie's chin wobbled. Oh God, she was going to cry.

"Josie," I said, "think of Tommy Lee. He could get mighty jealous, you looking so … ah … sexy and all."

She nodded, big-eyed and wobbly chinned. "You're right." To Jesse "Let's show me trying on the wedding gown and forget about this underwear scene."

"But it's—"

"You heard her, Jesse. Need some help getting into the gown, Josie?"

She shook her head. "No, I been practicing."

She ducked behind a corner screen, and to the sound of rustling silk, I said to Jesse, "Come out in front. We need to talk."

"About what? You haven't honored me with your presence be—"

"Save it, Jesse." I plunged through a split in the velvet barrier.

"So what's the problem?" he asked with a little smirk I wanted to slap off his face.

"I just heard Lenny Purvis telling the whole town you're airing the Velveteen Vixens Show."

"But—"

"If you do, Jesse, I swear I'll hire a lawyer and sue the pants off you."

"But Honey—"

"I'm giving you fair warning— "

"Whoa." He threw his hands up, palms out. "You've got it all wrong. I have no intention of showing the film in Hot Springs or anywhere else." He shrugged. "What good will it do? Two of the stars in the show are dead. You're the only one left alive. Ergo, there is no show. Simple as that."

He aimed a thumb at the curtain. "My new project's hot. Wait'll the viewing public sees it. It's got everything—a mom and pop business, middle-aged lovers, a wedding feast with a hot sizzling pig, and a cast of characters as big as the town. So not to worry. Let Lenny shoot off his mouth. Me, I'll just shoot my camera."

As he raved on, the air in my lungs whooshed out. I was about to apologize when Josie yelled, "I'm ready, Jesse. Come on in here and let's get going."

The man could sell igloos to Eskimos.

Chapter Forty-One

IN WINTHROP'S BACK lot, for the first time ever, I took the slot with a big 'Reserved For President' sign hunkering over it. As soon as I could get a hold of the building's handyman, I'd have him take down that boastful sign, but just this once, to see how it felt, I gave myself a taste of the high life. Actually, it didn't do much for me. Words, even fancy ones carved in wood were cheap. What you did was what counted and, so far, I hadn't even begun to earn a highfalutin title like president.

With the lunch bag in one hand, the Kate Spade over a shoulder, I climbed out of the Lincoln and hurried across to the agency's rear door. I'd about reached it when a "psst, psst, realty lady" stopped me cold. *No, it couldn't be.*

"It's me. Frankie Serrito."

It was.

I whirled around and spotted him, half-hidden behind a scraggly bush by the back door. He stepped out and inched in closer to me.

"What do you want?" I asked, backing up a step. Not waiting for an answer, I held out the lunch bag. 'Here, for you. Ham and cheese sandwiches."

"Oh good. You can be nice sometimes." He grabbed the bag like he hadn't eaten all day—or longer.

"I thought you were in the ... ah ... hospital."

"I was. They let me go."

I felt a cold trickle sneak along my spine. "You mean you escaped."

"No, nothing like that," peering in the bag. "But I was sure glad to get out of there, I can tell you. They treated me like a criminal or a nut case. And for what? Nothing."

"You had a gun in my face, Frankie."

"It was a toy gun. Plastic. I meant no harm."

"You could have fooled me."

"Yeah?" He perked up at that. "You believed me, huh? People don't believe ol' Frankie very often."

"You said you'd fix Barry McHale, and the same day his house burned down."

"Oh, if you say so." He took out one of the sandwiches, tossed the wrapper and started munching.

"Yeah, I say so."

"Too bad what happened, but like I told him, he should've had me house sit. Never would've happened if he did."

"You mean you wouldn't have torched it?"

Mouth full, he looked up, surprised. "Nobody torched it. The electric wires were all screwed up. Fire chief said so. I just found out a couple days ago," he said, ending with a wink.

"Is that why they let you go?"

"Nah, not really. After my sister posted bail on the gun charge, they sprung me. Well, sort of. I told the lawyer they gave me I'd stay with sis until my court date, but I'm a free spirit, they can't be—"

"Frankie, why are you here? What do you want with me?"

He leaned in closer, looked over both shoulders and dropped his voice. "I got some news for you." He pulled the plastic lid off one of the soda cups and threw the lid on the ground. In between gulps, he said, "Well, what I got is for the man, the McHale guy."

"Then tell *him*." I turned to the door.

"Don't know where he is, but I figure you do." The empty soda cup hit the ground next to the lid. "If you won't press charges over the fake gun scare, I'll tell you what I know. Otherwise, no dice."

"You're *threatening* me? Get off my property, Frankie, or I'll call the cops."

I yanked open the back door, but before it could close behind me, he said, "Tell the man I know where his brother Tommy's at."

Barry's long-lost brother? No way could I let Frankie walk off and not hear what he had to say.

"Okay." I let go of the door and, hands on hips, whirled around. "Where is he?"

"Not so fast. Tell him Tommy'll be waiting for him tonight in the woods back of the Tailgate Pub. And you better tell him not to waste any time getting there."

Chapter Forty-Two

As I walked inside, Mindy put the last stroke of Red Or Alive nail polish on her pinky nail before leaping up to greet me. Waving her damp fingertips in the air, she asked, "Are you my new boss?"

"Looks that way. The deal went through."

"Congratulations."

"Thank you. I'm pretty thrilled. Were there any calls?"

"Three or four. I can't remember for sure. I told everybody to call back."

"You get their names, numbers, contact information?"

She stopped waving her hands. "For two." She glanced at the desk and blew on her fingers but didn't touch anything. "They're here somewhere."

Uh-oh. Not good. Not good at all. "Have you had lunch yet?"

She shook her head. "I usually work through lunch and leave early instead. Is that okay with you?"

The phone rang. And rang.

"You planning on answering it?" I asked.

"Oh. Oh, sure." She picked up with, "Hi, Lorraine. I'll have to call you later. I'm busy right now. So," she said, putting down the receiver, "what do you want me to do this afternoon?"

"A fair question. That your car out in back? The yellow beetle?"

She nodded. "A present from Saxby. I moved out already, but he told me to keep it. A booby prize, he said."

"He's a generous man, turns out. Pays his way."

"Uh-huh. Why did you ax about the car?"

"Ask."

"Yeah."

"Okay, this isn't easy for me, Mindy. I never had anyone work for me before, so I may not say all the words right. But you want this job, and I want you to have it." I paused to catch a breath. "You agree so far?"

Her brows meshing, she nodded.

"So here's what I want for starters. I want us to be a top-notch team. Which means you're here from nine to five unless there's a good reason why you can't be. Take an hour lunch break. Pick the hour you want, and I'll plan to be here then. All incoming phone calls need to be written down." I pointed to an unused yellow legal pad without a mark on it. "Name, telephone number, property type they're interested in and any other info they care to give. Got it?"

"I think so."

"Good. Now for this afternoon, I want you to take all your manicure supplies out of your desk, drive them home and leave them there. While you're at home, I'd appreciate having you change out of that peek-a-boo blouse you're wearing—and the red bra too. You have a tailored shirt with sleeves?"

She nodded, not quite sure.

"Put it on and come back. There's lots more for us to tackle, but that'll do for now."

I felt guilty as all get out talking to Mindy that way. When it came to clothes and what the magazines called accessories, I was always in a dither about the right look and the wrong look. But I knew one thing: Titties and real estate didn't mix.

Without a word, just her lower lip poked out, Mindy sank

onto her desk chair and yanked opened a drawer. I sneaked a peek. She could run a salon with what was stashed in there.

"Oh, one more thing, Mindy."

She looked up, mouth hanging loose.

"As of today, you get a three percent raise. If all goes well, in six months we'll up it to five percent."

"Wow, that's wonderful," her mouth wreathed in smiles, she started in on the nail polish.

"Good. We're going to make a great team." I left off 'if it kills the both of us.' And then, a little tense, I strode over to Saxby's inner office and stomped in like I owned it,

Oh my. A bowl filled with bright red roses sat in the middle of the desk, and tied to Saxby's well-worn swivel chair, a red balloon swaying back and forth said, "Have a Happy Day!"

Except for the flowers and a leatherette binder, the desk top had been cleared of every knickknack Saxby had accumulated over the years. I flipped open the binder and read through a short list of pending leads written out in Saxby's big, round handwriting. The narrow center drawer had been emptied as well; just a few ink stains left to prove it had been used. Then having to know, just *having* to know, I yanked open the lower drawer on the right. The bourbon drawer. *Ha!* No Jack hiding out in there. In its place stood a bottle of sparkling water with a note taped to its neck: Don't drink this stuff all at once. It's poison. Good luck. SHW3

Well, my, my, what a good ol' boy Saxby had turned out to be. I sat back in the leather chair with the imprint of his behind in the seat and swiveled, just like a president was supposed to do.

A moment only and I brought the chair to a squeaky halt. I needed to get going not sit swiveling. Those leads had to be followed up before they got stale, but first, I had to reach Barry McHale. He'd been so upset about his missing brother that Frankie's tip shouldn't be put off a minute longer.

When I called Barry's cell number, he didn't answer, so I left a message. And another one an hour later. Finally, desperate to reach him I said I had urgent news about Tommy, his brother, and to please call back as soon as possible. In between cell calls, I used the agency line phone for those pending leads and set up two house showing appointments for later in the week. All good, but another hour passed and still no word from Barry.

Don't waste any time getting there, Frankie had said. Maybe he meant Tommy was getting ready to move on. If so, what a shame. Barry had been waiting for years to hear from him.

At quarter to five and still no word, I had a notion to call Andy and ask if he knew where Barry could be reached. But though my hand hovered over the cell, I couldn't bring myself to make the call. Barry had been plain enough; he didn't fancy having Andy messing in his business. But I'd never forgive myself if I didn't do *something*.

Chapter Forty-Three

"I NEED A FAVOR," I said.

"There are favors and favors. What do you have in mind?" his voice coming through the line kind of low and sultry-like.

"This is serious, Matt. I need your help."

He stopped the levity. "Sure thing. What's the matter?"

"Meet me at the Tailgate Pub in a half hour. I'll tell you all about it then."

"But—"

I hung up fast. No time for explanations. For a tramp through the woods, I had to get home and change out of my suit and heels. I grabbed my bag, yanked open the office door and stopped in my tracks.

Mindy was back.

"This okay?" she asked, pointing to her chest. Along with the white shirt, which she'd buttoned to the neck, she had changed into a black pencil skirt and swept her long hair off her face with a tortoise shell barrette. She'd even swapped out her killer nail polish for a darker coat. She held up her hands. "Prune Danish."

"Perfect, Mindy. Couldn't be better. We're going to get on just great, and you know something else? You look like a school teacher I once had. Third grade."

Her face fell. "A *school* teacher?"

"The kids loved her. Tell you all about her tomorrow. For now I have to run. Lock up at five and see you in the morning at nine."

In a half hour flat, Matt met me at the pub, his face full of questions. When I explained about Tommy, he frowned big time. "You want to go tramping through the underbrush back there, looking for some guy you don't know?"

"Yes, a stranger. Haven't you ever done that, Sheriff?"

Matt was out of uniform, probably expecting to have a heart-to-heart over a couple of cold Buds. So I guess I couldn't blame him for being less than thrilled. No wonder he ignored my question.

"Any idea what this guy looks like?"

I shook my head. "You know what I know."

"Given some lead time, I might have located Barry McHale. Had him join us." Definitely exasperated.

"There wasn't time. While you went looking for Barry, his brother could have skipped. Might have anyway. That's the problem. I mean, the guy's a missing person, not a criminal. So," hands on hips, "you game, or do I go in the woods alone."

"Over my dead body, and that's not an option. Okay …" with a sigh "… you win. Let's go."

In the piney copse behind the pub, the trees stood dense and tall with late summer undergrowth between the trunks. As we waded in, brushing aside branches and crunching on fallen pine needles, I sniffed the air. It reminded me of Christmas— until I looked down. Littered on the fragrant needles were empty beer cans and whisky bottles, old cigarette wrappers and rusty tin cans. I saw some needles, too, the kind that had nothing to do with pine trees.

A few feet in, Matt picked up a stout stick. He whacked at the undergrowth with it as we inched along. Twenty minutes later, he pointed to what sky we could see through the overhead branches. "The sun'll be setting soon."

At a rustling in the undergrowth, he put out an arm to stay me. "Listen."

Something, or someone, was hurrying through the woods, moving fast, not taking time to sneak away slow and easy.

"Did we scare somebody off?" I whispered. "I hope it wasn't Tommy."

"I don't know. Could be. There's a clearing up ahead. Once in a while a drifter's been known to camp out there and forage in the dumpster back of the pub. We'll check the clearing. If nobody's there, we leave. In fact, you shouldn't be in here now." He shook his head. "Call it a lapse of judgment on my part."

Anger at himself and worry for me etched lines across his forehead. A good man, Matt Rameros—something for me to remember.

"Come on, then," he said, whacking at another bush. "Let's make this fast."

The pines had thinned out, letting more of the late day sun filter through the branches. Pushing past the low growth, hot and sweaty now, we made our way toward the opening in the trees.

Nothing moved in the clearing. Nothing. Not even the blanket-covered mound in the center of the grassy glen.

"What's that?" I pointed to the blanket and whatever lay hidden underneath it.

"One way to find out." Leaving my side, Matt strode over to the mound. He lifted an edge of the blanket with the stick and peered down. For what seemed like a long time, he kept peering down. I started over to him, but he said, "Stay where you are, Honey. You don't need to see this. It's a body."

But I had seen enough to know it was a man's body.

Throwing the blanket off to one side, Matt knelt beside the corpse and patted down the pockets. When he came up empty-handed, he draped the blanket back over the remains. "No I. D.," he said, pulling out his cell and punching in 911.

"This is Sheriff Rameros. I'm in the woods behind the Tailgate Pub. There's a body here." A pause and then, "No, and as far as I can tell, no sign of foul play. It looks like natural causes." Another pause. "Not a problem. I'll be here."

While we waited for help to arrive, I sank to the ground at the edge of the clearing, my hands sagging over my tented knees. How sad, to die alone with pine needles for a bed and a moldy blanket for a covering. Worse, to die alone with no one in the world to ease your way.

But had that been the case? I glanced over at the mound. If this poor soul turned out to be Tommy McHale, maybe he hadn't died alone. Someone, after all, had covered his remains with a ratty excuse for a blanket.

"Matt?"

He came over and crouched beside me. "You okay?"

I nodded. "Yes. Do you think Frankie knew there was a dead body out here? Did he set me up?"

Matt shrugged. "Can't say for sure, but could be. Rigor mortis has set in. Whoever it was has been dead for a while."

"Frankie said not to waste any time getting here, Tommy would be waiting. Ol' fashioned horse sense tells me he knew. But why didn't he come out and say so?"

"There could be lots of reasons, but one really jumps out at me."

I looked up, fast. "*What?*"

"Revenge. He could blame you for blowing the whistle on him. And blame Barry McHale for having him arrested."

"You think that's it?"

"I think it's a valid theory. He knew finding a body deserted on the ground would be very upsetting, even traumatic. He probably enjoyed the idea of horrifying you and making McHale suffer."

I pointed to the blanket. "Then you think the body is Tommy?"

"We'll soon find out." Matt stood as two paramedics and the county coroner, the same tall, gaunt man I remembered from out by Carmen's pool, came into the clearing.

I stayed glued to the ground while Matt and the doc went over to the mound and lifted the blanket.

The coroner bent over the body. A few minutes only, and he straightened up. "I'd say natural causes. An autopsy will take care of any doubt, but from the look of him, the culprits were probably exposure and alcohol. Not in that order. Good luck finding his next of kin. When you do … if you do … he'll be at the county morgue. At least for a while."

"Right." Matt knew the drill and, sadly, so did I.

The paramedics came forward, raised the body onto a stretcher and carried it to the waiting ambulance.

Matt came over to me and held out a hand. "Come on, I'll help you up. Let's go."

"But the sounds we heard earlier … like somebody was running away. Do you think it could have been Frankie?"

Matt shrugged. "Who knows? Frankie could be long gone by now."

"But the sounds we heard … somebody was running away."

"Or some *thing*. Animals scavenge."

I shuddered. "Had they … had they …"

He shook his head. "I think we scared off whatever was about to." He peered up at the sky where a sliver of moon had begun to rise. "I'll check with the country probation office. If Frankie's skipped bail, we'll have to look for him. But first things first. Come sit in the truck while I make a call."

As I had done earlier, he tried Barry's cell phone number but got no response. Without wasting any time, he punched in a second number, and I didn't dare ask who it might be. I knew. As I stared through the windshield, he spoke into the phone, asked his questions then said, "Thank you for your help, Mr. Ballou." He hung up and glanced across the cab seat, one eyebrow quirked high. "McHale's staying at the Eureka Falls Inn."

Though he didn't say so outright, I knew he had a question on the tip of his tongue. Finding Barry had been so simple, why hadn't I called Andy myself?

Pretending I didn't notice his raised eyebrow, I took the Fifth, as folks say on TV, and continued staring straight ahead. Worry about protecting Barry's privacy wasn't the only reason I hadn't called Andy. The truth was the less contact I had with him the better off I'd be. For now, since Andy was Saxby's legal representative in the DeLuca sale, I had little choice but to deal with him. But as soon as Saxby signed on the dotted line, I'd make a point of finding me a new lawyer man.

Too bad, Andy being so elegant and all. But when you came right down to it, elegance was a frill. A real man was steadfast. Even if, from time to time, he looked at you with raised eyebrows.

Chapter Forty-Four

MATT FOLLOWED ME home in the Ram, and after checking around, warned me to keep my doors locked and the security code active—just in case. You couldn't be sure of anything in Eureka Falls right now. Not with a killer out and about. Or with a person as unstable as Frankie on the loose, though by now he could have hitched a ride to the next county.

After he left me, Matt had driven straight to the Inn, picked up Barry and taken him to the Yarborough County Morgue. Later that night, he called to say the body we found had been Tommy McHale after all. Barry identified the remains then broke down and cried like a baby.

Poor Barry. In a few days time, he'd lost his lover, his home, his brother, and from the look of things, the good will of his friend, Andy Ballou. Like Job in the Bible, he'd been plagued with one misfortune after another. How much more could a body stand?

I was about to find out.

THE NEXT MORNING, I fueled up for my first full day on the new job with Josie's old-fashioned grits and sausage combo.

Nothing green. Nothing veggie, just the way I liked it, topped off with a cheese biscuit and a large black coffee.

"The wedding's a week from Saturday," Josie said, leaning one elbow on the counter. "Jesse wants you to come early for the picture taking, around ten or so, okay? No need to fuss over a bridesmaid dress. Wear whatever you like."

"I have a blue sundress with pink roses on the skirt and pink high-heeled sandals. Will that do?"

She squeezed my hand. "Sure thing. You're what matters, Honey, not the clothes."

I squeezed back. "The bride's what matters, Josie. *You.*"

"Aw, come on, Honey—"

"How about a refill down here," somebody hollered.

T.L. slid my breakfast along the counter. I dove into it, and the bride went over to pour coffee for one of her regulars.

Done with the grits and all, I glanced at my watch. Was there time to make a run out to Moon Mountain and check on Barry's lot? Or would it make me late for work? Heck, I reminded myself, I was the boss now. *Imagine.* Besides, I did want to see how the land looked cleaned up with no charred chimneys or burned-out furniture laying about, for I planned to put an ad in some out of town papers—Hot Springs, Fayetteville, Little Rock, maybe even Atlanta. Attract big money from outside the area. Advertise the location as a perfect place to build a mountain get-away. The commission on the sale of Carmen's house would give me a nice cushion, so I could spend a little freely to grow the business.

Feeling full and perky, I drove to the Bluffs with the windows down all the way and singing along with Mariah. Life sure was good—until it wasn't.

As it turned out, I hardly got a look at Barry's lot. At the sight of the cars and trucks clogging Carmen's driveway, I screeched to a halt and pulled in behind them.

What on earth was going on? While I peered through the windshield, two men in gray coveralls came through the front entrance carrying dining room chairs. They stowed them in an open-ended moving van and headed back into the house, weaving around two other movers lugging out one of the great room sofas.

Good grief, the house was being stripped.

I put the car in park, grabbed my purse and went inside, only to be stopped at the foyer by none other than Deputy Zach. "Sorry, I can't let anyone in."

"Zach, it's me, Honey Ingersoll."

He touched a finger to his hat brim. "I know who you are, Miss Honey, but I have my orders."

"From Matt?"

He shook his head. "The U.S. Marshal."

I stood on tiptoe and peered over his shoulder but didn't see much, didn't really have to. What was happening was clear enough. Not only had the government seized Carmen's house, but everything in it as well. Every lamp, every pillow, every dish would be sold to pay off her creditors.

"Step aside, Honey," Zach ordered. One of the movers was easing toward the front door with a big padded rectangle in his arms, a painting, judging by the shape. Could it be the one I loved the first time I clapped eyes on it? All different shades of green with huge trees draping their branches over a house nestled in a clearing. Carmen had said all the art work came from South America. But the scene I liked so much spoke of home anywhere. Warm and welcoming, it would be perfect for the office. Between the picture and a fresh coat of paint on the walls, folks would see right off that a change had taken place.

"Where are they taking all this stuff?" I asked Zach.

"Little Rock. For a big sale."

"Do you know where? Or when?"

He shrugged. "Beats me. Maybe Matt knows."

"He's here?"

Zach nodded. "Inside somewhere talking to the marshal."

"I wonder if I could speak to him for a minute?"

Zach's stony face broke into the first smile I ever did see

him crack. "Well, now, if I said no, I reckon the sheriff would be mighty upset. So if you'll step outside for a while, I'll go fetch him."

I stood on the stone landing watching one pretty thing after another being carried out to the truck. No other oversized painting, though. Maybe it was still on the great room wall. All I needed was a little peek inside to see if—

"You following me, lady?"

I whirled around. Matt stood in the open doorway, grinning up a storm. "To what do I owe this honor?" he asked, the smile never leaving him.

"I came to check out Barry's lot and saw all the trucks. Couldn't help but wonder what was going on. Zach filled me in. Sort of. I think I'd like to buy one of the paintings ... if I knew when the sale would be."

"In about thirty days would be my guess. I'll find out and let you know."

"Now that I'm here, could I take a look at a painting I have a mind to buy, just to be sure?"

"Sorry, no visitors allowed. Marshal's orders."

Well, I didn't want to travel halfway across the state without getting a second look at that picture, but Matt had a no-nonsense set to his chin. He wasn't about to break the law for any reason and certainly not for a reason like mine.

"Oh, all right," I said, though it wasn't. What was I going to do, steal something from under the eyes of the law? *Men.*

Crooking a finger, I beckoned him closer. "I didn't want to let on the real reason. I need to use the wash room."

"Now?" his eyes narrowing.

"Yes. I'm not joshing, either. It's urgent," rubbing my thighs together and moaning a little.

He blew out a breath. "You suddenly have a bladder problem? Hard to believe, but go ahead. Don't take long," he warned as I hurried past him.

First I stole a look at the great room. A man in coveralls busy packing a collection of silver boxes into a cardboard container nodded and went on with his chore. My glance swept the walls. Only a single painting was left—a jungle full of monkeys and parrots. Not the one I wanted. Either the picture I fancied was already on the truck or I had seen it in another room and disremembered which one.

Trying not to make eyeball contact with any of the movers, I peeked into all the downstairs rooms—no luck. Upstairs, then. It was a long shot, but this had turned into a hunt, and I wasn't about to stop now. The stairs were clear, and up I went fast as my stilettos let me.

No luck on the second floor either. In the rooms I peered into, only little round hollows in the carpeting showed where the furniture had once stood. Though I didn't expect to see what I was searching for in Carmen's bedroom, I opened the door anyway and tiptoed in.

Oh my. It had been stripped of everything that made it so glamorous the day she brought me here to try on a bikini. No satin-covered bed against the far wall, no silk curtains at the windows, no mirrors throwing back images. And no Carmen.

All her beautiful clothes and shoes and handbags were probably gone as well, but something drew me toward that super-sized closet. Female curiosity, I suppose.

The closet's double doors opened to my touch, but it was so dark in there I couldn't see a thing. I fumbled for the wall switch and flipped it on. The sparkly chandelier in the middle of the ceiling flooded the room with light.

The breath whooshed out of my body. *Gone. Everything was gone.* Only bare shelves and a few empty hangers, not a rainbow of dresses or a boutique's worth of shoes. I opened the drawers in the island where she'd kept her bikinis and lingerie. A hint of jasmine perfume wafted out. Otherwise, they were as bare as the shelves along the walls.

At what I was seeing—or not seeing—brought the truth home to me like nothing else could. When the U.S. Government swoops in and sells your very shoes, your handbags, your underwear, you've broken some big time laws and created some big time problems. Up till now, I understood Carmen had bilked folks, but standing in a closet picked clean as a Thanksgiving turkey, the extent of what she had stolen hit with the force of a blow.

Had she been an evil woman? I didn't know. I only knew she had stolen money, a great deal of money, and then someone had stolen her life. And the reason for stealing her life, whatever it might be, *was* evil.

Phew, if only I could sit for a minute before sneaking back down stairs. But the tufted pink chair Carmen used to have standing beside the island, the chair that would have been perfect for tying on a shoe or for a girl friend to sit on and chat while you got dressed was, of course, gone. The dents it had made in the carpeting were still there, though, and a few stains as well. Like the rest of the carpeting in the house, it would have to be replaced or at least cleaned. Underneath where the chair had stood, the pile was slightly uneven too. I went over and pressed it down with the toe of my shoe.

Something crackled. I tamped the spot again. The same sound, faint but clear enough. Strange. Wall-to-wall carpeting should have nothing under it but padding and subfloor. I toed the area once more, harder this time. Again a crisp crackle like I was treading on papers. If so, they were hidden papers. For except to hide them, what other reason could there be to stash papers under a carpet?

Under a carpet … omigod … Carmen's dying words, written in blood, leaped into my mind. 'Under car.' I stood stark still, my pulse a piston throbbing with a crazy notion.

Carmen hadn't meant to say 'under car' at all. She had been trying to say 'under carpeting,' but died before she could finish the word. I pressed my foot on the area where the chair had stood. Once more, a crinkly sound rose up.

I stared down at the spot. How had Carmen managed to get papers under a carpet nailed in place from one wall to another? She couldn't have done so alone and then replaced it, not without help. But what if she *had* acted alone and trusted no one with her secret? Then there was only one possible way she could have managed it. And what one woman had wrought another woman could uncover. Or at least try to.

I dropped to my knees and, hands spread wide, pressed my nails into the plush pile and played touchie-feelie. My fingers probed the raised area but found nothing unusual, at least not at first. I was about to give up when the tip of one nail did find it—a slit in the deep pile.

Ah. I ran the nail along the cut edge. It was about four or five inches long, just big enough to slide in an envelope. Then smooth the carpet pile back in place, stand a chair over the spot and no one would be the wiser. Clever, very clever. But I shouldn't be so surprised. Clever was Carmen's middle name.

As I knelt there wishing I had a knife or a razor blade to widen the cut and see if my hunch was correct, male voices echoing in the empty bedroom froze me in place.

Oh Lord, the U.S. Marshal?

Silent as fog, I rose to my feet, grabbed my purse off the island and tiptoed over to the light switch. I flipped it to off and, hidden by the pitch black, I clung to the wall. But not for long.

The door flew open. "You sure you got everything out of here?" a man asked, and, in the next second, the lights blazed on.

Chapter Forty-Five

"WELL, CAN YOU beat this? Look what I found, Marshal."
The man doing the hollering had a clipboard in one hand and a pencil behind his ear. I tried not to notice the way his big arms were putting a strain on his shirt sleeves.

The marshal stepped into the closet right after him, kind of lively like, but stopped short at the sight of me.

"Who are you? What are you doing in here?"

"I'm Honey Ingersoll, your honor," my voice coming out sort of squeaky. "I'm a Realtor."

"That so? Answer the question. What are you doing in here? Didn't the sheriff stop you at the door?"

"Nobody stopped me." Oh Lordy, I was sinking into the rabbit hole. But how could I tell a U.S. Marshal the sheriff had let me in? Matt might lose his job, and it would be my fault. What was a little white lie compared to that?

"You have no business being in here. You're trespassing on government-held property." The marshal turned to the guy with the arms. "I want her taken in, Joe, and strip searched."

My jaw fell open. "You're kidding."

"Lady, the United States government is not in the comedy

business." Done with me, he said to Joe, "Take her downstairs and turn her over to the sheriff. He can handle it from there."

Joe aimed a thumb at the open closet doors, and I marched out in front of him, but not before I eye-balled the carpet. A body would never know I'd been messing with it.

All the way down the stairs with Joe right behind me, I wondered if I should have told the marshal what I suspected. Maybe then I wouldn't be in this mess. But my suspicions might amount to nothing, and I'd have to admit I'd tampered with government property. No, I'd best keep quiet and say my piece to Matt.

We hit the first-floor landing. Joe grasped my arm and escorted me over to Zach who was still guarding the front door. "You know this woman, Deputy?"

"Yes sir, she's a Eureka Falls Realtor."

"She's also under arrest."

"*Why?*" Zach's jaw went slack.

"Trespassing. You let her in?"

"No, sir."

True so far. I hoped to God Joe wouldn't ask for Matt but, of course, he did. "Get the sheriff out here, will you?" he said. Zach took off like he'd been greased.

"This is so silly," I began.

"Don't even bother, Lady," Joe said. "It's out of my hands."

A few minutes only, Matt, with Zach hot on his heels, came hustling out to the foyer. A brief nod in my direction and he turned to Joe, "What's the problem?"

"We found this woman hiding out upstairs. The marshal wants her strip searched."

"*Why?*"

Yeah, why? I'd like to know, too.

Joe shrugged. "What's with the question? Looks like she got past you guys, that's why."

"Not my fault, I didn't let her in," Zach said.

Joe blew out a heavy sigh. "You locals. Whatever. She might've found something in that closet our boys overlooked.

Take care of her, will you?"

"I'll personally see that she's searched." Matt reached for my arm.

"You will not," I retorted, yanking free.

"Figure of speech," Matt said between clenched teeth. "Hush up. You're in enough trouble already. Give Zach your car keys."

I threw my arms on my hips so fast the tote banged against my thigh. "No dice."

"I'm taking you to the station in the cruiser. Zach will follow in your car."

"No way."

"Don't force me to cuff you."

What? Was this the Matt Rameros who beamed every time he saw me? The man who had mentioned the M word to me more than once and who ... yes ... loved me? *That* Matt Rameros?

"It's serious, then, what I did?"

"You can sit in the back of the cruiser until we're ready to leave. The house is nearly emptied, so it shouldn't be long." He held out a hand, and I dropped my keys into his palm. "Come, let's go."

No smile lit his face, no hint that this was all a joke. Taking me by the upper arm, he marched me out to the driveway and locked me in the cruiser's back seat.

Arrested and by my very best friend. I slumped on the seat and closed my eyes. The first day on the new job and look at me. "Nobody's fault but your own, gal." Grandma Ingersoll again, loud and clear. "You had no business triflin' with the law and gettin' that nice boy in trouble."

She was right, too. If Matt drove down Main Street and let everybody in town gawk at me sitting in the arrestee's seat that would be fitting punishment. About the strip search, I wasn't so sure.

The car door opened and so did my eyes. Matt slid behind the wheel and peeled out of the driveway.

"I suppose you'll drive right through the center of town."

No answer.

"Even if you don't, this is mighty embarrassing."

No answer.

"You're not going to have me strip searched, are you? Does that mean what I think it does?"

Silence.

"Aren't you talking to me?"

No answer.

I huffed out a breath. We'd reached the bottom of Bluffs Boulevard. Two minutes and he hadn't said a blessed word.

"Matt."

Nothing.

"Matt, I'm real sorry for what I did … well, not so much for that … but for maybe getting you in trouble with the government men. Can you forgive me?"

I didn't go so far as to say it would never happen again, and neither did I tell him what l suspected lay under the carpet. He was already so vexed, I figured the less said the better.

"What you did, Honey, was foolish but not unforgiveable." Eyes straight ahead, voice stern. "What cuts is you lied to me."

"Well, I knew you'd never let me in to look around, and what harm was there in taking a peek at stuff?"

"That's not the point, and you know it."

"I'm sorry I lied to you. I mean it. Truly."

"Thank you."

We rode in icy quiet for a while. At the foot of Main Street, I scrunched down as far as I could. Any lower and I'd be flat on my fanny. "About the strip search?"

"Yes?" In the rear view mirror, I spotted a little smile perking up the corners of his lips.

"You're not really going to make me have one, are you?"

Half turning in his seat, he said, "Let me put it this way, when I sign the report telling the marshal his orders were carried out, I sign what I know to be true." The smile turned into a grin. "Not to worry, Deputy Ellie is so good at it she could be a gynecologist."

Chapter Forty-Six

N O KIDDING.

    Ellie snapped on her rubber gloves then went to work finding out everything about me a body could learn. Afterwards, she had me sign a paper which I did, though I was too flustered to even read it. On my way out of the station, she handed me my car keys with, "See ya, Honey."

"You already have," I said, stomping off in my heels without even bothering to put my panty hose back on.

Flustered, rumpled and vexed, more with myself than anything else, I finally hit the office at high noon.

"Don't even ask," I said to Mindy who was mouthing something I couldn't get.

I swept past her "but, but, buts" and hurried into Saxby's—my—office and slammed the door. I'd calm down, redo my makeup and put those hose back on ... no I wouldn't. I had a visitor.

"Andy," was all I could think to say. I leaned against the closed door. My knees were that wobbly.

"You're angry," he said, getting up from his chair. "I can see it in your eyes."

"It's been a bad morning, but I'll get over it. Why are you here?" I asked, wondering if my knees would carry me across the room.

"By having lunch with me to celebrate…" he waved his hands in the air "… your success. And by letting me make up for my neglect."

He came so close I could see the lashes fringing his eyes and the smile he wore most of the time—usually when he had a client in front of him. Anyway, I pushed off the door, got those knees to working and wasted no time putting the desk between us.

"Much as I would like to, I can't go to lunch today. Mindy out there hasn't had her lunch break yet and our agreement is she goes first. To be honest, I just got here and have a lot of catching up to do."

At that, his face fell as if all the fun had gone out of his day. I felt a mite sorry for him, but this wasn't a day for fun and games. Besides, it was bad enough to come home with your panty hose in your handbag, but to start out that way, well …

"Lunch isn't important, Honey," he said, retaking his seat as if he planned to stay a while. "If you weren't so busy, I'd gladly sit here all afternoon just talking to you."

A whole afternoon? Not a good idea. With no food or drink or music to distract him, Andy would soon find out how little I knew about most everything Because a body could sell a house now and then didn't mean she could carry on about art and books and politics and such.

So I sat there for a moment with my pantyhose stashed in my handbag, silently beating up on myself for not paying attention when I was in school. But then some of Nana Ingersoll's steel stiffened my spine: I got a grip and figured while there was no taking back those lost school days, there was no need to be so harsh on myself, either. True, I couldn't speak like a smart, city-bred lady on most things, but I could darn well sell properties, and I was loyal and truth-telling and honest. I had no slickness about me whatsoever, and that was a good thing, wasn't it? Why I didn't even dye my hair or wear falsies—and I'm not talking false eyelashes here—and I don't have a girdle to my name. When it comes to Honey Ingersoll, what you see is what you get, and what I say is what I mean. I figure those are valuable attrib… attributes in anybody's book.

So if an educated man like Andy who'd been to Vanderbilt and all would be bored with my chatter in no time, what difference did it make? For all of his book learning and educated ways, I didn't trust him. So let him go ahead and be bored with me.

Though Matt never was. But Matt didn't flaunt his book learning. Matt was calm and steady and honest right down to the ground, a fact that from here on, I intended to cling to.

Anyway, all these thoughts flashed through my mind in a second or two, and then to set the record straight, I said, "Andy, you already know a few things about me, but there's something you don't know. I barely squeaked through high school. My formal learning, if that's what it was, stopped there. Why I could no more carry on an interesting talk for a whole afternoon than—"

He held up a hand, palm out. "You know I'm an attorney, but do you know attorneys love to talk? It's how we make our living. So I'll do the talking if that makes you more comfortable."

"But—"

His palm came up again. "Case in point: I'm not through yet. Here's something about *yourself* that you don't know. You're a lot smarter than you think you are, Honey Ingersoll. You have common sense, the greatest form of intelligence the world has to offer. Plus an innate grace I ab—"

"What's that word you just used?"

He shrugged. "Innate?"

"Yes. See you just got started, and already I don't understand." I pointed across the office. "I think I'll put a chalk board up on the far wall over there and write down every darn word I don't know. Why that ol' board'll be filled up in no time flat."

He rose out of his chair and came around the side of the desk, his musky aftershave coming right along with him. "Let's consider this particular subject closed. What about dinner tomorrow night? The Eureka Falls Inn."

"I love to eat there," I said, "but isn't it a mite expensive?"

He laughed. "See what I mean? Common sense."

"I appreciate the invite, I really do, and the compliment, but I don't think so."

Judging from the set of his jaw, he thought on what I said real hard before replying, "Too fancy for you? Afraid you can't handle it?"

A challenge, like I didn't have any gumption or something? Well, that just wouldn't do. "All right, a business dinner at the Inn it is. Saturday at eight?"

"Excellent. See you then." Halfway to the office door, he swiveled around. "You're a wise girl, Honey. You'll always come out on top. Of that I have no doubt."

Well I had doubts aplenty, and he might, too, if he knew I was about to break the law. Again.

Chapter Forty-Seven

AFTER ANDY LEFT, I spent the next few minutes putting on my hose and inhaling the trace of aftershave lingering in the air. Then guilty about Mindy's delayed lunch break, I opened the door and peeked out. A note in big, round handwriting stood propped on her computer: Gone to lunch. Be back at one.

At one-thirty, clutching a diet soda and sucking on a straw, in she sashayed. Well, since she'd been alone in the office all morning and had on a buttoned-up shirt, I let it go. Besides, I had plans that needed her help.

"Mindy, can you work late tonight?"

"Sure can. You need something typed?"

"No, I have something else in mind."

AFTER DARK, WE drove toward Moon Mountain with the windows down and the radio off. Lush with summer, the air wafted sweet and warm as we headed up the rise toward the Bluffs. Mindy sat biting her lips and staring out the passenger side window. Already my conscience bothered me. I should have come alone and not mixed her up in this, but in case someone came by, I would need a warning.

The marshal had asked for my key to the house, and since I handed it right over, I hoped he hadn't changed the locks. He hadn't asked if I had a duplicate, but I did, so technically I wouldn't be breaking and entering. Even so, nervous as a hooker at a prayer meeting, I eased to a stop on Bluffs Boulevard across the street from the house.

"This won't take long," I said. "If anybody drives up and stops, call me on my cell phone. You don't have to do anything else, except for maybe one other thing. If I'm not back in ten minutes, contact Sheriff Matt at the number I gave you." I patted her hand. "Ten minutes, okay?"

"I guess." Her voice trailing off into a little wail. "It's so dark out here. Do you have to do this?"

"Yes, I'm trying to find out who murdered a woman. Maybe two women."

"Oh Lordy." In the dim light, the whites of her eyes shone like new moons.

"Raise the windows and lock the doors. You'll be fine."

Without waiting for her to tell me she wouldn't be, I climbed out of the Lincoln and hurried across the road. Carmen's front door had been padlocked, but using my realtor's universal key, I unlocked the door with no trouble at all, dismantled the security code and stepped inside.

For an instant, faced with black empty rooms, my courage folded like a limp hanky. I had to force myself to stand in the dark for a few moments breathing in the still air and letting my eyes adjust to the dim light.

Several feet ahead, the curved stairway rose out of the gloom and I went for it, taking the steps two at a time. At the second floor landing, I turned right. Not even starlight lit the upper hall, but this was a familiar trail, and I groped my way to the last door, Carmen's bedroom.

In the room's musty, eerie silence, I grasped the crystal handles on the closet doors, closed the doors behind me and snapped on the flashlight. The sudden flare had my eyes fluttering like moths then, *there*, right where I remembered, next to the island, four little dents in the rug.

I took the Swiss Army knife out of my pants pocket and knelt on the carpeting. With the narrow beam of light as a guide, I pressed my fingers on the space between the dents. Again, that faint crackle. Not much to go on. I blew out a breath. Not much to risk a breaking and entering charge for, either. The cold trickle slipping down my spine seemed to agree. Well, too late to be faint-hearted now.

Jumpy as a flea, I probed the area with my fingers until I found the cut in the pile. Using the tip of the knife blade, I widened the opening a bit and slid my hand inside. One tug and out came a manila envelope. 'To Whom It May Concern' was written on the outside.

I smoothed the slit edges of the carpeting together and fluffed up the deep pile with my palms until I was satisfied the cut couldn't be seen. Then I pocketed the knife and turned off the flashlight.

Plunged into a hellish dark, I sat crouched on the floor until I could see well enough to make my way out of the closet and along the hall without banging my shins.

Now get the hell out of here, Honey.

Keeping the envelope tucked under an arm, I crept down the stairs to the foyer, reset the alarm, padlocked the door and scooted across the street as fast as a fox with a hound on its tail.

Blowing out a sigh of relief, I slid onto the driver's seat and turned on the ignition.

"Lordy, I'm glad you're back," Mindy said, wide-eyed and pale in the moonlight. "Did you get what all you came for?"

"I think so. Didn't take time to look it over." I pulled onto Carmen's driveway, backed up and headed down Bluffs Boulevard. Only then did I turn on the headlights.

"Any cars come by while you were waiting?"

"No, none."

"Good. Thanks, Mindy. Knowing you were standing guard really helped me stay calm. I know you were scared. Me too.

But we may have found a killer tonight. Otherwise, I wouldn't have asked you to do this." I tore my attention from the dark road for a second to glance across the seat. "But no matter what, you can't tell anybody. Nobody at all, or we could both end up in jail."

She drew in a lungful of air and let it out real slow, kind of like it was escaping from a leaky balloon. "Too late, Honey. You were gone eleven minutes, so I called the sheriff."

Chapter Forty-Eight

*G*OOD GRIEF. WE were halfway down the boulevard, when the Ram passed by us going lickety-split up the hill. A peek in the rearview mirror showed Matt screeching on his brakes, doing a U-ee and coming after us. A second later, he was tailgating like mad and leaning on his horn.

"Oh, God, he wants me to stop."

"I'm sorry, Honey. You took so long, I thought you were in trouble. And you said ten—"

"It isn't your fault. You've been a peach. I'm just one of those people who can't break the law for love nor money." I put on my right turn signal and pulled over to the side of the road.

In cut-offs and a wife-beater shirt, Matt leaped out of his cab. Leaving his headlights on, he strode over to my driver's side window and leaned in. He nodded at us. "Evening, ladies. I see you're both all right. What's this about, anyway?"

"This." I held up the envelope.

"Explain." His cold stare lowered the temperature in the Lincoln a considerable amount. No wonder I felt a chill.

"I just found this envelope in Carmen's bedroom closet."

"Impossible. The marshal and his men went through the

house with a fine tooth comb. You mean to tell me they missed it?" His jaw, I'd swear on a stack of Bibles, had turned into concrete. This cold Matt had no warm smile for me. This Matt was a tough, strong-armed (the wife-beater shirt didn't hurt) man of the law—which I had broken. For the first time since I'd known him, I was a bundle of nerves.

"Well?" he said, "out with it."

"Remember Carmen's death note, written in her blood?" I think he nodded; the glare from his headlights had me so tensed up I couldn't be sure. "When she wrote 'under car,' I think she meant under carpeting." I patted the envelope, "I think this envelope is what she wanted the police to find."

"Quite a theory." *Phew, he was easing up.*

"A question: Are you the police?"

Or maybe not.

In the chilly silence, tree owls hooted into the dark. As I recollected, they killed at night. No wonder goose bumps were popping up on my skin.

"I'm waiting for an answer."

"No, I'm not the police."

"But technically, you are a thief." He held out a hand. "Let's have it."

"Not a chance, Officer, unless you have a warrant."

"You playing hard ball, Miss Ingersoll?"

"With you, Officer, no way. But I'm a peace-loving woman, so here's what I propose. Instead of standing here arguing while your battery wears down to nothing, why don't you follow me home so we can examine this document together? Then I'll be happy to turn it over to you for safe keeping."

"I can't say I'd be happy to turn you both …" his eyes slanted in Mindy's direction "… over to Marshal Dixon. But I'm considering it."

I figured he was joking at our expense, kind of punishing me for my transgression. But Mindy took his words at face value and busted … burst … into tears.

"Now look at what you've done," I told him.

"What *I've* done? I ought to haul for in for that crack alone."

"I want to go home," Mindy wailed, her face all wet in the moonlight.

"A sensible suggestion," Matt said. "Start driving, Honey. I'll be right in back all the way.

"ANY COFFEE?" HE asked, dropping the envelope on my kitchen table.

By the time I'd fired up the stove and put the pot on, Matt had already slid a knife blade under the envelope's sealed flap and tugged out a handful of papers.

"Well, I'll be." His lips puckered up and blew out a whistle. "Look at this."

In a fancy handwriting, full of loops and swirls, names, addresses and dollar amounts ran in a long line down one sheet and another and another. Ten pages in all. People from such far-flung places as South America, Europe, the Cayman Islands, and all over the U.S. from California to New York to Texas.

"Who are these people?" I asked.

"My guess is they're Carmen DeLuca's clients. The people she bilked. All arranged in alphabetical order. Very neatly and possibly very thoroughly listed. The question is why would she make such a list and then hide it?"

"Right. Isn't this information in her company computers?"

"Should be. That can be checked. Will be, in fact." He scanned one sheet and then another. "Interesting how many addresses are P.O. boxes and not all in the U.S."

"Meaning?"

He shrugged. "Who knows? An attempt to hide investment income from the IRS, a business partner, or a spouse."

"She must have been scared then. This was kind of an insurance policy. In case something happened to her. When something did, she wrote, 'under car.' If she'd lived a minute or two longer and finished the word—"

"We would have torn up every rug in the house." Matt

leaned back. Cradling his mug in both hands, he sipped his coffee. "I guess you could say, on one level anyway, that it's better you found the list the way you did. But I swear, Honey, you'll be the death of me yet."

"Meaning what?"

"This evidence has been compromised. It was removed from its hiding place. No telling if it was tampered with or not."

"Matt Rameros, that envelope was sealed tight and you know it," I said, pouring him some coffee, so vexed I nearly dumped it in his lap.

He raised his mug, eying me over the rim. "The envelope was sealed when you gave it to me. Was it sealed when you found it?"

"Oh, for heaven's sake. That's downright silly. I was in an empty house in the pitch black. Was I likely to start sealing and unsealing stuff?"

"Just being devil's advocate."

"Whatever that means. The way you found the envelope is the way I found it. No different. More coffee," I asked, hovering with the pot, changing the subject.

He nodded. "Might as well. Won't sleep tonight, anyway, wondering how to explain this sudden find to the FBI."

I nearly dropped the pot. "You have to tell them?"

"Of course." He scrunched his brows together like he couldn't believe what I just asked. "They're investigating her scam and may already know of these people. My hunch is there are also names on here that haven't come to light yet. So it might be useful to the FBI after all. Bottom line, whatever the victim did or didn't do, the fact remains she was murdered. Someone on this list might be the killer."

"Anyone? What an awful lot of people to investigate."

He nodded, sipping, and flipping through the pages. "Hey, wait a New York minute. Look at this entry, under M."

M? Oh no.

Barry McHale. Written out in the same fanciful hand but as clear as well water, and oh my, with a seven figure number following his name.

"Honey, can you get me a pad and a pen?" Matt asked. "Between us, we know most folks in town. Let's go over these names and make a list of the ones we recognize—even if they have an out-of-town address or a P.O. box. We might save the FBI a lot of aggravation. Might even keep you out of jail."

His eyes twinkled when he said that last bit, so I wasn't too worried about serving time, but I was mighty worried about Barry.

And then on page two, I came across another name, one with a six figure number following it. A name that sent all the blood in my body sinking to my feet.

Andarius Ballou.

Chapter Forty-Nine

THE COFFEE POT was empty, and I had the jangled nerves to prove it. Matt collected the lists and stuffed them back in the envelope. On the pad, we'd written only two names—Barry McHale and Andarius Ballou

"So overall, the DeLuca woman didn't hit on the locals," Matt said. He tapped the pad with a finger. "Except for these two. Why only them? They had the means to invest, but so did other members of the community."

"I have a notion."

He looked over at me, a devilish grin splitting his face. "Me too. You first."

"They were her lovers."

"Ah, great minds think alike."

"She seduced them into giving her money. Called it an investment."

"As an angle, it's not bad. But what about the rest of these investors? They're probably young, old, male, female. Scattered all over hell and back. She couldn't have seduced them all."

"Then suppose she didn't seduce any one. Suppose Barry and Andy asked her, maybe begged her, to let them in on what they thought was a good thing. She might not have wanted to. Stealing from strangers was one thing. Your next door neighbor and your attorney are another." I got up to pace the kitchen, hoping somehow that would help me read a dead woman's thoughts. "A Ponzi scheme has only one outcome, isn't that right?"

Matt nodded.

"Then maybe she planned to move on before it all unraveled. Though for the life of me I can't understand why she'd spend a fortune on a piece of property and fill it full of treasures if she knew it was nothing more than a house of cards."

Matt took a final gulp of what by now was cold coffee and stretched. "It's late. I should be going."

At the quick way he cut me off and was suddenly so ready to leave, I spun around. "What are you hiding?" I asked, ignoring the fake yawn he was putting on.

"Nothing."

"Matt Rameros, you're a worse liar than I am. What is it?" I plunked myself down at the table. "I risked a jail sentence tonight for Carmen's sake. I'm in deep, so why hold out on me now?"

He nodded, thoughtful like. "This is a little known fact, and it's not for public consumption. The autopsy revealed that Carmen DeLuca had a terminal illness. Her physician confirmed it. Said she had less than a year to live. Apparently no one knew. Not even McHale or Ballou ... though they do now."

She had been dying? A woman so alive she practically glowed with energy.

"So she threw caution to the winds and bought everything her little heart desired?" A vision of her boutique-sized closet flashed through my mind.

"Judging by the amounts she scammed from her clients, it would sure seem so," Matt said.

"Then why write this list? If it's all in her computer, what's the point?"

"My hunch tells me there are names in here not in the company computers. Maybe some of these accounts were loans, not investments, loans she defaulted on." He shrugged. "Some research can ferret out the truth. And who knows? The truth may be simply a matter of conscience. It's a long shot, but written in her own handwriting like this ..." he glanced up from the sheets for a second "... it could be a personal *mea culpa*. She might've wanted everyone she'd stolen from to be reimbursed, at least to some extent. There's also another possible reason: She might've been afraid someone on the list would seek revenge."

"But she was dying anyway."

"Hope springs eternal, Honey. Maybe she didn't want to be hurried on her way."

"True," I said, a heavy feeling settling over my heart like a cloud. Someone had hurried her along after all. It could be anyone—a stranger, a friend, a client, a lover. But I only knew of two people who had a motive for such an evil act.

Chapter Fifty

*S*ATURDAY MORNING. OH Lordy, tonight Andy would be expecting me for dinner at the Inn. Not that I'd forgotten our meeting or anything. I'd just buried it for a while, trying to get past the fact that he was a man on Carmen's scam list with six figures after his name. That was a lot of money to lose. More than enough reason to seek an eye for an eye, a tooth for a tooth. More than enough reason to pull a trigger and … I gave the alarm a squinty glance. Nine-thirty. Beautiful. It's what Saturday's were for.

I curled onto my side. The wisest thing would be to cancel. Beg off. He was not to be trusted. But what about Barry? His name was on Carmen's list too with an investment number double that of Andy's.

Though I hated to believe either one had harmed Carmen, somebody had. Somebody had killed Penelope, too, a girl who'd left no long list of people she'd scammed. She'd just been a pretty girl who wanted to go to New York City and shine like a star. Yet she was as dead as Carmen.

Last night, Matt admitted he couldn't be sure if the same person killed both women, but he did agree that Barry knew both victims. As for Andy, he'd met Carmen all right, but what about Penelope? When he visited the DeLuca house, which he probably did a lot, Penelope must have been there some of the time … or much of the time, so he would have known she lived alone. And so did Barry. Both men had a motive for killing Carmen, but why attack Penelope and leave her for dead? Had she seen or known something? If so, *what*?

With a groan, I kicked off the covers and sat up. Who could sleep while thinking about murder? Worse, I'd been putting two men on trial who might never have killed so much as a flea.

I sat on the edge of the bed, my head in my hands. What if the killer—or killers—wasn't on the list? I didn't know all of Carmen's acquaintances. I'd only met her once. One unforgettable time. Penelope I'd met twice. That day by the pool and again when I toured her house. At our third and last meeting, Penelope had been so damaged I couldn't bear to think about her—tied up like an animal and moaning …

Besides Barry and Andy, the only other person I knew who might be mixed up in all this was Frankie. After Frankie broke into Barry's house, he'd spied on Carmen and Penelope from across the lawn. Though he was creepy, true enough, it didn't mean he killed them. Even the state shrink said he didn't think Frankie had hurt anyone.

Then there was Sophie, gentle, quiet Sophie. For sure, she was no killer. She was a good, hard-working woman, nothing more. *Wait a minute.* Everyone has secret dreams and resentments. Was Sophie any different? She did manual labor for a woman who seemed to own the world. Could hidden anger have caused Sophie to kill her? And then to attack Penelope? No, no way. I put the wicked notion out of mind.

According to my reckoning, only Jesse was left as a likely killer which didn't make any sense, either. He wanted the Velveteen Vixens to be a smash success and boost him into a big-time career. He had no motive for harming either woman. The exact opposite, in fact.

The telephone broke into my conjecturing. Grateful for the interruption, I answered without checking caller I.D.

"It's a boy!"

"Cletus, how wonderful! Congratulations."

"Yup, eight pounds, three ounces."

"He's breaking records already. How is Amelia?"

"Beaming. Just beaming. She asked me to call you first."

"Give her a hug for me. And will you tell her I'll stop by the hospital this afternoon?"

"Happy to, Honey. Happy to."

We hung up, and I sat there for a moment, warming to Amelia's news. The phone shrilled again. Cletus calling back to tell me something he'd forgotten?

I answered on the first ring.

"Glad I caught you home, Missy."

"Saxby? I thought you signed a no harassment waiver?"

"I did. This is my first call since putting ink to paper."

"It's only been a few hours."

"This one doesn't count. The office is closed. Why I'll bet you're still in bed at this late hour."

"Don't start."

"Lord Almighty, Honey, ease up. You're like an aspirin that won't melt."

"Is there a reason for this call?"

"Matter of fact there is. I'm leavin' town."

"Oh?"

"Don't sound so upset. It's temporary. Goin' on a cruise with the Widow Farley. Remember her? Big blonde, big ... she bought the ol' place on Catalpa Street. The one with the wrap-around porch."

"No, I don't recollect the name. Or the description."

"No matter. She don't hold a candle to you, but to get through life a man's gotta compromise. Now here's the reason for this call. While I'm cavortin' on the high seas, the DeLuca auction will be takin' place. My experience tells me auction sales are tricky creatures. No way of knowin' how they'll pan out. So if anything goes sour, like a bidding war that sends the price sky high, or somethin', I want you to pull out and put a binder on the lot next door. Understand? I'm mailin' you a check for it today. Sending my top offer along with it. One way or the other, I'm bound and determined to live up on the Bluffs. Now I better hang up. I got a lot of packin' to do."

The phone went dead. I stared at it for a while and then, after some nail biting, I called Andy and cancelled our dinner at the Inn.

I REINFORCED MY determination with two fried eggs, coffee and a left-over biscuit, and suited up in cut-offs, a T-shirt and sandals. Good to go—actually feeling so blue I needed to get out of the apartment and keep busy—I drove to the Bluffs to check on the condition of Barry's lot.

As I drove, I lowered the car windows and dragged the piney air into my lungs, but I couldn't bother listening to any music. Not today, feeling a touch of guilt the way I did. For when I cancelled our dinner, Andy's disappointment had come zinging through the line, stinging me like the tail of a whip. Whether he bought my excuse—emergency babysitting for Amelia—or not, I didn't know. I said I'd see him at Josie's wedding next weekend. I wasn't proud of lying like that, but how could I do otherwise? How could I break bread with a man who, in my heart, I feared might have killed a woman?

So, no music today even though the sun shone as high and happy as ever. Like every day, Bluffs Boulevard had next to no traffic. Only one red convertible heading for town zoomed by with its top down. At the summit of the ridge, I passed Carmen's house on the left. It sure looked different in broad daylight with its windows sparkling in the sunshine.

I pulled onto Barry's land, parked the Linc and stepped out. The emptiness took my breath away for an instant. No more half moon drive leading to a gorgeous multi-million dollar mansion. No welcoming carved entrance doors. No tasteful plantings. No nothing. The demolition contractor had done a good job, scraping the ground clean of all rubble, right down to the bare earth. Out back, the pine trees edging the property still stood tall, and a few weeds had popped up here and there, but no hint remained of what had once been the closest thing to a palace Eureka Falls had ever seen.

I strolled the length of the parcel and gazed down the Bluffs. A few hikers taking advantage of the day were tramping around by the river far below. As breathtaking as ever, the Arkansas flowed blue and beautiful to the sea. Yes, this half acre was very saleable and should fetch a good price. One higher than the low ball figure Saxby probably had in mind.

On my way back to the car, I spied a wild flower springing out of the scorched earth. I had a notion to pluck it, but it looked so brave and so alone, I left it to the honey bee hovering nearby.

What a perfect day. Though I longed to linger out here in the open for a while, I had to get back to town. I had a new baby to visit.

Near the boxwood hedge bordering the two properties, an old familiar aroma, sweet as sin, wafted on the breeze. Carmen's gardenias blooming away. A few tucked under the ribbon on the blue blanket I was bringing to Cletus junior would be right nice. No one would miss a bloom or two.

I ducked through the opening in the hedge and caught my breath as I always did when stepping into Carmen's garden. Even now with fallen leaves sprinkling the pool's scummy surface and the shrubby gone wild, it could win a beauty contest.

I slipped off my sandals so my feet could feel the lush grass. Thick and green as ever, it tickled my bare toes as I hurried across the lawn to the other side of the pool where the gardenias, heavy with blossoms, grew taller than a standing man. Bees drunk on perfume buzzed all around. The one feasting on that scraggly wild flower over at Barry's ought to join the party. Careful to pick a spot where the bees weren't hovering, I plucked two gardenias, sniffed them and was reaching for a third when my toes struck something hard.

"Ouch!"

A sharp pain darted up my ankle. I glanced down and wiggled my stubbed foot. It seemed to be okay. What on earth had I struck? I didn't see a stone or anything hard where I'd stepped. Curious, I scuffed my toes in the soft soil and felt something beneath the fallen leaves. I toed a few more leaves aside, blinked and blinked again. *Omigod*. I dropped the gardenias. That was no stone.

Heartbeat hammering in my ears, I bent down and brushed off the rest of the leaves. Neat and snub-nosed, the gun was small—a lot smaller than the one Matt strapped in his holster. I straightened up, my eyes never leaving the weapon at my feet—at what my gut told me might be the first piece of solid evidence in Carmen's death. To keep it from being compro— What was that word Matt used last night? I couldn't recollect. No matter, I'd learned my lesson. I'd leave the gun right where it was and call the police.

I fingered my shorts pocket. *Uh-oh*. All I had with me were car keys. I'd left the cell in the car. For safe keeping, I toed a few leaves back over the gun.

A sharp crackle off in the distance shattered the silence. Nerves sparking like hot wires, ears cocked, I stood still, listening. There it was again, sun-dried brush snapping underfoot. Most likely a hiker climbing up from the river bank and tramping on the scrub growth.

A deep cough and the ragged breath of someone gasping for air told me the climber wasn't a seasoned hiker. Already jittery, I didn't know whether to run or stay and face whoever might be puffing up the hill.

While I dithered, dry twigs kept snapping away.

Run. Stay. Run. Stay.

I stood rooted in place until a man coughed deep in his chest and hawked spit into the wind. That wasn't anyone I wanted to meet.

Without wasting any more time, I snuck behind one of the

giant camellias, crouched down and held my breath. Peeking through the leaves like a wild critter wanting to see but not be seen, I watched the far side of the property. Magnolias separating the garden from the edge of the Bluffs began to sway. None too carefully, someone yanked branches aside, and the hiker hove into view.

Omigod. To stifle a gasp, I covered my mouth with a hand. In boots and shorts—did the man never wear pants?—his red ponytail blazing in the sunlight, came none other than Jesse Raidel. Winded, he took a second to catch his breath, glanced around over both shoulders, then headed straight for the very gardenia bush where I had plucked the blossoms.

I could have leaped up and yelled, "Surprise!" Made a joke out of bumping into him like this, but something stopped me. Fear, probably, and that demon, curiosity. What on earth was he doing here?

He dropped to his knees at the spot where I stubbed my toe and then did the strangest thing. He took a pair of rubber gloves out of his shorts pocket and pulled them on before running his hands through the piled-up leaves.

A grunt, a toss of his ponytail, and he'd found what he was looking for—the gun. Carefully brushing off some dirt, he lifted it up and cocked it. This time, I didn't catch the gasp fast enough. In the quiet garden my sucked-in breath sounded loud as a drum roll. Jesse's head went straight up and so did the muzzle of the gun.

He leaped to his feet, ponytail swinging. "Whoever's in there come out or I'll shoot."

Glory be, he meant it. "Hold your horses, Jesse. No need for any shooting. It's only me."

"Put your hands up."

I wanted to believe he was just playing cops and robbers, but something about his tone told me that wasn't the case. So I stood tall, raised my arms and took a few steps forward.

"Honey *Ingersoll*?" Sounding like it couldn't be, his eyes were lying to him. "What the hell are you doing here?"

"I was about to ask you the same thing."

He didn't bother to answer.

My arms were getting cramped but, keeping them raised anyway, I pointed a finger at the gun. "If that's yours, why don't you take it and high tail out of here?"

He laughed. "Some things never change. You've been a pain in the butt since the day I met you, and you still are."

"What are you getting—"

"Quiet. I let you go and you'll run to that sheriff boyfriend of yours and tell—"

"He's not my boyfriend." *Well, not exactly.*

"Shut up."

A sweaty trickle slid down my spine. The day was warm, but not that warm. He grasped the gun real good and aimed the barrel at my heart. One flick of his gloved finger and I'd be riding the air currents with the hawks. I couldn't let that happen. I wasn't ready to die. Not like this. Not here on this sunshiny day with so much of my life unlived. I had to distract him, but how?

"Can I step out a little more, Jesse? These branches are scratching me all to pieces."

Without saying anything, he tilted his head to the left. I came forward out of the shade. If only he'd say something ... if I could start him talking maybe I could ...

"Why are you so upset, Jesse? Because I saw you find the gun? It isn't a big deal. Just bring it to the police, tell them you found it and—"

"You a wiseass or something?"

"What's wrong with giving it to the police? They'll understand."

He laughed again, a bitter bark of a laugh. "They sure will."

Yes, they surely would. They'd know right off he had planted the gun under the leaves and had come back for it. But why had he hidden a gun in the first place?

The answer welled up from my soul. I tried to force it back down, but it refused to go away.

He upped his chin at the row of magnolias he'd just shoved his way through. "Start walking. We're going on a hike, you and me."

"I can't hike in bare feet."

"Too bad. Get going."

Good God in heaven, he intended to march me down the Bluffs and into the woods. That meant only one thing.

Chapter Fifty-One

So, GAL, YOU gonna let him march you off and kill you like you was some kinda scrawny chicken?

Now if that isn't Grandma Ingersoll all over, still after me to gain weight. Well, the answer is, "No."

"No? I guess you don't get the big picture," Jesse said, waving the gun toward the hiking path.

"Not if you're taking it."

"Honey, shut your sassy mouth and start moving before I shoot. And this is no camera I'm aiming."

The bully. I've had a gut full of bullies.

Then I swear I took leave of my senses, for with my heart leaping in my chest, I made a mad dash, raced across the lawn and jumped in the pool. A bullet pinged near my ear.

I dove for the deep end. A second shot hit the water, missing me by inches.

How many shots did he have left? Two? Three at most?

Stroking back and forth, I kept my body moving, kept the water churning. If I could get him to empty the gun into the pool, I might have a chance. It wasn't much of a chance or much of a plan, but it was all I had.

I swam for the curvy end where the water was deepest and as far away from him as I could get. Gambling on the notion that he'd race around the pool apron to take aim, I had to stay deep and keep him running from one side to the other looking for that good shot. But my lungs were screaming for relief. It was breathe or drown.

I broke the surface, gasped and turned turtle. A white streak whizzed by my eye. The bullet struck the far wall, ricocheted and fell to the bottom of the pool.

Legs scissoring, arms stroking, I did zigzag laps until the need for air forced me up again. This time, from the stinging in my thigh, I knew he'd got me. I kept on moving, a streak of red floating behind me like a banner. I had to get out of the water before the whole pool turned pink.

No need to panic. He had one shot left, no more.

No, not even one. I came up for a jolt of air and caught a glimpse of Jesse yanking on the trigger. *Ah, out of ammo.*

Now what? I couldn't swim forever, and I couldn't climb out. I was trapped. What a nitwit of a plan. But at least I could come topside and stay above the water.

I dog-paddled to the shallow end, careful to stay out of Jesse's reach. He stood guarding the narrow, pointy end of the pool, the useless gun grasped in his fist.

I pointed to the gun. "For all the good that's doing, you might as well hide it again."

He pocketed the weapon, stripped off the gloves and pocketed them too. "I can wait."

"Why wait? Come on in and get me."

No answer.

"What's the matter. Afraid? A big man like you. Can't you swim?"

If I could taunt him into coming in after me, get him to thrash around in the water, I might be able to climb out and make a run for the car. But could I run gun shot? I glanced down at the wound; it looked to be bleeding pretty bad. I had to get dry, and Jesse knew it.

"No need for any swimming," he said. "I'll wait. Catch a few rays while you bleed out."

"I'll keep you waiting for good long spell, Jesse. I'm in no hurry either."

Screech! Screech!

I treaded water and glanced up into the blue sky. A hawk circled high overhead. It couldn't smell blood, could it? The notion made me shudder. I had to do *something*.

"Jesse, let's talk," I said, kind of chummy like. "Why are you doing this? I haven't done anything to you."

"Not yet. Not like those other two. But you will if I let you go."

My feet sank to the pool's tiled bottom. "The other two? You mean Carmen and Penelope?"

"Yeah, so now you know. Makes no difference. Not with you bleeding like that."

"Why did you kill them? I don't understand."

He shrugged. "I got sick of being used."

I nodded, as friendly as could be. "I've been used, too. It sure is a rotten feeling. What's your story? As for me ..." I snorted "... I got used in the bedroom. I'm not proud I let it happen, but I did." My thigh had begun throbbing real bad. I tried to ignore it. I had to keep him talking, telling me stuff—in case I lived. "How about you? How did you get used?"

"Not much different from you, come to think of it."

That caught my notice, almost made me forget about the throbbing. "How so? I mean you're a guy. It's different."

"They liked being in the sack with me. End of story."

"That why you killed them?" Dropping the question like killing two women he had slept with was no big deal. Would he bite?

Yes.

"I wasn't just looking for a roll in the hay. I had an agenda." He shook his head. "They didn't respect that."

"I don't understand you, Jesse."

"Okay," he squinted up at the sun. "It's early. We got time

to kill." He guffawed. "I do, anyway. So here's the problem."
Talking kind of slow and chatty. "Carmen said she'd bankroll
the Vixens footage. It takes bucks, big bucks, to turn raw film
into a show. But the bucks never materialized. She played me
for a fool. Until she didn't."

I shivered. The water so sun-warmed a few minutes ago had
chilled. Goosebumps popped out on my arms and shoulders. I
glanced down at my thigh. The water around my leg was scary
pink.

"Yeah," he said, noticing. "I got time."

"Maybe not. Maybe somebody'll come along. Then where
will you be?"

"So why aren't you screaming?" He laughed. It sounded
dirty. Worse, he was telling me what I already knew. Nobody
would hear me even if I yelled my head off. So why waste what
energy I had left?

"While we're killing time, tell me about Penelope," I said.
"She didn't have the money to bankroll anybody."

"Not true. She had it, but she blew it even after I begged her
not to. If she'd stayed with ol' money bags a few months longer,
even a year more, she could have milked him. But oh, no, she
wanted out."

"You killed her because she got a divorce?" I had to struggle
to keep the shock out of my voice.

He shrugged. "No, not for that. She put the house on the
market. The money from the sale would have been enough
for the Vixens, but she had a little surprise waiting. Told me
she was leaving for New York. You could say I lost it then." He
pointed a finger at the water. "Enjoying your swim?"

"Yeah, it's great. Come on in."

"Nah, this is better. I leave the gun by the pool. They
find your body, and they find the gun. With that squatter's
fingerprints all over it."

"Frankie Serrito's?"

"That his name? Never did get it."

"How—"

"How did I get his prints? The day you had on the bikini? He came over after you left. I showed him the gun, let him handle it, said I'd use it on him if he caused any trouble. That night ... after ... I hid the gun for the cops to find. Trouble was I hid it too good—they never found it. So I come back to move it and what do I find? You." He shrugged. "No problem. The way things are turning out, I can leave it in plain sight."

As cocksure as the only rooster in the barnyard, he was making me real mad. "Well, Jesse, you sound mighty pleased with yourself. But you're forgetting something."

"Yeah, what?"

"I'm Josie's bridesmaid. Bet when she learns I've been killed, she'll cancel the wedding." I rubbed my goose bumpy shoulders. "There goes your second chance at making it big. Too bad."

"Nah, she won't cancel. Even if she does, I'll have the exclusive on a murder. Another beautiful woman killed. Another unsolved crime. I can play your death into a sensational video. You'll be all over the news. In your bikini." He grinned. "In that wet T-shirt too."

Talking with his hands, getting more and more excited, he moved near to the pool's edge. So near, the toes of his sneakers hung over the rim.

Screech!"

Closer now, perched on the top branches of a pine, the hawk spread its wings and waited. For what? For me? I shivered. The water felt icy cold.

"What's the matter down there?" Jesse taunted. "You look a mite pale."

I glanced up at him. Outlined against the sky, he cast a shadow across the pool. He was blocking out the sun, cutting me off from its warmth. Cutting me off from everything.

What right did he have? *None.*

The little heat I had left in my body rushed through my veins, fueling my anger. I'd be damned if I'd let him stand there and watch me bleed to death. Without thinking it through, without thinking at all, I swam near to where he stood and raising my head to the sun, I let out the mother of all rebel yells.

"YawwwEEE!"

The yell startled him right good and, in that split second, I reached up, grabbed one of his ankles and yanked with all my might.

It worked! It worked!

He fell, *kerpow*, but not in the pool as I thought he would. He tumbled backwards, striking his head on the concrete apron. Stretched out flat on his back, he didn't move a muscle. I eyeballed him carefully. Not even his eyelids fluttered.

Now.

I may never be forgiven for it, but as I climbed, shaking, out of the pool, I hoped I had killed him.

But no, his chest heaved up and down. He was breathing, dammit. I toyed with the idea of rolling him into the pool and letting him drown, but the water might wake him up and, besides, I wasn't a killer. I didn't even kick him in the ribs, a fact I'll always be a mite proud of.

What I did do is strip off the T-shirt, wrap it around my thigh and limp as fast as I could out of the garden. I had a phone call to make.

Chapter Fifty-Two

"MATT'S ALREADY LEFT the station," Ellie said. "He's on his way."

"How could he be? He doesn't know I'm here."

"Well, he knows something. A call came in a few minutes ago. Somebody complaining about gun shots going off up on the Bluffs."

"Sounds about right. Send an ambulance, too, will you, Ellie? The shooter got me."

I must have passed out, for the next thing I knew, someone was pounding on the car window, next to my ear.

Bang, bang, bang. "Honey, wake up. Wake up. Let us in."

My eyes slit open, but Matt had turned away. "Don't waste time fooling around with locks. Break the glass on the passenger side. Be careful. Don't cut her."

They were about to smash up the Lincoln. My wheels.

I released the lock and opened the driver's side door.

"She's conscious," Matt said. A strong pair of arms reached in, lifted me out and laid me on a stretcher.

"Step out of the way, Sheriff," someone ordered. "We'll take care of her from here."

"Is she? Is she … ?" Matt's voice trailing off.

"Her vital signs are good, but she's lost a lot of blood. We'll start an IV before moving her. She's lucky that shot didn't sever an artery."

"I knew it," I said.

"Honey, you awake?" Matt bent over the stretcher, his dark eyes filled with worry. Filled with love.

"Jesse Raidel?" I asked.

"We got him. He do this to you?"

I nodded. "He's the killer." Then fog swooped in, clouding everything.

THE NEXT DAY, I woke up in a room filled with flowers. A stack of newspapers was piled on the bedside table. The headline in the top paper, the *Eureka Star*, read: Local Realtor Nabs Killer.

That must be me. I closed my eyes. I'd read about it tomorrow. *Wait a minute!*

My eyes snapped open. I elbowed up to a sitting position in the narrow hospital bed and grabbed the paper off the stack. What had happened to Jesse? Had I killed him? Did they find the gun? The bullet holes in the pool? And omigod, when the EMS found me in the Lincoln, I'd taken off the T-shirt. They didn't photograph me like that, did they?

A quick scan of page one put my fears to rest. Well, most of them. The suspect in the killings, a Jesse Raidel, had been helicoptered to the Yarborough County Hospital. Currently in critical condition, he was expected to survive.

Good grief, maybe he was in the room next door. I eased back on the skimpy little pillow. No matter. He'd be in no condition to harm anyone.

A separate article said Detective Bradshaw of the Homicide Division of the Arkansas State Police was expected on TV sometime today to give further details in the case.

Honey Ingersoll, the woman who apprehended the suspect, has also been hospitalized for a bullet wound to the thigh. Her injury is not considered life threatening.

That was sure good to read in print, though my non-life-threatening injury was throbbing up a storm. Well, I'd survived, and at least the *Star* hadn't published any embarrassing pictures. Though there was a sad one of Jesse with his arms around a smiling Carmen and Penelope. The snake. And one of me from the time I went to work for Sam Ridley. A head shot in the serious, navy blue suit. What a relief. I needed to be seen as an upright, sensible business woman not as some bim …

The door eased open. I lowered the paper and glanced over at Matt in full uniform, holster, gun, hat, boots—the works—and carrying an armful of red roses.

"All right if I come in?" he asked. Not waiting for an answer, he strode to the bed, laid the roses on the blanket and took my hands in his. "You okay?"

"I think so. My leg hurts is all."

"The surgeon said you should heal without a scar." He flushed like a boy. "I thought you'd want to know that. Your legs are so—"

"Long they go all the way to the floor."

"Not quite what I had in mind." His hands tightened. "You could have been killed. The thought drives me crazy. You drive me crazy."

"Sorry. I only went into the garden to pick a gardenia." Tears pricked at my eyelids.

A pair of soft lips brushed my cheek. "Don't upset yourself, Honey. Save the details for Bradshaw. He'll be in to see you later. I've asked the hospital to notify me before you're released so I can take you home. In a day or two they said. As soon as they're sure you're stabilized."

"Thanks, Matt."

"And in case you're wondering, your car is sitting outside your apartment. Zach drove it back."

"So everything's been taken care of?"

"Pretty much. According to forensics, the gun found on Raidel is the one that killed the DeLuca woman. With the gun as evidence plus your testimony, there's no way he can talk his way out of this." Matt flashed a megawatt smile. "You solved the case, Honey. The whole town owes you." He glanced around the room. "From all the flowers in here, everybody knows it too."

"Something's still bothering me, Matt."

"The wound?"

I shook my head. "Why did Carmen use her last moments on earth to write about her will? Why didn't she write Jesse's name instead?"

"We'll never know for sure, but maybe revenge wasn't on her mind. Maybe she wanted to do the right thing before meeting her Maker."

"What a sweet notion, Matt. I hope it's true." I patted the paper. "At least there are no bikini pictures in the *Star* and, now that Jesse's been found out, no chance the Velveteen Vixens will be aired, either."

A big, badass grin spread clear across Matt's face. "Sorry to disappoint you, Honey, but Channel 8's broadcasting the pilot show tonight. Lenny Purvis claims he signed a legally binding contract for the rights. He showed it to us, and it looks bona fide. So with you in surgery, all we could do is threaten a law suit. But nothing we said could persuade him to cancel. He claims the show's the biggest one he's ever handled. The whole town will be tuned in."

My face went hot. "I never signed a release. Jesse forged my signature. And now he gets the last word?"

"No, what Jesse gets is a trial and then an orange prison suit. You get to be the most admired woman in town."

Unconvinced, I laid the paper down with a sigh. Still, a redhead in an orange jumpsuit sure would stand out in a crowd. And like those slick magazines claimed, orange was the new black. So the more I thought about it, the more I grinned. For whether he wanted to or not, Jesse would have his real reality show after all.

The bedside phone rang and I picked up. "Honey Ingersoll

speaking."

"Exactly the person I wanted to reach. So pleased to hear your voice."

I leaned back on the pillow like I was in a fancy boudoir or something. "Well, Lord Almighty, if it isn't Andarius Ballou, Esquire."

"Is this a good time? Are you able to talk?"

"Not re—"

"I just took a call from Lennny Purvis. He said the sheriff threatened him with a law suit over some bikini show you're starring in. Purvis claims he has your signature on the dotted line."

"That's a lie."

"I see. Well, you can get a restraining order and challenge Purvis, but that might result in a long, expensive court case. My advice is to let the show go on. Why, knowing you, I'm sure you look like a supermodel in your bikini. It could be Eureka Falls today and Hollywood tomorrow."

I blew out a breath and paused for a moment. "Thank you kindly for the call, Mr. Ballou, but the truth is you really don't know me at all. Sorry, but I can't talk any longer. Sheriff Rameros is here, and I don't want to keep him waiting.

Then I hung up—firmly—and turned, with a smile, to Matt.

Photo by Sharon Yanish

JEAN HARRINGTON SWEARS she ingested ink as an infant, for words are in her blood. Her first job was writing advertising copy for Reed & Barton, Silversmiths, and she claims she has the spoons to prove it. Then for seventeen years, she taught forms of discourse and English literature at Becker College in Worcester, Massachusetts. For several years, she also directed a peer-taught writing center at the college that was available to any student with writing problems. After Jean and husband John moved to Naples, she began dreaming of murder, and the award-winning, tongue-in-cheek Murders by Design Mystery Series is the result. She is the author of the Listed and Lethal Mystery series, which began with *Murder on Pea Pike*. Jean is up to her knees in dead bodies and loving every minute of it.

Jean is a member of Romance Writers of America, having served two terms as president of her local Southwest Florida chapter; International Thriller Writers; and Mystery Writers of America.

For more information, go to www.jeanharrington.com.